THE WHITE REVIEW

27

CELINE

TRANSPARENT THINGS
21 FEB – 03 MAY 2020
GOLDSMITHS CCA

NAIRY BAGHRAMIAN
CARLOTTA BAILLY-BORG
BECKY BEASLEY
GARETH CADWALLADER
NINA CANELL
MICHAEL DEAN
THEASTER GATES
DAVID HAMMONS
MARIE LUND
VLADIMIR NABOKOV
VIRGINIA OVERTON
LUCY SKAER
RENEE SO
KERRY TRIBE

GOLDSMITHS CCA
ST JAMES'
NEW CROSS
LONDON SE14 6AD
FREE ENTRY
GOLDSMITHSCCA.ART

PAUL P.
MARCH – MAY 2020

ERIK VAN LIESHOUT / MAAIKE SCHOOREL
MAY – JUNE 2020

GILLIAN WEARING
JULY – AUGUST 2020

MAX HOOPER SCHNEIDER
SEPTEMBER – OCTOBER 2020

Published by The White Review, March 2020
Edition of 1,800

Printed in the U.K.
Typeset in Nouveau Blanche

ISBN No. 978-0-9957437-9-3

The White Review is a registered charity (number 1148690)

The White Review, 8–12 Creekside, London SE8 3DX
www.thewhitereview.org

Supported using public funding by
ARTS COUNCIL ENGLAND

EDITORIAL

'People always say you can't change the past,' suggests Sarah Moss in her interview in
this issue, 'but of course you can change the past completely, because you can tell a different
story about it.' Moss's books, as Hannah Rosefield writes, 'negotiate the past and imagine the
future': she discusses optimism, fridge-magnet clichés, the dangers of nationalist nostalgia
(particularly in relation to contemporary nature writing), and how to 'perform love by work'.

Several of Moss's novels are written in the voices of children, a perspective – raw, unfil-
tered, perhaps unreliable, often seeking self-definition or belonging – which recurs throughout this issue of *The White Review*. In 'Fried Egg', a discomfiting story by Spanish writer
Sabina Urraca (tr. Thomas Bunstead), a woman who has retreated to a haunted house in an
attempt to disconnect from society recalls an incongruous childhood in a sinister anti-natal
commune. Elvia Wilk's essay 'Kids in the Field' dissects the knotty dissonance inherent
in growing up as the child of anthropologists. Her unstable memories of her childhood in
Belize – and her uncomfortable return – are interspersed with a nuanced examination of the
anthropological discipline's historical baggage, the sociological and emotional implications
of growing up in a culture not your own, and the possibilities and limits of 'assimilation'.

We publish new fiction – her first in two years – by Claire-Louise Bennett, a supermarket
reverie transporting us from the aisles of a suburban retail park to the velveteen splendour
of the Viennese opera. Fernanda Melchor's essay 'Veracruz with a Zee for Zeta' (tr. Sophie
Hughes) examines life in contemporary Mexico through a series of violent vignettes set in
its beaches, nightclubs, supermarkets, streets and homes. Readers of Melchor's explosive novel
Hurricane Season will recognise her propulsive torrents of prose, her polyvocal narrative style,
and her rage against power. 'Extremity' by Taiwanese writer Hsu Yu-Chen (tr. Jeremy Tiang)
is an acerbic and poignant story of queer desire and loneliness: although in May 2019 Taiwan
became the first country in Asia to legalise same-sex marriage, the elections of this January
were characterised by virulently homophobic rhetoric directed at President Tsai Ing-Wen,
who had signed the bill into law.

Rosanna Mclaughlin interviews artist Samara Scott, whose work collects and collages
used materials, from bath salts to Irn Bru, from fragments of glass to the 'gutter totems' of
cigarette butts and chewing gum. Scott's interest in the tension between abstraction and
representation, and in blending disparate objects, colours and textures to dizzying effect,
is complemented by series from artists Lisa Oppenheim and Zhang Enli. Following an
acclaimed live performance hosted by *The White Review* and DRAF in November 2019,
replete with projected gifs flickering on the walls, we present Johanna Hedva's Nine Inch
Nails hagiography 'They're Really Close to My Body'. Recalling their own experience
of seeking identity and community in the era of dial-up and VHS, Hedva's writing about
music and mysticism, devotion and desire, transcendence and the unknowable, takes us
to 'a world where a language made of words can't go'.

INTERVIEW   SARAH MOSS

Before I met Sarah Moss, in a tiny, cheerful café in the centre of Coventry, I visited the city's cathedral. I wanted to see it because Adam, the narrator of Moss's 2016 novel *The Tidal Zone*, is working on an audio guide to the building. The book's main narrative is interspersed with chapters describing the bombing of Coventry during World War II, and the architect Basil Spence's plans to build a modern cathedral from the ruins of its 700-year-old incarnation. Adam is also engaged in an act of reconstructive imagination. His teenage daughter collapsed at school, her heart stopped. She survived, but nobody knows why the collapse happened, or whether it will happen again. How does he move forward, honestly confronting what has happened and what may yet happen, but not allowing his family's lives to be dictated by this uncertainty?

How we negotiate the past and imagine the future – personal, social, national – is an overriding concern of Moss's six novels. A sleep-deprived academic struggles to write a book on the history of childhood while raising her own two young children (*Night Waking*). A Victorian woman grapples with the legacy of her mother's psychological and physical abuse as she trains to be one of the country's first female doctors (*Bodies of Light* and *Signs for Lost Children*). In *The Tidal Zone*, Adam is a part-time academic married to a GP, and his future must take into account not only his new awareness of his daughter's vulnerability, but also the years of austerity that have reshaped higher education and the NHS.

Born in 1975, Moss grew up in Manchester and earned a PhD at the University of Oxford. Her doctoral research examined the influence of polar exploration on the Romantic imagination; her first novel, *Cold Earth* (2009), followed a group of students on an archaeological dig in Greenland. Recognition for Moss's work has built steadily, with *Bodies of Light*, *Signs for Lost Children* and *The Tidal Zone* shortlisted for the Wellcome Book Prize in 2015, 2016 and 2017 respectively, testament as much to her deep engagement with science and medicine as to the regularity with which she publishes. Her most recent book, *Ghost Wall*, won wide acclaim as a tense and insightful Brexit novel, albeit one set twenty-five years before the 2016 referendum. The novel's teenage narrator, Silvie, along with her parents and a group of university archaeologists, is spending part of the summer attempting to live as the Ancient Britons did. Silvie's father, a bus driver, is obsessed with Pre-Roman Britain, and over the course of the novel's not-quite-150 pages we see that this obsession is rooted in the fantasy of a time and place free from foreigners, where women are controlled by men.

Moss is now a Professor of Creative Writing at the University of Warwick. Her teaching, like her fiction and *Names from the Sea* (2012), a memoir recounting the year Moss spent with her family in Iceland, is bound up with questions of place. *Place*, not landscape, she corrected me at one point: expanding what counts as interesting territory, she pointed out, is as politically important as expanding our understanding of the past, and that means carparks as well as mountains, cathedrals and shops as well as oceans and meadows. We met in early June 2019, the week after European elections in which the Brexit Party won almost a third of the vote. Pragmatically and determinedly ungloomy despite these results, Moss was committed to rejecting all forms of nostalgia and to believing in a better future.

HANNAH ROSEFIELD

TWR   The relationship between parents and children is at the centre of almost all your work. What is it about that relationship that you find so interesting or fruitful?

SM   Well, it's the one thing absolutely everybody has in common: we all have parents. After *Night Waking* came out, it was to some extent reviewed as a kind of mummy book, as if parenthood were some minority interest. The idea that raising the next generation, or having parents or having kids, is something that only a few people do is a very strange one. My career as a novelist has overlapped almost exactly with my kids' lives. I was writing my first novel when I was on maternity leave with my first child, so those arcs, of being a novelist and being a parent, have been identical for me. When I wrote *Night Waking*, there was very little representation of parenthood in contemporary fiction. A lot about family life from the child's point of view, but very little from the parent's. That's changed over the last five years, but at the time it seemed an odd gap in the story.

TWR   And then in your next two novels [*Bodies of Light* and *Signs for Lost Children*, both loose sequels to *Night Waking*], you did switch to writing from the child's perspective.

SM   Yes. Worrying about what parents do to children and what children do to parents. Because it's a narrative idea, isn't it? The whole post-Freudian idea of parenthood is essentially narrative, that your ancestors are telling their stories through your life.

TWR   Why did you decide to make the narrator of *The Tidal Zone*, who's more or less a stay-at-home parent, a father rather than a mother?

SM   I was interested in masculinity. In some ways masculinity is much less interrogated than femininity at the moment, and because I'm raising sons, I think about that quite a lot. And I don't think feminism and raising sons are in tension or incompatible in any way, but that project makes me much more alert to the damage that patriarchy and ideas of masculinity do to men. So *The Tidal Zone* was partly an experiment with masculinity and patriarchy. What does the good man look like? Can you be a good man and not work? What happens to your masculinity if you take on conventionally feminine kinds of work? All those questions were interesting to me.

TWR   Do you think that people responded differently to the novel because the narrator was male?

SM   Well, it's interesting that nobody assumes it's autobiographical, as if the experiences of maternity and paternity are so different that you couldn't possibly put your own experiences into a different set of clothes.

TWR   You've spoken elsewhere about the idea for the novel coming to you when, on the same day, a children's hospital in Syria was bombed and a boy at your son's school collapsed on the football field. Did you know instantly that the narrator of the novel would be the parent of the child who had collapsed?

SM   I started with Coventry Cathedral, actually. And then yes, with that moment, standing in the kitchen listening to the news, and then later hearing about the boy collapsing on the football field, and then those things came together, but it was part of a much bigger project of thinking about trauma and rebuilding, and that question: What is art for in the face of violence? To which I don't have an answer, but Basil Spence [the architect of Coventry Cathedral] has an answer.

TWR   I looked round the cathedral before I came to meet you, and it was amazing to see how central those questions are in the building.

SM   It's a building about war.

TWR   Yes. And seems to have continued to be about wars, ongoing wars, rather than specifically a memorial to World War II. Maybe that connects to a question I had about the way that several of your novels take place in multiple time periods. At what stage does that doubleness or multiplicity come in? It sounds like with *The Tidal Zone* it was there from the beginning.

SM   It's always there from the beginning. And even when it's not so explicit, with *Ghost Wall*, say, where that past is almost silenced, just filtering through, it's still my starting point, always.

TWR   You're an academic by training, and you studied Romantic literature, which is not something you've written about, or a time in which you've set your novels. Is that deliberate?

SM   No. Maybe it's partly that those Romantic ideas are so deep in the way I think about writing and place, and often in the way that I question ideas about writing and place. I think Romanticism is often very badly misused in the service of nostalgia and nationalism. The classic sublime is very exclusive in ways that I don't like, and we inherit it in ways I don't like. But those conversations about the relationship with land and place and writing... I almost don't need to address them directly. I address them directly in my teaching, but in my writing they can just bubble along underneath.

TWR   In *Ghost Wall*, there are tremendous problems with the way that the narrator's father and the archaeology professor think about the land, and the way they go about doing experiential archaeology, but the novel also suggests that there are good things about being deeply connected to the land, as the teenage narrator clearly is. I wondered whether you have a positive vision of what it could be to feel you belong to a place, and whether it could be something that doesn't necessitate excluding other people.

SM   I hope so. It's probably one of my long-term projects, as a teacher and as a writer, to find a way... I think of it as belonging without ownership. A very democratic idea of belonging that keeps it open for different kinds of connection and is not rooted in some property-based or genetic claim on the land. But that's always going to be a practice rather than an achievement, for whoever is doing it. That's very much a part of how I teach writing about nature and place: the writing *is* the practice of belonging. And often knowing about a place is the practice of belonging as well. I've moved around a lot, mostly within the UK, so when people ask where I'm from, I can say Britain, but beyond that I don't really have an answer, and depending on the motives of the people asking, even saying Britain will collapse under interrogation, because on my father's side there's a classic European Jewish diaspora story. I fit in perfectly well in Britain, but that idea of a kind of ancestral connection to place – when I'm teaching, we end up talking about 'from-ness' – is not one that I know. There are lots of places I like very much and feel connected to, but I think none where people who feel that other kind of connection would recognise my right to be there or to have feelings about the place.

TWR   Thinking about the dangers of nationalism and nostalgia, I wondered how you feel about

historical re-enactment of the kind that happens in *Ghost Wall*.

SM   I'd make a distinction between re-enactment and experiential archaeology. The latter is an idea that I find very appealing: that you can learn through practice. It can never work on its own, but in conjunction with other kinds of archaeology you might learn about artefacts or objects and material ways of being, through making and remaking. I know some archaeologists like that idea more than others, but I find it enormously appealing, because it's back to the very material, embodied idea of a creative practice that continues to fascinate me.

TWR   And that's continuous with, or an intensification of, something like going to a museum? That is, you're talking about any kind of engagement with the tangible or the material rather than with narrative.

SM   Yes. Narratives usually come out of it for me, but it's not where you start.

TWR   One thing that struck me when reading all your novels together is how much space is given to... not the domestic exactly, because in some of them the characters are outside all the time, or camping, but to the work of cleaning, and mending, and preparing food, and so on. I know some of that was part of your academic work too. I'm interested in what function the description of this kind of labour has in your novels, and how it relates to their more plotted aspects?

SM   I don't think they can be separated from the more plotted parts of the novels. I think those practices are how we experience and perform most of our relationships in daily life, particularly in a family with kids. It may also be that I was brought up in a family where you didn't go around saying 'I love you' all the time, but you kind of know that you're loved when there are clean clothes in your drawer, and a meal ready when you need it, and someone to collect you when you need collecting. And I was very aware, particularly when my kids were younger and most of the work of parenting was embodied and material, that it doesn't really matter if you think you love your kids and you say you love your kids, if you don't behave as if you love your kids. You perform love by work. And that's less so in adult relationships, but I still think that in any long-term cohabiting relationship, the bedrock is much more to do with practice than speech.

TWR   Do you think of yourself as writing in a particular novelistic or generic tradition?
SM   That's probably not a question a writer is ever going to be able to answer. It's more for readers to say. I try to read as broadly as I possibly can, and of course, my academic training and background will always shape the way I think.

TWR   Does that mean your fiction will always be something that requires a lot of research?
SM   I don't know. I've just finished writing something that didn't require very much, quite a mad little book set now or in the near future. And although there was a lot of research behind *Ghost Wall*, much less of it actually made it into the novel than has previously been the case. I think I may be moving away from those very intensely researched novels. It's not a conscious decision, it's just where it's going. I was surprised that *Ghost Wall* was short. I think it's something to do with getting older, and more confident, and outgrowing that undergraduate need to hit the word count... again, it's this Yorkshire thing of feeling like you mustn't give short measure, that people somehow measure novels by weight or by metre, and you can't call it a novel if it doesn't weigh a certain amount. One of the things about getting older has been casting off some of those constrictions of wanting to be the good girl and the good student and to be the one who gets top marks all the time, and instead just thinking screw it, let's see what happens.

TWR   Can you tell me about the book you've just finished?
SM   It's called *Summerwater* and will be out in September 2020 in the UK with Picador, and in the US with FSG, probably sometime in 2021. It's set on one very wet day at a holiday park in Scotland, and the narrative moves from one cabin to another as the hours pass, starting with a woman who gets up at dawn to run and ending with someone holding a party in the early hours. I started to think of it when we spent a week in just such a park three years ago. It rained heavily all the time, every hour of every day, and the park was at the end of a long, narrow road and there were no indoor activities for miles; people go there for hiking and watersports. We went out and climbed mountains anyway – being able to get dry at night is why you rent a cabin rather than camping and I like running in the rain – but there were several families who seemed to be sitting inside all day.

No one spoke to each other, but I think we were all watching and judging, and certainly by the end I was making up stories about everyone else, trying to work out where they were from and why they were there.

TWR   In another interview, you said that your first drafts tend to be much shorter than the finished version. I was struck by this because it's something you rarely hear: whether it's academic work or fiction, people usually say they write masses and masses, and after the first draft realise that three-quarters of it is trash or whatever.
SM   Well, I realise some of it is trash too, but there's not usually masses of it. It's not always the case that I write very short drafts, but certainly as a student, I used to write these very intense two-page essays on John Donne, say, and then think that's it, that's everything there is to say about him, I have nothing more in me. And then I'd go back and unpack it and open it up. Sara Holloway, who edited my first couple of books, used to tell me to give it more light and shade, give it room to breathe. It felt almost like letting something rise. Let it expand, let it spread, give it room to grow a little bit.

TWR   So that process happens once you've shown it to someone?
SM   Not since the very early days. I think I'm doing a lot more of that work myself.

TWR   Because you feel more confident?
SM   Yes. It's not that I feel I know how to do it. I always think you only learn from writing a novel how to write the novel you've just written, which doesn't particularly help with writing the next one, but I probably am getting more confident in my own editorial judgement after the fact. I love editors, and I love detailed line-editing, and the great joy of a good editor is that there's someone who cares as much as you do about whether or not that semi-colon ought to be a comma. So it's not that I don't want or like editing, but I think I can do more of the structural, large-scale stuff myself these days.

TWR   When did you start writing fiction? Is that something that you were always doing alongside your academic work?
SM   Yes. My mother said that I was writing fiction before I could read, which can't be true,

but I did learn to read very late.

TWR   Did you ever feel that writing fiction was in tension with your academic work?

SM   No. I mean, my academic prose was never very academic, and that was one of the reasons I ditched it with great relief. When I told my school that I wanted to be a novelist, they said, 'Yes, dear, that's nice' and told me to do English at university. And then I stayed on and did the doctorate, just because I could, really. I had funding, I didn't know how to get a job. It seemed like the natural thing to do, and having done that then there wasn't anything to do except stay in academia. And it was fine, you know, I felt myself ambitious as an academic, but I was always writing fiction on the side.

TWR   Universities are very present in your novels, although not in a campus novel kind of way. Is that because it's the world you know, or is there something about universities that allows you to do particular things in your novels?

SM   Probably a bit of both. They're still places of ideas, just about, or one of the nearest things we've got to places of ideas, however impoverished and enmeshed... Teaching is really fundamental to my sense of purpose, and where I do some of my best and fastest thinking. The need to stay ten minutes ahead of a room full of very bright 20-year-olds is really fun and I enjoy it enormously, so I suppose I can't separate the practice of teaching from the practice of writing or the practice of thinking.

TWR   There's a moment in *The Tidal Zone* where the narrator says that 'History is the enemy of fiction.' I'm assuming that that's not your own view, because you're a writer of fiction and Adam isn't.

SM   That's right. 'Fiction is history with ethics' is another thing he says.

TWR   And that's also something you wouldn't subscribe to?

SM   I don't know. I think the risk of history is that you tell it as if it has ethics. That's what you mustn't do. Fiction needs an ethics of some kind, I mean it needs a structure.

TWR   How do you see historical fiction fitting into this? There are plenty of people who read historical fiction but don't read history, so fiction *is* the way they learn about history.

SM   I think historical fiction is always from and for the moment of its writing, rather than the moment it's describing. It's a kind of meta-history about how we narrate the past, what we want to inherit. At worst, it's nostalgic. That's always the risk of historical fiction. At best, it's a reflection on the stories that don't make it, and it challenges the reader to think about their idea of the past. People always say you can't change the past, but of course you can change the past completely, because you can tell a different story about it. And I worried about this... I had been doing a very lofty post-structuralist thing, you know, there's no such thing as reality and all of that stuff... and then after Trump's election I thought, bloody hell. You don't want this to come into popular culture as a belief that there are as many versions of the truth as there are people, and that it doesn't matter if you lie. I think it's really important that everyone's absolutely clear that there is truth and there are lies, and they're different. Which is an odd thing to say as a novelist, because obviously I make my living by telling lies... and I think that's just one of those difficult things to think about. I would be very worried about somebody who claimed that denying the Holocaust is a kind of historical fiction, and that's a fine thing to do because it's only a story. Clearly that's a story that's not fine: there are certain historical realities that it's imperative to recognise. So I don't have an answer here, and I don't have a set of rules for historical novelists. I think you just have to know what you're doing.

TWR   When you were writing *Ghost Wall*, which is set in the early 1990s, did you think of yourself as writing about another era? What made you set it during this period?

SM   I did a bit, yes. That's the era of my own adolescence: I was born in 1975, so Silvie's a little bit older than me, but only by a couple of years. It's weird now to think that the 1990s were a moment of hope, but looking back, that's what it was. My adolescence was so much marked by the Berlin Wall coming down, and Europe opening up. My generation was born as Britain joined Europe, I mean it was the Common Market at the time, and we were taught in school that we needed the languages, and we needed to understand European politics, and we should read European literature: that this was our future, and there were all these schemes and opportunities and that we were going to grow up to be citizens of Europe. And I think, for people like me – and I mean that in class terms – we thought that was the future, and we grew up believing that that was how the world was. So I was thinking about that phase of opening and excitement in the 1990s. It wasn't just the Berlin Wall coming down. I had spent a lot of my child-hood summers in the 80s driving deep into the Soviet Bloc with my parents. I'd go back to school and say I'd been to Bulgaria, and people would say, now don't tell stories, nobody can go to Bulgaria. I remember my mother saying, 'Look at this and remember it. This won't be here when you're grown up, and you'll be one of the last people to have seen it.' I don't know how she knew that – I should ask her about it now – but she did. I used to play a game with myself on those journeys, from West Germany to East Germany, or Austria into Hungary, where I'd shut my eyes for a few minutes and then open them and try to think: if I didn't know where I was, how would I work it out and how long would it take me? And I always knew if we were in Western or Eastern Europe. You could tell immediately, always, and I would ask myself, *how* did I know? Because if you were in Austria, or Hungary, the architecture hadn't changed very much, and the landscape hadn't changed. The language of course had, but it was something about the volume of traffic, the kinds of cars, the way people stood... There was something that was very recognisable about those border crossings. So then in the early 90s to have it all go was... extraordi-nary. In my teens I had a German exchange partner who became a good friend, so I spent a lot of time in Germany, and the difference as the Wall came down and the country reunited was really palpable. So I was thinking about the contrast between that excitement of my teens and the despairing sense of borders closing and walls going up and everybody retreating into nationalism today.

TWR   Though, in *Ghost Wall* at least, that nationalism was really present back then too.
SM   Yes. Partly because it's a novel of now, but yes.

TWR   Many people who voted for Brexit, say, feel this kind of nostalgia for what I think you and I would both say is a kind of false history, whether it's a history of the Iron Age or the 1950s, and that seems dangerous. But then it's also hard not to be nostalgic for a time before we were aware that so many people felt this different kind of nostalgia, and wanted to detach from Europe, and so on. It seems like there are negatives to wanting to return to that state of ignorance, but there also has to be something good about remembering the sense of openness that existed when you were a teenager. So I'm curious as to how you handle that. Is there a good kind of nostalgia? Can we find it in fiction?
SM   The problem with the idea of a good kind of nostalgia is that nostalgia is locating all desirability in the past. And because you can't get to the past, that's making it impossible to get what you desire, and setting in train a regression. And it is clearly the case that whatever your political persuasion, countries go through better times and worse times. I'm very aware of this talking to my American friends: you know, Trump is not forever. And there's deep despair at the state of things at the moment, but also a deep knowledge that it won't endure forever. Demographic change, apart from anything else, means that this cannot go on, and a lot of harm is being done and can be done, and a lot of that harm is irrevocable... but it won't last forever.

TWR   Hopefully there's enough of a world left when it *is* over.
SM   Yes. I think we mustn't be nostalgic: I grew up with parents who were always a bit nostalgic for the 1960s, they were baby boomers and they were hippies at exactly the right time and in the right place, and they had a great time, but... Especially for women like my mother, middle-class, profes-sional women, inequality was more obvious and entrenched in the 1960s and 70s than it is now. And then there's just the basic stuff to hang on to: antibiotics, clean water, access to healthcare – well, maybe not in the US – but people are living longer and in better conditions now than at any previous moment. These times of despair feel very long when they're happening, but if you look at the longer duration of history, they're really not. A catastrophic Presidency is awful if you live through it, but it's four years, maybe eight years, and out of a hundred that's not very much.

TWR   So you can remember the good things that were in the past and try to bring them back, but you also need to keep in mind that on balance there are lots of things now that make our lives better.
SM   Yes. And I think that's just a survival

strategy. I mean, it's also perfectly obvious that if all of us don't change our behaviour, there isn't going to be a world to live in at all, in my children or my grandchildren's lifetime, and that's horrible. But it's also true that we're all going to be dead at some stage anyway, and that's also horrible. So... I think there are things that you need to know, but you don't need to know all of them all of the time because it's completely paralysing. And even if the world is definitely going to overheat and end in forty-five years, my kids need their dinner on the table tonight. So in a little while I have to go home and cook, and I think partly for me that's why those rhythms of domesticity in my novels are always a counterpoint to the broader narratives of fear or hope.

TWR   I've read you say that writers like Paul Kingsnorth and Robert Macfarlane, who write non-fiction about landscape and the environment, are engaging in a kind of nostalgia that you're not interested in. How can you write non-fiction about landscape in a way that isn't nostalgic, and how can you do that in a time of climate change?
SM   Well, I think Kathleen Jamie is a shining example here of how to do it intelligently and sensitively and realistically. I absolutely love her writing. It's interesting that you ask about this because one of the things I might do next is a non-fiction place book, another one after Iceland. Kathleen Jamie does it by knowing how complicated it is. She's not looking for these grand overarching narratives about how it was better in the past, or how it's going to be better in the future, she's just observing very closely and with ferocious intelligence what's actually there, and making connections with the deep past in a knowingly fragmentary way, with as much attention to what we don't know as to what we do. And I think that kind of agnosticism is the only honest way of doing it. Do you know her essay 'Pathologies'?

TWR   I don't.
SM   It's one of my favourite pieces of writing. It starts off being about wildness and wilderness and how to write them, and of course she's deeply suspicious about the idea of wilderness. And then she visits a pathology lab in a hospital and she watches things through the microscope and she's thinking about wildness on a cellular level. Is cancer not wildness? After all, it's something natural that we can't control, you know, there are

the cells doing their thing and we can't stop them. Is there a sublime of oncology? It's brilliant. I love that change of focus, and it puts the things that matter squarely in the everyday. Because the problem with Robert Macfarlane is that the important landscapes are always far away. He's not interested in towns or cities, and the special experiences are always solitary. That's all well and good, but if the only way to have an authentic experience of landscape is to be alone somewhere remote, that ego's taking up an awful lot of space on a crowded planet. So I think you have to relocate the idea of places that matter to accessible places. We don't all have to drive off to the Lake District in order to have an authentic Wordsworthian experience of landscape. You know, look up, look down, get your microscope out, get your telescope out, go into a carpark. And it doesn't have to be in splendid Wordsworthian solitude – and by the way, he usually had Dorothy with him anyway. It can be a communal, social experience. And I just worry that that kind of modern sublime writing of landscape is fundamentally exclusive, because it's an idea of primacy, solitude, standing on top of everything and looking down. It's not about community or collectivity, or sociability, and I think those are the ideas that might save us.

TWR   Is that kind of collectivity representable in fiction, or is fiction too much about individuals?
SM   No, I think fiction can do that. That was part of what I was doing at the end of *Ghost Wall*: what saves Silvie is not some solitary hero. It's women collaborating.

TWR   So when you say collectivity, you're thinking about five or six people working together rather than at a bigger scale.
SM   Absolutely. That's the scale at which it works in fiction, anyway. No, what I meant there was an understanding that we're all interdependent.

TWR   There are several communes in *The Tidal Zone* – which is a different kind of collectivity. You've spoken elsewhere about your interest in institutions as a substitute for the family, and the commune seems a kind of intermediate space between the institution and the family. What role does the commune play in that novel, and how do you think about communes as models of community or collectivity?
SM   It's partly a response to Adam's devotion to

the domestic... Or maybe Adam's devotion to the domestic is a response to having been raised in a commune. It's about alternative ways of living together, on every scale. And those communes aren't bad, that was important to me: they're not cults where people are harmed. They're sometimes places where young people get things wrong, in the way that young people do get things wrong, but they're fundamentally benign.

TWR   Most of the commune parts of the novel are set in America. It sounds partly an autobiographical choice to make Adam's father American, and Jewish, but I could imagine a version of the novel where that wasn't the case.
SM   Well, I was thinking partly about legacies of war again, particularly the Second World War, and responses to trauma. The dangerous bit with that novel is always the implicit comparison between the trauma of nearly losing a child who gets excellent medical care and the trauma of actually losing a city, and then silently and several generations back the trauma of the Holocaust. If I appear to be making equivalences between those things, it's disastrous. So the challenge for that book was to think on all those different levels about trauma and reconstruction, and what you do in the aftermath. What good thing can you do in the aftermath? Given everything that you've lost, how can you make the aftermath better than what you had before? And you must do that, because otherwise everyone is mired in nostalgia forever, but how do you do that without trying to repress the loss?

TWR   I don't know whether you would agree with this, but it seems like *The Tidal Zone* and *Ghost Wall* are kind of symmetrical, in that *The Tidal Zone* is all about the aftermath of something terrible, and *Ghost Wall* is all about the lead-up to something terrible. Did that create different challenges for you when you were writing them? Or did you feel like you'd done one and wanted to try the other?
SM   I hadn't quite thought about it that way, but it's interesting because one of the things I was trying to do in *Bodies of Light* was a kind of impressionist technique where the main events were always offstage. You get the thing before and the thing after, but you never get the main thing neatly framed. I hadn't thought of *The Tidal Zone* and *Ghost Wall* as continuous with that, but maybe there is something in those novels too about the

bits round the edges being more interesting than the central drama. In *The Tidal Zone*, what they're dealing with all along is something that didn't happen.

TWR   Right, and at the end of *Ghost Wall*, the worst thing actually doesn't happen.
SM   Because happening isn't really what's interesting to me about fiction. There are occasional complaints about both of those books that nothing happens in them, but I think if you want happening, read the news. If big events are your thing, if you want explosions... read something else.

TWR   One of the things in *The Tidal Zone* that interested me was Adam's realisation that a lot of clichés are true, even if they're not entirely liveable. If what you're trying to do in fiction is present some kind of truth, that seems like a real challenge because of course you don't want to be writing clichés. How do you deal with that in your own writing?
SM   I think they're different kinds of truth. The clichés that Adam's thinking about are the kind you find on fridge magnets. Which are clichés because they're true – most clichés are, that's why they acquire that kind of currency. Adam's just a bit sad and pissed off that in the depths of despair what you actually learn is that the fridge magnets are, broadly speaking, right. That's almost the opposite of the kind of complexities and double negatives that I'm interested in. When I'm teaching, what I'm really hoping to do is bring the students to the point where they seem to be standing between two completely incompatible truths, and then you do a little feint and a dodge at the last minute and that's the point at which you can start writing. So for example, it's true that Wordsworth is appropriating women's voices and repurposing them for his own glamour, but it's also true that Wordsworth is very interested in attending to women's voices. So those things seem to be completely incompatible, but it's that incompatibility, that tension, that makes it interesting. If he's just another bloke who's appropriating female voices, we've got no shortage of those, that's the kind of fridge magnet moment. If he's an elite white male poet who's seriously interested in women's voices... That's a different kind of fridge magnet, maybe, but it's still a one-sentence summary. If both of those things are true, which is what I believe, that's where your interesting

reading is going to start. And similarly, thinking about Coventry Cathedral, if it's true both that to repress the trauma of the bombing and pretend it never happened is wrong, and yet to sit in the ruins and mourn perpetually is also wrong, what do you do? It's wrong to remember and it's wrong to forget. How do you get round that? And how you get round that thing is the angel screen [the glass West Screen of Coventry Cathedral engraved with dancing angels, designed by John Hutton], which is one of the most beautiful and constructive acts of memory I can imagine. I think those angels are Holocaust victims. I'm not an art historian, but given that at the time Hutton was making those drawings the Nuremberg Trials were happening, and all of those images [from the concentration camps] were coming out and all of those conversations were being had, to imagine the apotheosis of angry skeletons... I don't know that that's what he's doing, but for me that's what he's doing. And that seems to be the most honest possible response to those incompatible imperatives to mourn and to remember but not to allow the obliteration of those people to be the obliteration of the future as well. That's how you do it. You don't pretend that one of the things is true. They're both true, and they're not compatible. So you live with the incompatibility and you make something out of it. So I guess that's where I come to the idea of the truth and the clichés: that only one kind of cliché at a time can be true, but when you hold them together there's an energy there, it's like holding magnets together. When you take them apart you don't get that energy; it's when you push them together that you feel the force.

TWR   One thing I noticed reading your novels in a short time frame was... it would be too much to say that they all have optimistic endings, but they all end in a moment of tentative stability, or safety, or hope, and I wondered whether that's deliberate or whether it's a political stance or a formal stance, in terms of how you think a novel should end?
SM   Both. Probably more a political stance. I don't *think* I think that's how novels should end, formally, at least I certainly like novels that don't end in that way. But I think if you're going to leave your reader in a howling wilderness, you need to be damn sure that you mean it, and that there's no other possibility. And there are howling wildernesses, and there are reasons to leave people in them, but I've always been able to see a slightly lighter way to end. I mean, there is *so* much evidence for despair, but despair is also not very useful, and I'm fundamentally pragmatic. I'm not normally an Updike reader, but there's a lovely thing he says: 'Optimism isn't a philosophical position; it's an animal necessity.' I think that's right.

H. R.,
June 2019

KIDS IN THE FIELD
ELVIA WILK

ESSAY

As we cross the border, the smooth, four-lane Mexican highway collapses into a winding, undivided, pockmarked road. Scraggly underbrush takes the place of manicured trees. Swathes of farmland are punctuated by swamps. Cows and goats wallow in the middle of the road and flat-bed trucks laden with bundles of sticks rattle past, pumping gusts of black smoke behind them. No speed limits, no zoning, no side rails. A sun-bleached billboard implores us: *Belize it or not!*

My friend T is in the passenger's seat. Technically, she knows how to drive, but she doesn't want to try here, and I can't blame her. She's German – she learned to drive on the Autobahn, the highway of all highways. Me? I'm fine on these roads. I know what I'm doing. I'm the one who planned this trip. I booked us the flights to Cancun, I rented us the car at the air-port, and I'm in charge of getting us to my parents' house another seven hours south, at the tip of the peninsula that leans off the Belizean main-land into the Caribbean Sea.

In lieu of cops, Belizean roads have what are called 'sleeping police-men', irregular speed bumps at random intervals that appear without warning. It becomes T's job to point out when a bump is on the horizon so I can hit the brakes in time. Sometimes a bump turns out to be a spot where the paving has simply washed away. As we jostle around I start to realise that our Chevy rental may not be cut out for this terrain. I make a lame joke about what would happen if our car broke down. T nods, spits out her nicotine gum, and lights up a duty-free Gauloise.

The road suddenly plunges into thick green jungle and we're both shocked by the overwhelming beauty, the lush wetness and the size of the trees arching overhead. T asks whether the rest of the drive will be like this, and I search my memory for an answer, but find it's blank. My dad told me that I'd taken this route with him many times before, but I can't remember a thing about it. To tell the truth, I'm not even sure we're on the right road. Casually, I ask T to check Google Maps – she bought a roaming package before we left, while I insisted I could get by on my wits – but she can't find a signal.

Now that we're alone on the empty road in a shitty car, I'm not sure which is worse: confess that I have no idea how to get where we're going, or keep pretending that I do. I'm about to suggest that we call someone for directions, but then the air conditioning shorts out and we have to roll down the windows to breathe – and I'm hit in the face with a smell so nostalgic I can barely exhale. Dirt and white rocks mingled with sweat: a smell that reminds me that I know this place. My amnesia is supplanted by déjà vu.

*

I can trace the smell back to the early 1990s, to the place my family usually calls 'the site'. The site is the Mayan ruin called Chau Hiix where my mom led an archaeological excavation for two decades. The smell is the scent of sweat-drenched graduate students and workers picking with axes and tapping with trowels at taped-off squares of rubble that never looked to me anything like a pyramid. The smell of adults working in the dirt was oddly libidinal to me even then, dark and exciting and upsetting: the aroma of things my child-brain didn't understand. In my mind, it is intermingled with other Belize sensations – the stomach-churning taste of crushed malaria tablets and the sweet stench of overripe cashew fruits on the verge of rotting, which is the best time to eat them.

To access the site from the nearest village, Crooked Tree, you have to

cross a lagoon in a boat during rainy season. As a baby and a kid I lived
alternately between the site and in the village with my parents during
their fieldwork stints, spending weeks or months at a time in either place.
My dad is an anthropologist who studied the living people of Belize,
while my mom – as the joke goes – studied the dead. Like most jokes, this
is both true and false. They were actually trying to bridge those kinds of
disciplinary divisions in various ways: by working with the people who
lived in Crooked Tree, by involving the locals in their academic study, by
living together as a family in the field. By stretching the confines of their
professions through what I now recognise as an unusual level of social and
political engagement. But I did not know this at the time. I only knew, or
felt, the part of it that concerned myself: that I was somehow important to
the endeavour. That I was, in an oblique way, wrapped up in its successes
and failures. That I was supposed to like being there, but that I didn't.

Anthropology has a lot of historical baggage to contend with. Both
anthropology and its corollary field, archaeology, were built around an
eighteenth-century concept of an anthropological 'subject': the passive,
fixed, and separate Other located in distant space and time.[1] Even living
subjects were set in the permanent, unchanging, unadulterated past.[2]
The ethnographic framework was a colonial instrument that contributed
theoretically and materially to the European expansionist project – a
process of gathering data about the natives to validate and inform their
'conquest'. On the other hand, my dad tells me, the historical description
of anthropologists as 'unwitting tools of imperialism' is overly simplistic.
'As far back as Malinowski,' he says, 'anthropologists have been providing
medicine and advice, bandaging injuries, acting as mediators in disputes.
A lot of anthropologists were radicalised … and were doing their best in
a horrible colonial situation. Many have always seen themselves as caught
between a colonial power and indigenous people, and often they were the
only people who spoke for the indigenous.'[3] My dad explains the inevitable
breakdown of 'professional' boundaries in practice, of the existence of aid,
activism, and friendship – even where these stories are missing from the
historical record.

Anthropology, like most of the social sciences, finally underwent an
explicit postcolonial turn (crisis) in the 1970s and 80s, a process of reckoning in which the anthropological gaze flipped to regard itself. The struc-
turing dichotomies of home and field, observer and observed, global and
local, colonial handmaiden and colonial subject, Western and Other, all
came into question. Can 'we' study ourselves? Can indigenous anthropologists study 'us'? Is it possible to do away with cultural relativism without

1 Most universities in the United States place archaeology as a subdivi-
sion within anthropology (along with three other subdivisions: physical
anthropology, linguistic anthropology, and cultural anthropology – the
last of which is my dad's field). Although archaeological methodologies
are distinct, for this reason I'll use anthropology as an umbrella term.
2 For some classic reading on how the anthropological Other is situated
in a permanent past and distant time, see Johannes Fabian, *Time and the
Other: How Anthropology Makes Its Object* (New York, NY: Columbia
University Press, 1983).
3 The Polish anthropologist Bronisław Malinowski, sometimes called
the 'father of modern anthropology', advocated for the importance of
living closely among one's ethnographic subjects as a 'participant observer'
in order to understand the world from their perspective. His best known
research is his early 1900s work on gift exchange systems in Melanesia,
a foundation stone for later work on kinship and reciprocity.

also doing away with human rights?[4]

Today, academic papers often begin with complex acrobatics trying to justify a methodology that the author acknowledges is, no matter how self-aware and deconstructionist and postcolonial, a permanent descendent of colonial dispossession. The inclination to perform this contortion is exacerbated by the fact that, with the disintegration of academia as a reliable support structure, many, maybe most, trained anthropologists find themselves working on behalf of today's engines of accumulation via dispossession: corporations, militaries, and governments.[5] Each new generation of politically inclined anthropologists and archaeologists is faced with the question of whether they can reinvent the tools of the trade to ally with the struggles of their living subjects (or living descendants of their subjects) – or whether the tools just might be too dirty to wield at all.

In 2003, my mom wrote a list of 'Principles for Community Engagement for Archaeologists', where she laid out her own position. 'No amount of archaeological data is sufficient to justify claims about the past that compromise the human rights of living people,' she writes.[6] (For instance: discovering that an indigenous group's 'real' genetic ancestors didn't occupy the same territory the group now lives on. This sort of ancestry data can be easily mishandled or misconstrued, in service of governments seeking any 'scientific' premise or excuse to dispossess indigenous groups of their land.) Until recently I had not actually read this document, but I've heard most of its lines repeated like mantras throughout my life. I was very young when she first explained to me that she did not 'discover' Chau Hiix in 1989 – the year I was born – but was invited by the Crooked Tree village council to come and excavate, with the goal of creating sustainable infrastructure. The hope was that visitors would be doubly attracted to the area, to tour the local wildlife reserve and the ancient site. With tourism as a long-term source of income, the village could resist both the sale of artefacts and the destruction of the rainforest – the twin decimation of heritage and ecology to which so much of the world's population has had to resort in order to survive.

In a 2014 article, my mom explains further: 'I described my project as effecting a compromise among the preservation needs of the archaeology (the government mandate), the needs of the village (economic development), and the needs of the wildlife.'[7] She also explains that the relationship between the village and the site is a complicated one, since

4 On the problems of humanism and 'doing good' beyond cultural relativism, see Carlo Caduff, 'Anthropology's ethics: Moral positionalism, cultural relativism, and critical Analysis', *Anthropological Theory* 11 (2011), pp. 465-80; Joel Robbins, 'Beyond the Suffering Subject: Toward an Anthropology of the Good', *JRAI* 19 (2013), pp. 447-462; Didier Fassin, 'Beyond Good and Evil?: Questioning the Anthropological Discomfort with Morals', *Anthropological Theory* 8 (2008), pp. 333-44; Miriam Ticktin, 'Transnational Humanitarianism', *Annual Review of Anthropology* 43 (2014), pp. 273-289.
5 I'm focusing primarily on the United States in this discussion. In 2018, the USA Bureau of Labour Statistics reported that 26.74 per cent of anthropologists work in 'Management, Scientific, and Technical Consulting Services'; over 23.42 per cent in 'Scientific Research and Development'.
6 K. Anne Pyburn, 'Anne Pyburn's Principles of Community Engagement for Archaeologists', 2003. <cademia.edu/5129190/Anne_Pyburns_Principles_of_Community_Engagement_for_Archaeologists>
7 Pyburn, 'Preservation as "Disaster Capitalism": The Downside of Site Rescue and the Complexity of Community Engagement', *Public*

the inhabitants of Crooked Tree, roughly 500 at the time, identify themselves as Creole, or Afro-Amerindian, not direct descendants of the Maya
who lived there over a thousand years ago. (Another thing that drives her
crazy: the common belief that the Maya are 'extinct', when there are more
living Maya now than there ever have been – just another way of keeping
the colonial Other in the perpetual past, and disavowing the rights of
living populations.) We lived in a few places in Belize when I was young,
but the one I remember most is Crooked Tree.

*

My memories from Belize are fragmented, distorted, and disordered.
When I compare them to my parents', they don't usually match up.
I recognise many of these memories as clichés that I can't be entirely sure
an early therapist didn't implant – basic feelings of 'not belonging' and
'abandonment' that seem to unfairly hinge on my mother having been
absent a lot while working. In my late twenties I finally started to try
to string these memories into a story, a real one with places, names, and
dates. I spoke with my parents many times while writing this essay, the
conversations ranging between mock-formal interviews, nostalgic chats,
arguments, and lectures (for the first time I was grateful that a late-night
phone call could turn into an articulate 45-minute explanation of Mayan
land rights). I was continually surprised by how far our narratives diverged
– mine from theirs, and theirs from each other's. At one point my dad
started digging through photo albums to check the dates on Polaroids.

Nearly twenty years have passed since our last family stint in the
field. I don't want to make too much of my amnesia; childhood recollec-
tion is notoriously unstable, invented and reinvented as life goes on.
But the opacity of the memories has begun to bother me, the difficulty
I have in distinguishing them from archetypes that don't quite apply. My
question is not exactly why I can't remember details, but why I've been so
resistant to filling them in. Until recently, I have categorically refused to
contextualise or revise my memories from an adult perspective: to really
think about what Belize is and was, or what my parents were doing there.
I haven't read the dozens of articles and books they've authored on the
subject. I haven't been able to think about the *big picture*. I turn inward.
I can only think about myself.

Most kids think the universe revolves around them, and the rude realisation that parents have their own lives arrives only in retrospect. In this
case, though, I wonder whether my memories have adhered to the sticky
core of personal feelings for so long – where everything that happened
was about me – because in some ways, my parents' intellectual and political project *was* about me. Bringing your kid into the field fundamentally
changes the nature of fieldwork. It also shapes the nature of the kid. The
kid becomes both little anthropologist and native informant; research col-
laborator and research outcome; observer and observed. The kid becomes,
in a word, complicit. And therefore the kid's feelings have to constitute
their own form of ethnographic evidence.

One feeling that emerged over time was resentment. I resented that

Archaeology Vol. 13 Nos 1–3 (2014), pp. 231–2. She explains: 'the village collaborated with the Massachusetts Audubon Society – a New
England conservation organisation – to create the Crooked Tree Wildlife
Sanctuary. As stewards of this sanctuary, the residents can continue to use
their resources as they have for 300 years, but keep outsiders from doing
unsustainable commercial extraction.'

my childhood was also a political project, that my success as a person was tied to the success of the field. What is that resentment evidence of? One thing is simply the dumb fact that growing up between cultures and navigating difference is hard. Of course, anyone in a minority position can tell you that much better than I can. I'm reporting from the position of whiteness and privilege. The only unique aspect of my privileged position is that I *knew* it was my position from the very start, and I felt guilty about it. Putting me in a situation to be acutely aware of my own privilege was exactly what my parents wanted to do. They wanted me to become a person who did not see herself as the default, as the centre of the world. And shouldn't every white kid experience that? On one hand, this project was successful: it worked. On the other hand, what does it mean that my main responses to this awareness were resentment and guilt? That I held the secret selfish belief that the world's inequality was my fault?

At the age I am now, when my friends are starting to have kids, my perspective is shifting. Much of the resentment is giving way to incredulity, awe, and respect. Much of the guilt is giving way to my own political projects. I can finally recognise what my parents did for its effects far beyond our family. I can understand what a brave, ambitious, idealistic endeavour it was. Heading into the jungle with an infant? Mom digging up a pyramid while dad takes care of the baby? Converting centuries-old colonial methodologies into contemporary social justice work? I wonder if I could ever be so ambitious.

*

As we slow to a crawl to pass through a village – smiling, but not stopping for the kids holding sacks of mangoes and coconuts up to the car window – T asks me about the country's demographics. Again, I'm at a loss and ask her to check Wikipedia, but there's still no signal. The only factoid I can recall off the top of my head is that Belize was the longest lasting British colony in the Americas, gaining full independence from colonial rule in 1981.

If my parents were here, they would explain this through anecdotes dating back to the 1970s, when they first started out. My dad was an archaeologist at first, making his first expeditions in the 1970s with an archaeologist named Norman Hammond. I have always known Hammond's name without knowing him, because my parents fell in love while my mom was on a Hammond excavation in 1985. By that time my dad had become exasperated with the field's myopic view on the distant past and switched over to cultural anthropology. He wrote in 1997: 'I felt hypocritical and helpless talking to people about recovering the past, when their children were dying from measles.'[8] In 1985 he was on hiatus from academia and was working for the international development agency USAID, hoping to make governmental policy more effective in protecting the rights of the indigenous. Meanwhile, my mom had committed to trying to change archaeology from within. She wanted to run an excavation on her own terms. My dad wanted to support her. His support was necessary; there weren't a lot of women running excavations at the time.

I tell T a sketchy version of this story, messing up all the dates, and then apologise to her for not being a solid tour guide. Of course, she knows the

8   Richard Wilk, 'How research can go astray and harm the people it was meant to help', preface to the second edition of *Household Ecology: Economic Change and Domestic Life among the Kekchi Maya of Belize* (DeKalb, IL: Northern Illinois University Press, 1997 [1991]), p. 2.

situation. She's my closest friend and, on some level, she realises this isn't strictly a beach holiday. I'm here to try and get a grip on my memories, to place them in context, to try to define my position. It's a pilgrimage of sorts, the kind you make in an effort to attain adulthood.

The pilgrimage is confused further by the fact that we're not returning to the village or the site, the meccas of memory – instead we're heading to my parents' beach house. Ten years ago, they bought a plot of land in a resort development with beachfront properties owned by a friend, and built a two-bedroom home with a wraparound porch. A few weeks out of the year they can be found on the porch with glasses of iced tea, grading dissertations and hosting visiting academics and family. My mom's final fieldwork season at Chau Hiix was in 2007 and my dad does ethnography elsewhere now, but their involvement in local politics and education hasn't slowed. Mom brings undergraduates on field trips and takes them to sites and villages. The two of them work with a Mayan high school, making visits, discussing curricula, sending computers, installing washing machines. Recently they spent a weekend with indigenous leaders who had invited social scientists specialising in Belize to discuss how to work toward a more autonomous and sustainable future.

Another family joke: the anthropologist is never not doing ethnography. My dad sometimes makes this joke when I interrupt his third-person commentary (at a restaurant: observe how that couple is distributing food between them! at the airport: observe how many of these tourists carry pillows!). But it's undeniable that sometimes these two social scientists, my parents, are now *also* sometimes on vacation in Belize. There's no inherent contradiction between the roles of vacationer, academic, expat, local, activist, philanthropist, spouse, and parent – 'helping and studying are not diametrically opposed,' my dad tells me when I press the point – and indeed, showing how these roles can coexist is a political endeavour in itself. All the same, there must be cases where the interests of these roles do not neatly align. When they don't, which comes first?

*

One therapist told me there was a name for my type: the Third Culture Kid. An American sociologist named Ruth Useem coined the term in the 1950s, when she and her husband were living in India with their children. They were surprised to discover that their kids had learned to identify both with their parents' culture (the 'first' or 'home' culture) and the culture where they were being raised (the 'second' culture) – leading to the formation of an idiosyncratic 'third' culture all their own.

Useem's original TCK categories were: Foreign Service Kids, Corporate Brats, Military Brats, and Missionary Kids – that is, children of post war families living in 'exotic' locations abroad, typically within Western enclaves, performing various versions of postcolonial colonialism. The unspoken premises of the original 1950s TCK theory were that both parents were white Westerners venturing into foreign (less white) territory, that cultures can be separated and reduced to monolithic and quantifiable entities, and that kids who live abroad acquire 'cultural experiences' that are impossible to get in a supposedly monocultural home society. In other words, many of the same premises on which anthropology was founded. The premises my parents were trying to dismantle by bringing me into the field.

According to Useem, who went on to survey other families in similar situations, children raised in these environments grow up to exhibit a common set of personality characteristics. Hallmarks include always feeling like an observer; constant meta-questioning of social interactions; difficulty forming attachments and making commitments. General ongoing identity crisis, tempered by an unusual capacity for adaptability. These easily describe my issues, but the category has always felt wrong.

In their 2001 book *Third Culture Kids: The Experience of Growing Up Among Worlds*, sociologists David Pollock and Ruth van Reken picked up and expanded Useem's theories for a wider audience.[9] The book was popular with people who saw their neuroses laid out for them in tables and diagrams, their experiences finally given a taxonomy. But by the 2000s, in light of globalisation and postcolonial study, the colonial psychodrama underpinning this construction had become all too apparent, and Pollock and van Reken received a healthy dose of criticism.

Why was the default TCK white? Why didn't TCKs feel inclined to 'assimilate'? Is there no implicit hierarchy between the first and third cultures? Does 'third culture' not imply 'third world'? If the TCK always has the ability to return to the first – home – culture after living safely abroad, could such experience be universalised at all? Does the term not in fact refer to children made complicit in forms of domination over the third culture? Doesn't the grouping of diplomacy, military, corporation and missionary suggest that they may all have something in common, something like colonial legacy? When so many people are raised in cross-cultural environments, why is TCK a category at all, unless it's based in race, class, and privilege?

In 2009, Pollock and van Reken published a revised edition, in which they attempt to address these questions. In the updated version they try to temper the racial/class specificity of the TCK, not by expanding the category itself, but rather by introducing an umbrella term, Cross-Culture Kid (CCK), which includes the TCK and several new categories. The new categories include the children of domestic or seasonal workers, refugees and international adoptees. That is, those who leave (what remains implicitly categorised as) the 'second' culture for the 'first', likely out of necessity rather than choice. This addition seems to reinforce rather than flatten the cultural hierarchy at play. If the TCK is the temporary expat, the CCK is the precarious migrant. The TCK asserts and preserves dominance through difference, while the CCK is pressured to assimilate into the host culture, to eradicate any difference perceived as threatening, to become invisible, to pass.

Nowhere in the list of categories does one find Children of Anthropologists.

*

Five hours into our drive, T and I have to make a decision about which route to take for the final stretch. Either we turn left on the Coastal Highway and head directly east, towards the sea, or we continue south on the Hummingbird Highway, which swoops east at the last minute. I should know the answer, but I don't. We pull over so T can walk around by the side of the road and search for a signal. The iPhone insists, with certainty, that we'll cut an hour off the trip by opting for the Coastal, so we do.

The further we get down the Google-endorsed road, the less like a road it becomes. Tamped earth gives way to pits of loose gravel, jagged

9 Pollock and van Reken, *Third Culture Kids: The Experience of Growing Up Among Worlds* (London: Intercultural Press, 2001).

and rocky. Then there are the wet, sandy holes, followed by at least a mile of miniature ridges like tiny sand dunes, then more gravel. I'm only going at ten miles an hour, but red dust is flying up from all sides and mosquitoes are splattering into a layer of black guts on the windshield. Assaulted by insects, we roll up the windows despite the heat. We consider turning around; we resolve to forge ahead.

There's no dusk to signal the transition from day into night, and in a matter of minutes we find ourselves in total darkness. Craggy mountains, looming in an undefinable distance, fade into menacing silhouettes. I'm dripping sweat, my hands slipping on the steering wheel, body arched as far forward as possible, shoulders clenched to ears. Jolt after jolt. I can't see more than a few feet ahead. 'Did the tyre just pop?' I shout. T shouts back: 'Are you sure the headlights are on?' She has her nose glued to the screen of her phone. 'Why isn't the blue dot moving?'

Later we will learn that *everyone* knows not to take the Coastal Highway. It hasn't been printed on official maps in ten years. This is not information that anyone thinks to convey any more, because it's common knowledge. Only I – and apparently Google – could be so out of touch. And I was out of touch enough to assume that by now Google would know Belize. Either Google doesn't care enough to update the map, or the landscape somehow resists access.

To be fair, I did ask someone besides Google. Before we left, when T and I were planning our trip, I called my dad to find out if there was anything we should know about the drive down from the border that we wouldn't necessarily find online. He said yes, and then gave me very detailed instructions about where to find his favourite tamale stand by the side of the road. It didn't occur to him that I wouldn't remember the most obvious thing, not to take the bad road. Everyone from Belize knows that.

*

TCK case study one: I'm in first grade at the village elementary school and all the kids are reciting the Lord's Prayer at the start of class. My parents have taught me how to recite the prayer so as not to offend anyone, but they have also told me to quietly replace the word 'god' with 'dog' so as not to unwittingly convert myself with the incantation. Another family joke in retrospect, but I took it seriously at the time. One day, feeling rebellious, I decide to try saying 'god'. No difference.

TCK case study two: it's my birthday, and I'm wearing a ruffly pink dress. I'm surrounded by a circle of village kids playing Red Rover – the game where the chosen person in the middle has to charge at the edge of the circle to break the chain of hands and escape – but for some reason I can't figure out what to do. I'm embarrassed in my fancy dress, which was supposed to make me feel special but instead makes me feel stupid, and I can't understand the instructions everyone is shouting at me. Somehow, I've never learned to speak the local Creole well, even though I picked up rudimentary Spanish easily from a caretaker I had as a baby. I know everyone is just trying to include me, but I also feel like they're making fun of me. My mom notices I'm on the verge of tears and has to bail me out of the circle.

TCK case study three: I'm in the yard of my house, eating a stewed chicken foot given to me by a family friend from the village. Patty, a teen-ager, is pretty and kind and loves to feed me things. I'll eat anything she gives me – it's my way of trying to impress her. My dad cheers every time he hears about a new unusual item I willingly eat.[10]

TCK case study four: unable to heed my mother's admonishments not to bite my fingernails, I've finally gotten the dreaded worms. In the middle of the night I run into my parents' room writhing as I feel them wriggle out into my underwear.

*

T and I arrive at our destination three hours later than planned, rattled and exhausted. The house, true to expectations, has been undone by the tropics: there's gecko shit smeared all over the beds, the rust from the fixtures has settled into a fine dust on the floor, and the screens in the windows have been torn by animals, letting in spiders and who knows what else. The internet and phone connections are patchy.

I take T on a tour in the dim light. The house is painted sea-blue and plastered with Mexican Talavera tiles. From the veranda we can hear the sound of waves, but the ocean, only a few metres away, is hard to see in the dark. Instead of maintaining the white, sandy beach coveted by expats the world over, my parents ask the gardener to leave the forest untouched in front of the house, so you enter the water by walking through dirt and pine needles and then wading through half a metre of seaweed washed up on the shore. *We are no tourists*, the place says. *This is no beach cabana!*

Until now the housing development has been quiet, with only a few single-family homes. But by the coming autumn the resort down the beach will finally be finished, complete with spa, yoga studio, two restaurants, and a poolside bar. My parents have put up a good front, but soon any pretence of their living like locals or fieldworkers will be hard to maintain. From the perspective of a passerby, they will be vacationers in a gated community. Their distaste for the situation is palpable. Increasingly, they debate selling the house. But they don't. It means too much.

*

T and I throw our stuff in the house and get back in the car. I drive us to the nearest restaurant, at a hotel a few miles away. After we order, I attempt to explain Third Culture Kid theory to her. Shovelling in bites of coconut-battered shrimp, I tell her how TCKs are supposed to take on a 'representational role' or 'system identity' on behalf of their parents. They become creepy 'little ambassadors', 'little missionaries' and 'little soldiers' parroting their parents' beliefs. Little zealots, little proselytisers, little salesmen.

The problem, I explain to T, the reason I don't fit, is that the system identity of the Little Anthropologist is to be aware of those system identities: to deconstruct system identities as such. Like the TCK, you're supposed to stay separate – not because you think you're superior, but because you understand your own position of privilege and the impossibility of ever fully becoming Other – and yet, like the CCK, you're supposed to fit in. If the anthropologist parents are good anthropologists, the Little Anthropologist will be a TCK masquerading as a CCK. Or something. T looks sceptical.

10 One of my dad's special areas of studies is food and eating practices, and for a period he researched 'picky eating' on the part of children of middle-class families. See Wilk, 'Power at the Table: Food Fights and Happy Meals', *Cultural Studies ↔ Critical Methodologies* Vol. 10 No. 6 (June 2010).

A new waiter appears at the table to ask if we want refills on our Piña Coladas. I do a double-take – I recognise him, he recognises me. Ten years ago, when my parents were building their house, we stayed at this hotel for a week, and I made friends with him. He flirted with me constantly in Spanish; my Spanish was fluent back then. (By now, I've spent years in Berlin trying to learn German, and my other languages are all rusty.) As a teenager, I struggled not to seem like a rich gringa who wouldn't give him the time of day, while also not giving him the idea that I was interested. The Little Anthropologist should treat everyone like an equal human but should not breach the boundaries of the field. I wondered whether my parents would be angrier if I were rude to him or if I hooked up with him.

I stand up to hug him, awkwardly, and we make small talk. He asks where I've been all this time. I try to explain. To college in New York. To be an art critic in Berlin. He asks what those places are like. I stutter, as if in the last decade I've completely forgotten not only Spanish but also how to find common ground with someone who doesn't share my cultural vocabulary. We're both too old for pretend flirtation now, grown-ups too aware of our difference. The extent of my privilege has only become magnified in the intervening time. I feel the age-old shame. He stayed here. I left when I wanted, and didn't come back.

*

My parents were by no means the first anthropologists to bring a kid into the field. A book of essays by other field-parents was published in 1987. Joan Cassell, the editor of *Children in the Field: Anthropological Experiences*, explains in her introduction that the 1980s saw an uptick in researchers bringing their families along, in part due to women's changing professional roles. In her essay for the collection, anthropologist Christine Hugh-Jones agrees, with some irony: 'If we have decided that it is a good thing that women are involved in fieldwork, a sleight of thought persuades us that it is virtuous and liberated to take our children along as well.'[11]

Hugh-Jones suggests that, especially for women, choosing to bring the kids was partly about making a point: family and job are not mutually exclusive, I can have it all, etc. Of course, no one can have it all, and it's not like heteronormativity or patriarchy disintegrate upon relocation. Doubling down often meant doubling up, and women researchers probably ended up shouldering the burden of care while working, instead of having spouses or others step in.

The fact that gendered caregiving is itself a social construct often becomes unavoidably obvious in the field. In a paper from 2004, my mom describes trying to hire a babysitter for me while living in a Creole village. The babysitter she found couldn't seem to keep an eye on me, and it took a long time for her to figure out why the woman appeared so neglectful. Eventually she noticed that single adults don't often mind children in Creole culture; instead children watch each other, in conglomerations beyond family units, and there's no assumption that childcare is the responsibility of an adult or biological parent, much less a female one.[12]

For her part, my mom took me along to the site when she could and otherwise handed me over to my dad to stay in the village. We talked a

11 *Children in the Field: Anthropological Experiences*, ed. Joan Cassell
(Philadelphia: Temple University Press, 1987).
12 Pyburn, Introduction to *Ungendering Civilization: Reinterpreting the Archaeological Record* (New York, NY: Routledge, 2004).

lot about this fact. They wanted me to feel proud that my dad was often the only father among mothers in line to pick me up from school, that my mom was brave enough to head into the jungle for weeks at a time without phone connection, that I had short hair and was not afraid of bugs. (This is another myth. I hate bugs.) I felt my mom's desire to make these points acutely. Most of the time, I wasn't sure who she was making them to. Herself? Her colleagues? My dad? Me? It would have been easier if leaving me behind didn't make both of us so sad. At the same time as she knew her work was the right thing to do, she couldn't get out from under the age-old female guilt. More to the point, she missed me.

The attitudes of the parents in Cassell's book vary from self-satisfied and oblivious to tortured and guilt-ridden. Some claim that the experience of having their kids around was domestic bliss; some relay stories of culture clash as situational comedy; others worry they've scarred their kids – physically, as in testing positive for tuberculosis, or in less tangible ways, as in becoming withdrawn and depressed. One parent says she was eager for the opportunity to 'immunise' her children 'against complacency'. In turn, having your kid in the field gives you a whole new subject to study. Family dynamics became part and parcel of the research. One woman in Cassell's book reports that, while working in Northeast Brazil, she asked her children to write daily journal entries and interviewed them regularly. I remember my dad questioning me in a way that I understood to be more than just parental curiosity. The questions made me feel special and smart, but also like I was under constant observation.

Almost everyone in Cassell's book seems to agree that bringing their kids was helpful for their work. There's nothing like a toddler to highlight cultural common ground. In one essay, Renate Fernandez, a full-time mom who accompanied her anthropologist husband to Asturias with their two children, observes that children 'accelerate the ongoing social dynamics in the field community', and that 'a child's encounter in the field, witnessed by the parent, may create an emotional charge powerful enough to redirect the investigation'. Experiences of parenthood may not be universal, but parenthood forges social relationships that wouldn't exist otherwise. My parents describe toting baby-me around during interviews and chats, and say that people tended to be more open when I was around. In his early fieldwork, my dad says, people thought it was strange that he *didn't* have children. Most Belizeans he talked to already had families by their mid-twenties.

One essay from *Children in the Field* is a tragedy. The author, in this case a non-anthropologist, went with her husband to rural Nepal with their three kids in tow. Early in the trip, their youngest son fell sick with an undefined illness and suddenly died. The author writes of her attitude upon arrival: 'We knew we would have to share this way of life to begin to understand it. Yet, to be honest, we knew we would not be sharing *it* all the way. We would not have to face bedbugs without DDT. We would be very sorry if the rains did not come to the cornfields, but we would not go hungry. We also knew that two years was not a lifetime. Still, we never dreamed our sharing would be so complete.' The situation embodies one of the basic paradoxes upon which anthropology is built: how to become an insider to report back as an outsider; how to get an authentic experience without assuming too much authentic risk. Her story starkly outlines both her family privilege and its limits.

My parents struggled with this, too. How to protect me from malaria, but not give daily tablets to all the village kids? How to send me to the village school while keeping me on the college track? How to let me wander in the jungle with the others but make sure I didn't step on snakes? Any theoretical conundrum becomes unavoidably practical when you're parenting someone. The needs of the kid direct where you look, who you talk to, change your priorities.

Before leaving for a month of fieldwork when I was 3 or 4 (depending on who's telling the story), my mom, to her credit, asked me if I wanted to come along again. She wanted to know how I felt, because she knew my feelings mattered. I told her I did not want to go. I explained that 'there's no ice cream in Belize' and I asked to stay with my grandparents in suburban Texas instead. My grandparents' house was air conditioned, they had ice cream, and they gave me all their attention. I was allowed to stay for the whole month. I loved it.

*

In the morning I walk down the beach to the neighbours' place, to ask if their housekeeper might help me and T get my parents' house in order. The neighbours are expats who run a restaurant in the tourist town a few miles away. As I approach, their 9-year-old daughter rushes out of the screen door to meet me. She tells me all about her dog, a big Labrador who's chewing something in the bushes, and then she announces without prompting that this isn't her real home; her real home is California. She says proudly, pointing to her own arm, 'I live in Belize, but I'm not Belizean – see, I'm white!'

I squint down at her and try to see myself at her age. Blonde hair braided in an approximation of corn rows, scalp burned at each parting. Barefoot, seashell anklet. Yep, there I am. But I'd never have said that. I knew I was white, and that I was a minority in Crooked Tree, but I did not think this negated my being Belizean. One story that gets told and retold is my confusion upon returning to the USA after living in Belize as a toddler: I wasn't used to being surrounded by white people, and I panicked in the airport to see so many at once.

No, this kid I'm looking at is a true TCK. Her system identity is Little Restauranteur, and she seems fine with it. As far as I can tell, she isn't trying to figure out which is her first culture, or feeling embarrassed about her nice house with running water. She feels like the majority, even when she's in the minority. She isn't trying to decide whether her maid is her friend or her employee. She'll go back to California and act the same.

When my parents weren't doing fieldwork they were on tenure tracks at a university in Indiana. Just as foreigners usually describe Belize in relief – not as touristy as Mexico; not as dangerous as Guatemala – people sometimes describe Indiana: not as Republican as Kentucky; not as diverse as Michigan. At my not-very-diverse Montessori elementary school, I was a novelty just for having been on an aeroplane. Word got out on the playground that I spoke another language, and the kids wanted me to perform.

Then they got suspicious. Why did I get to skip school to go somewhere else? Did I think I was so smart? How rich was I? Did I think I was better than them? I fell for it, and I bragged, wanting to feel special, showing off what I knew. In Belize, where I was unavoidably more academically advanced than the other first-graders, who had not received a Montessori education, I definitely did not brag. I tried very hard not to show off.

*

T and I fail to reach the Jaguar Reserve as planned. We don't even get close. We take the wrong turn yet again, and, unable to reverse on a narrow, rocky road flanked by jungle, we get our Chevy wedged in a chasm on a dirt road on a mountainside. It's idiotic, and it's the last straw. When we finally make it back home – having been towed out by the son of a family friend – I finally give up: no more self-guided adventures. No more pretending I know where to turn. For the next week and a half, I decide to descend, or rise, to the level of tourist.

Yelp tells us where to find a yoga studio and a massage place in town. We make dinner reservations at the neighbours' restaurant. We spend a day at the resort down the beach, which is owned by the Coppola family, and burn ourselves in the sun, reading novels and drinking from coconuts served to us by people who I don't check to see if I recognise. We have long conversations and take long naps. We watch reruns of reality TV in the evenings. Shirking my system identity, it turns out, is fun.

As an experiment, one night I take us to a restaurant in a little house on stilts in the Garifuna (Afro-Amerindian) village nearby. My dad takes me to this place every time I visit, and he always takes a moment before we order to demonstrate his familiarity with the menu – as I've said, one of his anthropological specialities is food. Sometimes he asks the server where he or she is from and what his or her family name is. The server is usually obliging, acting pleasantly surprised if my dad knows an aunt or grandfather. It's not unlikely that he does; he's been working here for forty years and the country is tiny, but I'm embarrassed either way.

This time, I tell T, I want to try eating at this restaurant, where tourists never go, without acting like a tourist *or* a little anthropologist. In other words: I want to try to split the difference. This proves awkward because I want to order the speciality, stewed pig tail. The waitress frowns and stares me down. It's OK, I say, I know what it tastes like. Pig tail is actually one of my favourite dishes. She wants to know: Really? When have I eaten pig tail? I shrug. I should have known this would require some explanation.

It dawns on me that the question of what I want to eat has never really been a question about what I *want* to eat. It's been a demonstration, a performance. But of what, and to whom? And what do I really want? What I want, I think, is not to perform at all.

*

On our second-to-last day I sign us up for a snorkelling tour of a nearby reef. Our companions on the boat trip are a South African couple on honeymoon and a group of four retirees from Texas. Our Belizean tour guide is friendly but bored, chatting on his phone while he steers us out to the reef, where twenty boats will converge and unload their tourists to eat barbecue on a small sand dune, then paddle around in the shallow water, ogling the diminishing species of fish. The sunscreen that we've rubbed on with fervour during the ride out will end up as a thin, oily scrim on the surface of the water that washes up on the sand.

I successfully resist the urge to make small talk with the guide at any point, signalling to him that I'm not one of *them*, the honeymooners and the retirees. I pretend I don't know the names of the fish he points to in the water; I pretend to be scared of the nurse sharks. At the same time, T and I desperately try to separate ourselves from our tourist companions, who are insufferable. While they chatter about the local bars, she and I exchange glances that say *we've taken this tourism thing one step too far.*

On the ride back to the mainland, Fran, a former nurse from Dallas, passes around a bottle of Belizean rum she's brought to share. When I accept a sip, she starts to chat at me. She describes her travels with her friends; they've been all over Europe and they especially loved Germany. I lie and tell her that I'm German, like T, and she seems convinced.

'Isn't the ocean here fabulous?' she shouts at me above the sound of the boat's engine. 'This is our first time in South America!' With one hand she's clasping her purple visor on her head to keep it from flying off in the wind and with the other she's smearing sunscreen on her upper lip.

I look out to the horizon. The water is a brilliant green, with tangled patches of seaweed rising to the surface. I can smell the gasoline of the boat's engine, which is leaking behind us. The sun is raw and ferocious in a cloudless sky.

I don't tell Fran that the Caribbean isn't an ocean. I don't tell her that we aren't in South America. I don't tell her that she has sunscreen in her moustache. What would I be trying to show, and to whom? Today is not the day, and she is not my audience. I take a gulp of warm rum, nod at her and say, 'It's my first time too. Isn't it so authentic?'

ZHANG ENLI

A tablecloth, floating disembodied; an empty bucket cast in shadow; a hollow bathtub, concentric circles of white interrupted only by the dark abyss of the plughole. Zhang Enli's elegant paintings from the mid-2000s examine everyday domestic objects, depicted with a quiet beauty and satisfying attention to geometric detail. Born in 1965 in Jilin Province, China, Enli's early works considered urban life in Shanghai, from its public toilets to its meat markets. He has more recently turned outwards to natural forms, evoking the texture and subtle movements of skies, gardens, trees and leaves; as with Samara Scott, also featured in this issue, Monet's studies of Giverny have offered a reference point. Enli's newest paintings, recently debuted at Hauser & Wirth Zürich and shown here in a second series, move away from concrete objects to explore abstraction through free, dynamic spools of colour. Though their shapes and patterns conjure nature, their titles – *The Single Mother*, *A Young Man*, *The Boss* – situate the works within figurative as well as abstract tradition. Enli is known for his 'space paintings': three-dimensional installations painted directly on to walls, floors and ceilings, engulfing the viewer in colour. His work is always immersive, rooted in place and physical reality, yet imbued with an imaginative energy that appeals to all the senses.

PLATES

I

III

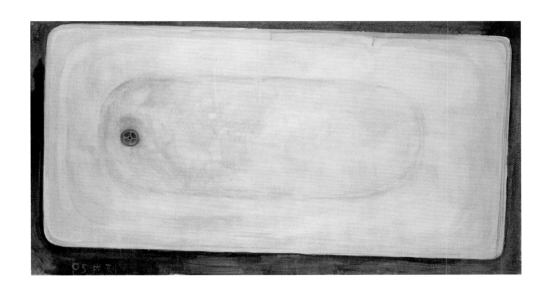

VII

II

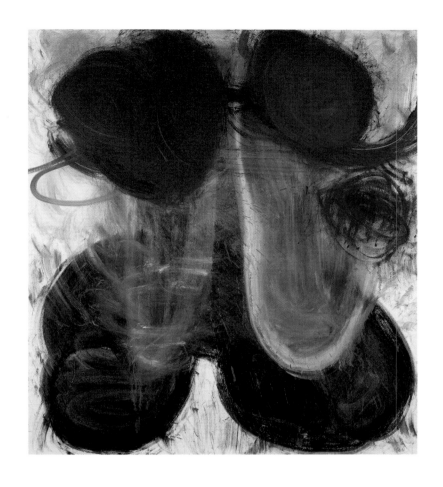

VIII

IX

X

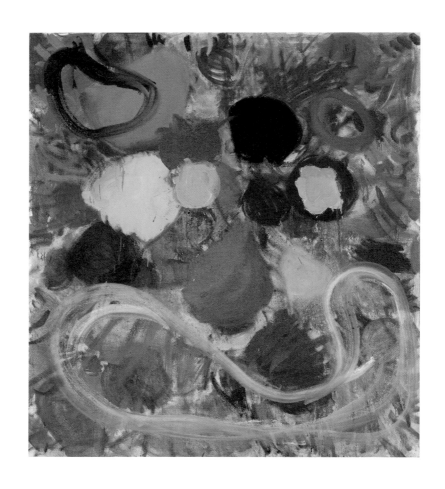

XI

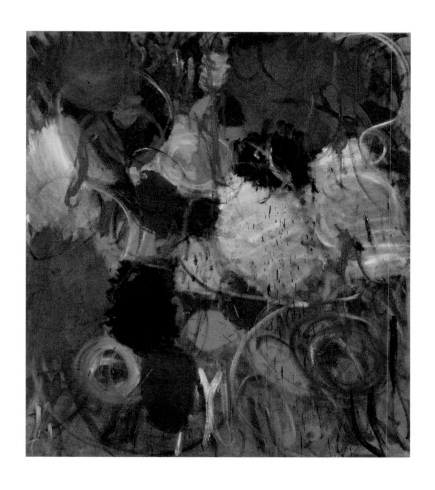

XII

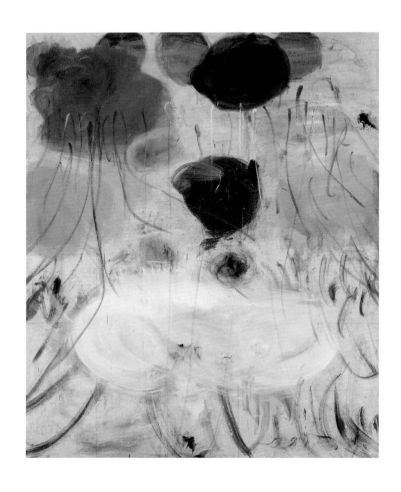

XIII

FRIED EGG

SABINA URRACA
tr. THOMAS BUNSTEAD

The woman who looks like Sara is crying.

She and I are at the top of the valley trying to thumb a lift, standing by the side of the road that descends from the snow line into town. We need matches, candles and bread, and the town is the closest place to get them.

Really it's me who needs these things. The candles and the matches in particular. Boars have been digging up the earth around the house and they've damaged the cables that bring electricity from the adjacent property's supply. The past two evenings, the house has been plunged into darkness from sunset to sunrise.

The woman who looks like Sara is just coming with me. There's nothing she needs to buy. And her tears are because of the state of her life: she's broke and has nowhere to live, and now, for reasons I haven't ascertained, things have come to a head. She lives her life sleeping on people's couches, waiting for something to come along, some instantaneous cure for all of life's ills. The kind of character you see quite a lot of in the valley. They drift in for a while, they drift out.

As a 12-year-old, on trips to the beach with my parents, I would let them walk on ahead and once they were out of sight, in a sudden romantic outburst, take a stick and write in the sand: 'Something, somebody.'

I was calling on events and people, or at least an event or a person, to magic me out of that listless pre-teen time, to kick-start real life on my behalf.

This woman must be in her early forties, but that's precisely what she is doing: gazing up at the sky, running her fingers over a necklace of Buddhist worry-beads, crying endless tears. Her skin is slightly sunburned and she has grey-flecked hair: like Sara the last time. She has never been pretty because she's never seen herself as pretty and because no one's ever told her she's pretty. I know nothing about her, just that at this particular moment in time I am her only hope. I have access to the internet, I have a mobile phone, and these make me her means of contacting the person whose number is written on the crumpled slip of paper she keeps on taking out of her pocket, continually checking it's still there. Each time, I feel certain a gust of wind is going to pluck it from her hands, and with it her last hope in all the world.

Flurries of wind accompany the passing of cars, but the piece of paper does not fly away. Neither does anyone stop. I stand, legs braced, brow furrowed and thumb pointing in the direction of town. She, sitting on her rock, still crying, holds out a thumb as well. The more she cries, the redder her face becomes. I pat her on the back, but avoid the embrace she keeps trying to gather me into. I make her drop her thumb, folding her arm down as though she were a doll; no one's going to stop if she carries on like this. And my priority, the only important thing for me right now, is buying bread, candles and matches. Candles and matches in particular.

I can't do another night of complete darkness, I wrote to a friend on Facebook.
I'm terrified something I say is going to manifest... The house is haunted.
as in? haunted how?

A haunted house is somewhere events have taken place which the current inhabitants find impossible to contemplate. In my case, the deaths of a young boy and a young girl at some point in the past, about which I was told soon after renting the place.

Falling asleep afraid is new to me. For any terrifying situation in my life, there has always been somewhere to run, someone to turn to, a light to turn on. No such thing in my tumbledown farmhouse. Run outside and you're immediately in deepest forest.

I sense them when I'm on the cusp of sleep, and I see them – playing on the carpet – in my dreams. Sometimes she's alone, although a knock on the door will always follow and then I know he's come as well: he wants to join in. At this point I need to be able to open my eyes and see straight away that there aren't in fact dead children in the room. Hence the matches and candles. Candlelight can add to the ghostliness of a place, but I'd still rather have these ghosts look straight back at me than constantly have to listen to their little feet running off into the darkness.

None of the cars stop. The woman who looks like Sara is still crying. I kneel beside her to try to calm her down.

And then she gets her consoling embrace. She seizes me with a single hand and pulls me close. With my head on her shoulder, I look down and see her other hand clutching the piece of paper at her side. I feel her large, sagging breasts: no bra. She's wearing a very thin cotton blouse, semi-sheer, and her nipples brush a little way beneath my own breasts. Like Sara's, the last time.

Sara and Joan had a name for me. They used to call me 'Fried Egg'. And the way they said it was always slightly sneering, as though I were a bald Barbie doll of which they were secretly very fond.

But they treated me well. They let me do whatever I wanted.

'Hey, Fried Egg, don't worry about finishing your soup. Why don't you go and have a run-around in the orchard?'

Or:

'What are you up to in there, Fried Egg, all quiet, all alone? We thought you'd died.'

That kind of thing would make me cry.

Joan was sometimes hard on me, always seeming to want to test me in some way. He would put his foot down in the Land Rover and keep on accelerating, faster and faster, until I couldn't stand it, and then tell me off for crying or shutting my eyes. He made me try Tabasco sauce. He had voted against me being born, and the fact I had been born meant I then had to earn the right to exist.

Sara, on the other hand, was sweet with me, caring in the extreme.

There were games she and I played. Like the 'Welcome Home' game. I would leave the house, mini suitcase packed and a red rain hat on my head: off on some long journey. Then, after a short time doing nothing outside, I'd go back and knock on the front door. Sara would throw it open, drop to her haunches and fling her arms out wide, crying tears of joy. I would collapse into her: what a terrible journey I'd had, how awfully I'd missed her.

We could repeat this same scene endlessly over the course of an afternoon.

Sometimes my journey through the garden would last less than a minute. I would go out, put the hat on, turn around and knock on the door again.

At the climax of one of these homecomings, with the outpouring of hugs and triumphal cries at its height, the door swung open to reveal Sara red-faced, dispensing a kind of furious joyfulness. Arms outstretched, her fingers straining, and her eyeballs wavering with the overwhelming energy of this return, something in her expression was too much for my young self. I stepped back – I couldn't help it – and ran off to hide in the towel closet.

Chickens were kept at Casa Grande. A coop made of old doors and chicken-wire, and speckled hens leaving their eggs here and there on the straw. You had to be careful when you went in not to step on the eggs.

'Off you go now, Fried Egg. Time to get the eggs for breakfast.'

I nodded sleepily from the bed as Sara opened the windows: my signal to get up. She would rub my tummy and do little raspberries, making me giggle. I liked being treated like a baby. I liked it, but she loved it. She once said to me:

'The littler, the better.'

I started taking longer to wake, moving now a single finger, now a toe, coming round very gradually, feigning immense surprise at the fact of the world. There were days when I played at not having learned to speak. Upon getting out of bed I would be mute, and over the course of the day re-learn all the words I knew. I sat at breakfast making baby noises, pointing at the things I wanted. Then it would be time to get the eggs, and sometimes I would deliberately fumble one, letting it drop from my clumsy infant hands, just to watch it crack on the ground. By midday I knew my name, and Sara's, as well as 'water', 'wee-wee' and 'bread'. I became a sponge for the second half of the day, my uptake accelerating, and when Joan came home from work I would be chattering away once more, like a very precocious child who knew everything and wanted to make sure everyone knew it. If it had been Joan looking after me, such games would never have been allowed. And so each evening, by the time he got home, I had to revert to my usual wise-little-dwarf self again.

Only before going to sleep would I cry a little, unsettled at the prospect of the departure into unconsciousness.

It seems to me that my fear of sleep was due to the fact that, at five years of age, I was still so close to nonbeing: five years earlier I did not exist in the world. That was little different to being dead, a state intermediate between life and not-life. So recently had I been acquainted with what it was to not be alive, that there was now something, an enzyme, a hormone, prompting me to grab on to this new life, to scream at the night not to take me away. Sleep was the closest

I ever came to the non-existence that continued to pulse in my small, soft brain.

Sometimes, I'd be deep asleep and wake suddenly, frightened by something. Images of non-life came to me, of the dark pulse that precedes the formation of the zygote, when the sperm forces its way into the ovary like a hyperactive worm. And they kept on coming, until sleep overwhelmed me once more.

My mother told me about these sudden wakings later on. And I then thought that if I'd made a concerted effort at the time to travel back into the darkness previous to life, I would eventually have arrived at a pinprick of light, voices. A dimly lit room, eight people sitting around a messy table, and six of them voting for me not to be born. There were options: go and see a woman in a nearby village, or go over the border to France to have it done more expensively, but more safely.

Of the six opposed to my birth, Joan was the most vociferous. Sara sat at his side, nodding gravely.

But life in that commune unfolded at the same slow pace at which the peaches ripened and fell from the trees in the orchard before rotting on the ground. A dilatoriness around decision-making that gave me time to take shape: my hands, my eyes, my legs, my mouth. There were no gentle hands to support my mother's smooth, burgeoning belly, the shining hot air balloon that would eventually set me down upon the earth.

And like hot air balloonists, my parents left the commune in search of a safe nest in which to land the white sphere of flesh, then to incubate it.

If I were to go on looking back, I would see the Land Rover departing Casa Grande, jolting around on the rutted earthen track. Joan is the grudging driver, and my parents are sitting in the back.

Nobody came out to wave them off because there had been heavy rain the previous night and they were all trying to save whatever they could from the flooded orchard. Hands feeling around for roots in the muddy water, feet sunk deep in the squelching earth, while the sound of the Land Rover engine grew faint in the distance. The soft, aqueous creature that was me squirmed at each bump in the road. My mother held her aching belly. Are these early bumps and jolts the reason my eyes wander in the moments before I go to sleep – as my friend Olivia once laughingly pointed out they do?

Dropping my parents at the train station, Joan did not even get out to kiss them goodbye. He sat in the driver's seat, ashen-faced, eyes fixed on the windscreen ahead. Unbeknownst to him, within a matter of months the other couples in the commune would begin leaving as well, all eventually going back to the city. Some had changed their names on arrival at Casa Grande, calling themselves after meteorological phenomena, Indian gods, accidents of geography. In the years after their return to civil society, they gradually reassumed their former names. This was followed by a general surrender to the idea of bringing children into our degraded, overburdened world, one to which all had solemnly sworn never to add a single soul. Everybody left Casa Grande except

Sara and Joan. Everybody except Sara and Joan went on to have children.

In the seven years of the Casa Grande commune, Sara became pregnant three times. She spoke of the abortions as purifying experiences. After the last one, as Sara left the clinic, a female nurse smoking on the pavement made some remark. She said it in French, and under her breath, but to Sara it sounded very clearly like a curse, a great accumulation of scorn condensed into a few short words. She turned to face the woman. But the nurse was looking off in the other direction, exhaling a plume of smoke at an oblique angle. That nurse became a frequently referenced figure in the commune, a clear example of prevailing double standards around abortions. When in reality – in their view of reality – the criminals were everyone else, all those people bringing new lives into this 'toxic world'.

I remember seeing a flyer in a drawer in Joan's studio that showed a picture of a woman and her newborn baby. Behind them, a planet earth crowded with small yellow figures – so crowded that some of them were falling off into space. It said in yellow lettering:

WHY? WHAT FOR?

And beneath that:

FIRST SPANISH ANTI-NATAL CONFERENCE
SESSIONS RUN BY: JOAN MASCARELL

Every now and then, when it was possible for me to slip into the studio, I went and took out this flyer, and I would spend the ensuing hour feeling troubled and upset, without knowing precisely why.

Joan would swing me around sometimes, but quite roughly, and I would be overcome with the sensation that I was about to fly off into space.

Perhaps it was my fragility, the ease with which I could crack and break – 'I can't drink Fanta, Sara, the bubbles hurt my mouth' – perhaps because for them I would always be the unformed chick that would never reach term, but whatever the reason, 'Fried Egg' stopped being a joke and for all intents and purposes became my real name.

A long time after all of this, in the midst of a disastrous one night stand, hunting down an elusive orgasm, I asked the guy I was in bed with to stop pulling my hair and call me 'Fried Egg' instead.

It wasn't perversion, it was just so cold in that room, and I had felt the wrench of a former love. He laughed at my request and went on with what he had been doing. When it was over, he let out a silent fart that stank out the room. We never saw each other again but after the 11/M attacks I got a text message from him: 'Tell me you're OK,' it read. 'Tell me you weren't on those trains.'

Any time we came across stray or injured animals, Sara always took it upon herself to gather up the mangiest, most unfortunate-looking one and bring it home. The hens she bought had next to no feathers and terrified eyes. One of the men in the commune once came across some raven chicks fallen from their nest. Sara had no hesitation in pointing at the one with the big bald patch on its head. When we got it home, on closer inspection we found that it was infested with tiny lice. Joan said to put it in the bin. Not in the garden, where a rat or snake would eat it and it would pass back into the natural cycle, but the bin. This was Joan Mark 2. He had gone on to take a job in marketing and went around with a ponytail and linen suit, up-to-date with the latest in nanotechnology, his withering humour always blacker than black.

Only Sara had stayed on in the world they previously shared, and only at night would her former companion return, coming back to massage her feet with essential oils, he who had been the one to hug and rock her lovingly on the night the raven chick finally died.

On the summer afternoon when they came to pick me up from the airport, Sara was expecting to find a self-centred, wilful little girl. Since I'd been raised in the city, they had attributed to me all the ills of the capitalist child. They were taking me in for a period of three months as a favour to my parents, who were going through a difficult patch. In spite of the bitter send-off, and cross words in the past, Sara and my mother had never stopped calling or writing. A painful but unbreakable bond existed between them. That was why she convinced Joan to let me stay, and what brought them to the arrivals hall that day, nervous, fearful even, about this new addition.

But instead of the insufferable brat they had imagined, an animal arrived of the kind that Sara loved best.

She would give me baths. She cooed over my soapy body, the miniature fingernails, the round tummy, my shoulder blades, which she used to call my 'little wings'. When, to her horror, she spotted lice in my fine hair, she doused my head with vinegar and wrapped it in a towel. She blended up garlic and echinacea and gave it to me as a drink. 'It's a milkshake, honey, and you'll grow big and strong if you drink it all up.'

Throughout the process of picking out and killing the lice, Sara's hands trembled and her face had the blanched pallor of someone about to lose a loved one.

And after the lice episode, she took me out to the garden to meet the children for the first time.

There was a boy I had a crush on as a teenager, a brilliant and sparky peer at my school, and he introduced me to the ethno-folk groups that, little did I know, ruled the airwaves in the 1990s: El Bosco, Los Indios Americanos. I remember the intense, gleeful look in his eyes as he said to me, litre bottle of beer in hand: 'We never knew, but they've helped us to see: there's a spirit we're supposed to tend to. All we've ever known of spirituality is Santa Claus and reindeers!'

I, though, had found this out long before, one weekend when Joan was away on a work trip and Sara took me to the bottom of the garden to introduce me to the children. They were three large stones. They had not even been fashioned into human forms, which was what I had expected. Just three lumpy grey blocks. I gave each of them a kiss, as instructed by Sara.

Then Sara made a small bonfire, and I burned three of my toys on it. She told me to choose really nice ones, because I had so many, and the children had none. I did as I was told, suddenly overcome by a kind of zeal I had never known in myself: I watched as the plastic face on my favourite doll melted and eventually disappeared in the flames, giving off a plume of thick black smoke.

It was then that Sara worshipped me for the first time, on the round table in the living room. The table was small and red, with small motifs of animals and intertwined plants climbing up the legs. Sara lit candles as I lay naked on the table: my round 5-year-old tummy, my big cheeks, my bob. I remember being entranced by the various moving shadows cast by my fingers across my body. She sat on the armchair and watched me, her head and neck emerging from a large shawl that covered her entire body, as far down as her muddy sandals.

The phone rang, and it went on ringing. The only movement Sara made was to lean forward and kiss my small feet.

I was exhausted from the evening's emotions, and curled up there and then on the table to sleep. I called out, saying I was cold. The smell of burned plastic hung on the air. Sara gathered me up in her shawl and began to rock me. Half asleep, I felt her take out one of her large breasts and guide the nipple into my mouth. And as I began to fall asleep, before slipping away completely, I felt a lukewarm substance fill my mouth.

The following day I felt an unusual fortitude course through me. I wasn't afraid of fire any more, and I decided to make a French omelette on my own. I went to crack the egg but the moment I did so Sara, standing beside me in the kitchen, whipped it out of my hands. But I saw it nonetheless: the watery albumen containing, suspended, the beginnings of legs, beak and eyes. A semi-formed chick.

If I ever did anything to get in Sara's bad books, a wall of silence would descend between us. She would say nothing for the entirety of the day, just go on working in the garden, hanging out the washing, getting supper ready for Joan's return, or putting the leftovers in a container should he not arrive before she went to bed. If the phone rang, she would pretend not to hear it. I was the only other person there. Even when we heard the growl of the Land Rover coming up the hill, and Joan appeared in his sweat-soaked linen suit, all he would get was a detached kiss on the cheek, before Sara returned to whatever she had been doing, as if still alone.

I only once saw them unite over a cause that wasn't emptying the compost or agreeing that a daily shower was overkill (for the fact that it broke down the epidermal energy). It was a Sunday and I had spent the morning playing in the orchard, making swimming pools for the ants. I felt incomparably happy playing on my own at Casa Grande, and it was only then that it became apparent how exhausting it was to spend such long periods alone with Sara. But a few hours of solitude was enough, I would be ready to return to her side, primed and anxious to please. I looked down at the shape my fist had left in the soil and, feeling a stab of nostalgia for Sara, prepared myself for a real game of 'Welcome Home'.

I found the rain hat and the suitcase and walked back to the house. I knocked on the door and waited, but no one called out to tell me to go in. Confused, I pushed open the door. The house seemed very quiet. Joan's trainers, covered in mud, had been kicked off in the hallway.

I tiptoed into the kitchen. Lunch preparations had been curtailed midway through: a pan full of water stood on the gas hob, which was off, and on the table were a few partially chopped carrots and a half-drunk cup of coffee. Sara's grey woollen cardigan hung on the back of a chair, the sleeve rippling in the through-draught from the open window. I brought my face close to the wool and took in the smell of her; a little of her body warmth remained in the fabric too. My thought as I went through into the bedroom was that, if they weren't there, it meant something had come and lifted them away from planet Earth, and they would now be off floating in outer space. But there they were: sprawled side by side on the bed, motionless, eyes closed. I stood in the doorway at a loss. I said their names, quietly, then a little louder. I approached slowly and, heart pounding, laid my hand on Sara's forehead.

'Sara, let's go and eat now,' I whispered.

Her face looked peaceful. I began hugging her and saying her name, louder and louder. I climbed on top of her, tears pouring down my face. Joan was lying close beside her, and I nudged him with my foot. I thought I saw his face move, but when I said his name he lay completely still.

I gave up shaking their bodies, and curled up between them instead. They did not feel warm in the normal way, but neither were they stone cold. Then it occurred to me that maybe they weren't dead yet, maybe I had arrived in time to call the doctor. I jumped down from the bed and ran into the living room. When I picked up the phone, its sound alone broke the heavy silence in the house, and I was so taken aback that I dropped the handset. It fell to the floor with a clatter and, with that, laughter exploded from Sara and Joan's room. Still laughing, Sara came running in, swept me up and lay down on the floor with me in her arms.

'Don't ever change, my baby, my little Fried Egg.'

The woman who looks like Sara gives me a triumphant smile. Her situation is sufficiently dire that someone offering us a lift seems like huge headway, a giant leap towards a different life.

The German couple giving us the lift do not speak Spanish, and neither of us speaks German, and in the silence of the car she smiles across at me and winks continually. She pumps her fists covertly in the gap between the front seats, as if to say: *We did it, we did it.*

She reaches out and puts her arm around my shoulder. Her breast bulges into me, bumping repeatedly against my arm.

They let us out at the entrance to the town. My phone has signal now, so I hand it over for her to make her call. She walks a little way off with it pressed to her ear, but comes straight back, handing it to me with a sheepish look. It looks like I'm stuck with her until her friend decides to pick up.

A sign on the roadside announces that it's fiesta in the town. The fiesta of the Christ of Órgiva. We hear a banger go off somewhere, and the strains of a brass band starting up.

She is beaming. She takes my arm and does a little dance, a dance of sisterhood, as though the two of us were buddies from a dance class, or something of the kind: off to the fiesta, off to see if we can bag us a man. In spite of her obvious tribulations, it strikes me that this absurd woman's chances of finding happiness actually seem less remote than my own.

One night, Sara found me hiding behind the door in Joan's studio, in tears. Two days earlier she had taken me to see the stones at the bottom of the garden again. But I did not want to kiss them, had kicked one of them instead, and since then she and I had been keeping our distance.

The one television in the house was in Joan's studio. He had left it on after going out for a drink with some work colleagues. When I came across it, I sat down on the floor and spent the next four hours watching a *Simpsons* marathon on Antena 3. Before that I had only ever seen the odd movie, a random assortment of past and present: *The Muppets*, *Little Lord Fauntleroy*, *Meet Me in Saint Louis*, *Mary Poppins*. An inoffensive patchwork, all part of my parents' good intentions in the formation of my innocent young brain. The sight of the television stopped me in my tracks, like a road accident from which it is impossible to avert one's eyes. Half-abducted, half-seduced, and my heart in my throat, I had been imbibing the Simpsons' capers, the endless silliness of their familial strife.

When Sara found me behind the door, I was crying and trembling from head to foot. It was half an hour before I finally told her what was wrong: sitting on the kitchen counter, cradling a glass of almond milk, and with my breath still ragged, I pointed in the direction of the studio, where Bart could be heard squawking after Homer had given him a slap on the neck:

'Sara,' I said. 'Are they never going to find happiness?'

The woman who looks like Sara and I make our way into the centre of town. At the bakery, I buy a large loaf of bread while she tries to get through on my phone again. Her clumsiness is starting to aggravate me, her seeming ineptitude in all facets of life.

We go to some other shops, her trailing after me, talking on the phone to someone who seems not to be giving her the answers she was hoping for. She also seems to be asking forgiveness for something, or things, that happened in the past.

The woman in the grocers gives me her usual devilish smile. The woman who looks like Sara is still on the phone. There is a large, lanky German man in front of me in the queue, the kind of foreigner in camping apparel that has also become a feature in the valley. He wants a bag of sweets, nothing else.

'Oh, sweets, OK,' the shop woman says. 'I'll give you a sweet one, don't you worry...'

The German gives her a confused smile. She takes his money and hands over the bag with a wink.

Once he has gone, her expression changes. Turning serious, she points at the door through which the man has just disappeared, saying confidentially:

'He's a very important scientist, you know.'

The woman who looks like Sara might not have succeeded in convincing her friends to let her stay, but she can't hang off my elbow all day, and she definitely can't stay with me. With a face of pure innocence, she says:

'Why not?'

'Because,' I say.

My lack of sympathy, I can already see, might be precisely because of her resemblance to Sara. She thanks me, several times – 'For all you've done' – and says she's been waiting a long time to meet someone like me, someone 'who knows about solidarity' and 'actually gives a shit...'

I don't let her finish. I have to get going. I know we'll never lay eyes on one another again. She throws her arms out wide, expectation in her eyes, and hauls me into one final embrace. Just as it's about to happen, I feel very aware of the imminent contact with her breasts. I quickly extricate myself. And when we have parted, once I have put considerable distance between us, I picture her still standing in that same spot, on her own in the middle of the street: waiting for someone, or something, to save her.

When I was 19 I went on a trip for the first time with my new Madrid friends. We were going to make a stop in a town not far from Casa Grande. A few hours earlier, my mother told me over the phone that I had to go and visit Sara and Joan. 'They'll be thrilled to see you. They haven't seen you since you were tiny.'

Sara was standing in the doorway when I arrived. She wore her now-grey hair in a bob. She threw her arms out wide, as though I had the little suitcase with me, and the rain hat, as though we were still playing the old game. I felt her breasts against my body, saggier than before, less substantial.

She asked me how everything was going, and I said good, that I was living in Madrid now. She raised an eyebrow at this, as if living in Madrid were the most absurd life-decision a person could make. I asked after Joan but she said he was sleeping and that she didn't want to wake him.

We sat across from one another at the red table and I told her about my studies, about not really enjoying the course, and that I'd been going out drinking a lot. I kept my hands on the tabletop and fingered the beading at the edge, my mind starting to wander. I thought about my friends waiting out in the car. And I thought about myself, lying on this very table, small and naked.

She asked me whether I meditated; I said I got high. This drew a reproachful smile, a shake of the head. She said I needed to meditate. Looking at her hand, I noticed how small her silver wedding ring looked, how it was pinching her finger. I pointed this out, and asked if it didn't bother her, and she then also noticed how tight it had grown; it was stopping the circulation. We tried getting it off with soap. Our hands came together under the tap. The second there was physical contact, I no longer felt like helping, and went to move away. But she grabbed my hands, squeezing them, and, looking me in the eye, whispered my name. There was something in this that I could not accept, the charge of her sentimentalism. I pulled my hands free and told her to go to the jeweller's, they would cut it off for her: the same thing happens to old women all the time, I said.

'I have to go now.'

I could feel how crushed she was. Though it did not register in her face, I could tell. I couldn't go, she said, not until Joan got up. I was sorry, I said, I had to. And as I made my way to the door, Sara following behind, all but begging me to stay, I came out with a series of things that would destroy her idea of me as the little Fried Egg, once and for all. As I passed the bedroom and caught sight of the empty bed, no one lying in it, I unleashed a torrent of details about my life of late: about my nights out, about the unprotected sex I'd been having, about the night I fell from a rooftop and ended up in hospital. But I could tell from her face that she'd stopped listening, that she had identified something more urgent than the words I was saying.

We made it to the door and, before going out, I ceased my crazed speech. I turned to face her for the last time and, trembling all over, lifted up my top, baring my body to her. And she gasped, and it was as though my breasts had struck her with the same force as someone kicking a stone that was not a real child.

I decide to join in the fiesta. The sun beats down on the town square, which is alive with the packed bodies of the revellers. I feel differently about the candles. I feel differently about my night fears. I suddenly feel as if I will be able to bear the darkness when the sun goes down.

Later, with the fiesta finally coming to an end, I set off back to the house on foot. I lift my thumb every now and then to passing cars, but with little conviction. I no longer mind the prospect of the three-hour walk.

As I walk I tear pieces from the loaf of bread and pop them into my mouth. High above in the distance I can see the snow-capped peak of Mulhacén. A man on a dappled grey horse comes past me, typing something on the keypad of his mobile phone.

ON MEAT ROUNDTABLE

A roundtable 'On Meat' may seem, at first glance, to mark a divergence from the subjects that have, until now, characterised TWR's roundtables: Work, Universities, Class, Translation, and Housing. Yet like where we live or work, what we eat exceeds questions of production and sustenance, bleeding into superstructural questions around religion, morality, ritual, and the aesthetic. Meat plugs us into networks of metaphor, embroiling us in global market 'cowspiracies' whilst also remaining deeply mundane – that wet, minced substance lurking in your pet's bowl. This discussion arrives at a moment where politicians and celebrities lean in to 'Meat-Free Mondays' (as if 'mindful' consumption, not policy, is the best way to mitigate against climate collapse!), and Big Business bends the knee for plant-based consumers. It took place in an airy, white-walled room, secreted in the bowels of the ICA, just six days after a General Election result which put pay to any notion of a government with a green mandate that would enshrine non-human welfare. And yet, for many, meat floats free of the political altogether, yoking itself to murkier territories of luxury or pleasure. (Perhaps it's simply what lines your scotch egg at St. John.) This detachment can feel more pronounced in a climate where the political and ethical vim of veganism risks being defanged by corporate appropriation, and certain strains of holier-than-thou healthism.

Captured in the faddish uptake of 'Paleo' diets is the essentialist sense that meat will always, to quote E.T., *be right here*, occupying its rightful spot in the food-chain, and the cultural imaginary. Though supermarket aisles confront us with a packaged product continually on the brink of expiry, meat lays claim to a peculiarly elastic temporality; it's easy to conjure a narrative lineage that starts with hunter-gatherers disarticulating a carcass and ends with Homer Simpson chowing down on a cartoon T-bone. But what is meat, if not a thoroughly modern institution? Though it predates the 'horrors of capital', meat cannot be divorced from them. Any purported opposition it has to modernity is made ludicrous by a slick, technocratic industry, which has formed a blueprint for modes of oppression that continue to thrive – both within and across species. As this conversation reveals, meat opens up on to questions of individuated morality. But it also intersects with state-level questions of bio- and necropolitics, of what lifeforms and lifeways do or don't get to 'count'.

Whether or not we choose to consume it, our proximity to meat's circulation – not to mention our own meatiness – implicates us all in the lives and deaths of non-human others. What follows is a rangy discussion that covers questions of access, gore, erotics, class, gender, cliché, the politics of care, and the radical possibilities of interspecies harmony. Whilst reading, we must hold in mind the uneven distribution of violence – not just among animals themselves, but among those who labour alongside, or in close proximity to them. We should remain vigilant, too, to the relative impossibility of keeping the blood off our own hands. Dig in.   CECILIA TRICKER

ROBERT MCKAY   When did people first know what meat is?

RACHAEL ALLEN   I became vegetarian when I was 9, but not because I was concerned with an animal. I became vegetarian because I was really aware of Mad Cow Disease. And that shaped my ideas about eating animals or not eating animals way more than respecting them or loving them. It was a fear of what they were going to do to my body if they were diseased.

PATRICK STAFF   I think that it's interesting to consider how things enter into our consciousness via crises. My first question to myself and to everyone is, how do we define our terms. It feels like we need to establish exactly what we mean by 'meat'.

MCKAY   One of the things that meat discussions tend to do is create a kind of slippage between knowledge and ideology, though. So even the question, 'When did you first know what meat is?', prompts the response, 'When did I see through cultural discourses about it to what it truly is?' Which is essentially a point of trying to *read* meat as an ideology. When did you know that meat was 'meat'? When did you know that the thing that you eat was this kind of cultural force? This is part of the question, I guess. But then there are other ways of thinking of meat, right?

REVITAL COHEN   For me it's a really visual memory. There are two images from around the same time, although I don't really remember which came first. One of them was seeing an open van next to the butchers with sheep carcasses. And the second, I had just started reading by myself, I was reading the newspaper and there was a story of a little girl who was murdered and pieces of her body came ashore. Something kind of mixed in my head about all these pieces of bodies, and I haven't eaten meat since.

MCKAY   And you saw a connection. So the connection there is to do with the meatiness, the way the human body suddenly becomes seeable as meat?

COHEN   Maybe also a feeling of vulnerability. Suddenly seeing this, this personhood in these pieces of meat in the van, and understanding that we could all be these pieces at some point...

MCKAY   There's a philosopher called Matthew Calarco who coined the term 'indistinction' for this thing that you're talking about. That it's not quite that humans are the same as animals – which is what quite a lot of pro-animal rhetoric might say

– in the sense of being on a biological continuum, which is questionable for lots of reasons. But it's also not that we are radically different to animals in the sense of them being absolutely, singularly, other to us. Instead, there's some place in between these where it's sometimes possible to recognise these sort of 'indistinctions', he's called them, where you can't maintain the distinction that you might want to maintain or that the culture asks you to maintain.

STAFF   I think the horrors of being a child in connection to meat are really interesting. Daisy, you grew up on a farm, right? Was that a horror-laden experience?

DAISY HILDYARD   Not at all. No, and I think I can't remember a moment of recognition of meat as a thing. Following Rachael talking about this kind of slide from BSE (Bovine spongiform encephalopathy) to all meat, perhaps what we are thinking about here is a mistrust of something that you can't see. If BSE is a thing, if there's horsemeat in your lasagne, then any meat could be anything. And if you don't have any direct experience of the animal – which most of us don't – then the moment you see reason to mistrust a part of production, it becomes logical to mistrust the whole.

The one thing I can remember from early childhood was that at my village primary school we had meat every day and it was no doubt unethically produced. But this is the closest I can get to some kind of recognition of the idea of meat – I remember that one day it would be pork, one day it would be sausages, one day it would be beef, and then one day it was *sliced meat*. We didn't attach it to an animal, it was just like: 'it's meat'. I remember feeling there was something spooky about that.

YOU'D EAT THE PRAWN
BUT NOT THE SHIT

STAFF   Growing up, my dad was a policeman. And part of being a policeman, in a very small town, was just knowing everyone. Much more than solving crimes or anything serious like that. It was a community role. I hated all of his friends who were policemen. He was also very good friends with all the men working at the butchers. And so part of the circuit of walking around this small town with my Dad was to stop in and visit his friends, including the butcher's, who I also just remember hating as a child, but for no real reason. But going into the butcher's was a horrific experience. You'd go through the plastic hanging curtains and it was one of those ones where – I think this is in your book, Daisy [*The Second Body*] – where the floor is that particular stone or tile, designed in such a way that meat or blood or whatever could go on it. So there was something very sensorial, a kind of haptic horror about it. And it smelled terrible.

ALLEN   It's so functional. There's something so brutal.

STAFF   Much more than eating meat, I think about the experience of entering that space.

MCKAY   Meat and butchering somehow insist on a lack of modernity, or refuse it. So this demand for cleanliness, or an expectation that things must not have muck on the floor, is shown up as a peculiar twentieth- and twenty-first-century reality. It's certainly part of a modernising trend to try and make life cleaner, more ordered, more organised. And when you go through the plastic curtains, it's almost like you're passing out of this...

STAFF   Crossing the threshold.

MCKAY   Yeah, crossing the threshold. But then you enter a zone where matter is out of place. One of the things you're saying is that your way into knowing meat comes first from being trained into being well-modernised, and expecting the world to go along these lines.

COHEN   I actually read the cleanliness as the moment of horror. When Patrick is describing the butcher's shop, for me, that is the terrifying thing about it. It's this perceived 'nothing to see', which is so uncomfortable.

MCKAY   Well, don't we expect there to be no remainders that you have to see or deal with? So that the process can completely provide you with ordered, packaged meat?

ALLEN   I remember if you get prawns – I don't eat prawns – but sometimes they have a black line in them, and I remember asking my mum, 'What's this?' And she said, 'Oh it's just the shit.' You'd eat the prawn but you wouldn't eat the shit.

STAFF   The first ever argument I had with my boyfriend was when we were talking about meat. And I said to him that I didn't understand why he would be comfortable to eat the animal, but not fuck it. And he was just like, I just don't get why you'd ever say that. But it feels like the same thing to me. It feels like a very arbitrary moral equivocation.

ALLEN   That's funny, I went to a conference on Animal Studies on Sunday, and everyone got very focused on bestiality. There was all this discussion about bestiality, and then someone was like, there are ham sandwiches sitting over there! There are these expected ways we consume or use the animal, and expected ways for their usage to disgust us or to sit outside of societal norms, even though morally each may be as abhorrent as the other.

AN ASS LIKE TWO STEAKS

STAFF   Is it worth talking about our conception of meat in relation to flesh but also to consumption? Because that's also an integral part of being aware of what meat is or what it does. One of my first times in a gay bar, an older guy said that I had an ass like two steaks...

MCKAY   Is that a good thing?

STAFF   ... which is like horrific and amazing! I think I just giggled. But, I bring it up because meat can mean many things. Like getting to the 'meat' of an issue.

ALLEN   Like, all the idioms around meat? How we position meat through the language that we use.

STAFF   At some point, we may become a piece of meat, whether we consent to it or not. Whether through death, or dispossession, or some sort of libidinal economy.

HILDYARD   I remember years ago seeing a documentary about Germaine Greer. She had a book cover which was a big piece of meat with a fertility amulet on it. She was being filmed with her publicist, who was saying, 'I don't think we should have meat on the cover because it might offend vegetarian readers.' And Greer bluntly said, 'They're all made of meat, even the vegetarians.' It's stuck in my head, I suppose because it poses a difficult question about the extent to which we are talking about ourselves when we talk about meat. Do we think about ourselves as flesh or some other alternative?

MCKAY   I think there's an interesting slippage across the thematics that are attached to meat. Even just in the conversation we've had, there's a strong sense of the down-to-earthness of it, the absoluteness of it. There's this idea of, 'Well everyone is meat, we're all fundamentally meat.' One of the things that's happening in that move is that we're saying: if we cut through all the cultural claptrap, the fundamental truth is meat. But then, in your example from the bar, Patrick, part of this idea spills over into a sense that meat is what is desirable, erotic. So the connotations of meat are that it is something that necessarily has to be eaten, something that must be desired, or something that will be good for you if you eat it, because it is somehow fundamental and real.

HILDYARD   The conversation around our pernicious engagement with non-human animals, particularly in the meat industry, tends to focus on an essential separation between humans and animals, and I think there's space for developing narratives of engagement that aren't necessarily to do with either slaughter or companion species. I suppose what I'm talking about in a practical sense is an actual engagement, rather than a conceptual engagement, with animals – because everybody *is* involved in entanglements with many other species, but much of that can pass unnoticed.

ALLEN   Sometimes I feel like people who farm are closer to the animal, obviously, to animal morality, than I am, despite the fact that I'm someone who is vegan.

MCKAY   That kind of argument is part of thinking that there's no other way than modernity for humans. That this is what we are now, modernity has taken us away from the animal. But there are little pockets of life that aren't modern, like farms. And over there, it's *real*, and over here, with us, it's cultural bullshit. But I think farms also produce cultural ideas of what animals are, not least in the lives of animals themselves. An animal isn't born going, 'Please cut me up and eat me. It is the truth of my life to be cut up and eaten.' A cow doesn't have to move between field and byre, or stall and slaughterhouse. Yes, its life will be made into that. But the farmer could wake up one day and say, 'Let's go for a stroll.' Or something completely other. It's not impossible.

STAFF   Yes. Like any number of other things, you know, it's very easy to assume that our only relationship to animals is consumption through the mouth, through food or whatever, when it actually feels multi-layered and often highly technological, as we see in Revital's work, whether it's in the engineering of genetic code for reproductive ends, or the mechanics of the racehorse industry.

THE LOGICAL END TO A PUG

MCKAY   So before, Patrick, you were asking us to think beyond just food. Can you give us some other ideas of ways that we would look beyond meat as food? The rhetoric of meat is really important in religious practices, for instance. I was thinking that my own first encounter with meat would have been through religion – my father was a Church of Scotland minister, about as far away from Catholicism as you can get in Christianity, but still, there was a communion once a month or so. And I can remember being completely freaked out – not quite by the transubstantiation itself, but by the idea of it. I can particularly remember the people in the choir drinking the red wine out of these cups and just thinking, that's blood. Is it blood?

COHEN   But that is so interesting, because it's actually not a body at all, but still has the same power.

STAFF   I've been trying to figure out, while we've been talking, the ways that non-human, interspecies interaction can be a modelling process. By which to say, we model a larger picture of the world through these supposedly more insignificant interactions, or forms of kinship. Thinking about that very first question, I think the conception of meat requires a definition of the animal, which is dependent on how we define the human. And the definition of the human to me seems dependent on many forms of racialised and gendered violence; mass incarceration, white supremacy, imperialism, colonialism.

COHEN   Yes. In my work I often try to stay away from meat, because I feel that my opinions are too strong for me to say anything of interest. So I've been looking for moments where the body of the animal appears as an object made by culture, but not for eating – most recently following the bodies of thoroughbred racehorses, which are created and sustained by the ecology and economy of gambling. Our latest film follows thoroughbreds collapsing on Ketamine, and we will soon be documenting their breeding procedure which traditionally take place on Valentine's Day. I'm really curious by the status or presence of these creatures which are so completely created by humans. And what is our relationship to them? They seem somehow to be more precious than the animals used or made for eating. But then they also get discarded quite quickly.

HILDYARD   There's a construction, or even actual creation or breeding, of an animal as a resource of some form. And meat is a prevalent example of that, but we also constitute whole landscapes or peoples as resources. Have people always been kind of libidinally mining other beings as resources, or not? Is it essential to humanity? I don't know.

COHEN   Yes, I think so. It's just a question of which species, and what it is worth to somebody at a certain moment.

ALLEN   You can see it most visibly in dogs, I suppose? They're the things that we assume to be closest to us, but we've deliberately created them to have that bond with us. This master/submissive relationship. And then when you look at something like a pug – like, what's the logical end to a pug?

MCKAY   Just an arsehole.

ALLEN   It's so broken. It's absolutely monstrous.

COHEN   But that's really a process of design using organic matter that happens to be alive.

ALLEN   What's the agency there? It's like a really slow violence towards the animal.

COHEN   Absolutely.

MCKAY   Part of the horrible strangeness, though, is that it produces other forms of affect at the same time. For example, various kinds of pleasure both for the pug and for pug owners. There's an ownership of the life future, or the genetic future, of these beings, there's a taking hold of that and shaping it in a self-centred way. But this doesn't necessarily produce only abject dominion. Life would be much easier if every horrible action produced nothing but awfulness. I mean, you could just work out what they all are and then ban them.

COHEN   Maybe cruelty is just part of our nature. Maybe cruelty is just how we deal with the world around us, which is actually an excuse for a lot of people who eat meat. Saying, 'This is nature and we're the top predator,' which I don't actually agree with.

HUG THEM TO SUBMISSION

STAFF   To return to the concept of the animal and meat as a modelling tool, I'm thinking about my friend the writer Che Gossett, who has written about the entanglements between animal rights, necropolitics and anti-blackness, racial slavery and racial capitalism. Che has talked about how prisons have used animals, from dogs to bees and more, since the 1970s to 'humanise' incarcerated people. And how perversely, using inhuman violence to restore an idea of humanity is a carceral logic.

MCKAY   I'm trying to think of a way to connect this aspect of the discussion back to meat, in particular. So, one thing I think is significantly challenging here is divergent cultural practices around meat. When you offer a straightforward or an undifferentiated position *against* the consumption of meat, you risk closing down all kinds of cultural heritage. And that's part again of this opposition that keeps coming up in this discussion. Something like this: meat is the body of an animal and the animal should own that body. That's one way of thinking about meat, a critical way of seeing meat as an ideology. But meat is experienced all over the world in different ways: foodways, ways of making meaning with meat, ways of forging community or closing community down with meat and through meat. So you have, on the one hand, animals' own flesh, and on the other, cultural practices, which are deeply felt and very meaningful. But when you're talking about horse racing, which appears in Revital's work, it simultaneously objectifies equine natures *and* produces a possibility for many different kinds of leisure activity, community activity, all these kinds of things.

COHEN   And it's not necessarily a bad thing. And that's why it's interesting. I mean, we've been doing lots of filming in the Horse Hospital in Newmarket where, honestly, horses receive medical treatment that any of us could only dream of. These are the most expensive horses in the world. They have eight nurses per animal who treat them with love, and hug them to a kind of submission when they go under anaesthesia, and cradle them as they come out of it. It's actually really, really beautiful. So these so-called 'pieces of meat' are actually treated as animals who are deeply loved and respected.

MCKAY   Yet I guess that's indistinguishable from the workings of capital that are part of that love. They're getting medical treatment some of us could only dream of – there's a really interesting relationship between capital and speciesism right there. So there's a speciesism that's putting horses, particular kinds of horses, above lots of humans, as well as above lots of other animals. Capital doesn't straightforwardly have a hierarchy – humans, this kind of animal, that kind of animal. It's much more jaggy than that.

COHEN   Yes. And when you say that, I think maybe a lot of the horrors of meat are actually horrors of capitalism. I'm fine with the idea that someone will raise an animal and at some point slaughter and eat it. It's the horror of the mass production of the factories, of the animals that might become a product that no one buys, and expires and goes straight to the bin. That's different from a one-on-one relationship, even if it includes violence, and one consuming the other.

SOFT SACRIFICE

HILDYARD   I have a question about the dairy industry and the meat industry, with that in mind. I think it's difficult to know whether it's better for an animal to live a life and then be slaughtered quickly, or for the animal to not express certain central life processes, so for an individual to be separated from their young within minutes of birth, or, another example, to be castrated. I once saw some bullocks straight after they were castrated, and they looked distressed. Like: I'm not angry with you, I'm just disappointed. They were dejected in a way I've never seen another animal look. In animal behaviour and in farming there's a move towards anthropomorphism in the assessment of animals, towards saying if an animal looks happy it probably is happy. I'm interested in the moment of death versus the experience of life, I suppose.
COHEN   The scale of the system is horrifying. I am really interested in the way industrial practices (scale, opacity, disconnection) allow for slow or structural violence to happen. A few years ago, while making work simultaneously in electronics factories in China and fish farms in Japan, we kept going back to Sigfried Giedion's writing on mechanisation, for example, how Ford's first assembly line was inspired by a butcher's disassembly line. I feel that any thoughts I have about meat come from this tension between a living creature and the industrial complex. I mean, there were moments during the footage in Patrick's show [*On Venus*, Serpentine Sackler Gallery, November 2019-February 2020] where I had to look away. It's super powerful, especially as you made it less graphic. It's psychedelic, and the colours change, and you're not sure what you're seeing. I don't know what the cows are suspended by, but there are all these hydraulics and steel and lots of people and everyone is on this kind of mission to transport this body through some kind of a process, a production process. Which is the kind of thing that we try not to see as much as possible.
ALLEN   Yeah, it's interesting thinking about the ways we adapt animals. Like my friend has two

rabbits, and one of them is a girl rabbit. And it's really hyperactive. And he keeps being like, I need to get her neutered because once she's neutered she'll calm down. She's in her natural manic wanting to breed state, but to improve her quality of life with him in the home he's going to alter her.
HILDYARD   Yet with the history of breeding and the circumstances in which she's living, it's hard to get at what really is a natural expression of what she's like.
MCKAY   There's a scholar I know called Julie Ann Smith, and she has rabbits and other animals. She has this essay where she talks about how she lives with these rescue animals, in such a way that they don't kill and eat each other. And it's an interesting example of a kind of decolonial thinking. She's not trying to say, 'I can create a peaceable kingdom in my house.' Rather, we've got these actual living beings with these actual life histories and actual ways that they live now. So how do you do your best to allow for the life of these animals? She literally built big fences right through her house. She's making certain kinds of soft sacrifices against the human right to live comfortably. But to me what's interesting about it is the move away from a kind of idealising, utopian kind of thinking. And instead to say, well, there's going to be certain things that this one doesn't get to do, if that one's going to get to have its freedom. But what kinds of compromises can be made in human lives in order to get a couple of steps forward for those animals' lives?
STAFF   But the ultimate move away would be to let them kill each other, right?
COHEN   I think so too.
MCKAY   But you know you're in the relationship even if you take the decision to leave them alone. You know, if you make the decision to have them in a place, or if the decision is made for you by the way they've been treated by the world, they've still made their ethical demand on you, you're held by it. Once you've actually got the animals, you don't get to say, well, I can just ditch the ethical demands by leaving them to it.
ALLEN   Because you've made the space in which they will exist.
MCKAY   You've made the ontological space as well, you know, for the rabbits to live in.
STAFF   Maybe the ultimate move would be for her to let them try and also kill her. And to kill them back!
ALLEN   True meat. Absolute meat!

CANNIBAL'S AFTERBIRTH

COHEN   Daisy, I was really blown away by what you said in the emails we exchanged before today, about how a midwife once told you that 'we're all cannibals until we're born', and that 'a cloth screen is erected compulsorily during a Caesarian section, so that the pregnant body can't catch a glimpse of its own offal'! I think perhaps pregnancy is a moment where a woman becomes or feels suddenly like meat or like a body first, and where all these visceral experiences become stronger than ideas. And the foetus is actually eating you up inside.

ALLEN   Well, it's like a parasite being, it's like a parasite meat.

COHEN   But that doesn't mean that it's without love.

ALLEN   Does it love you, though?

HILDYARD   The loving parasite is an attractive idea.

COHEN   The parasite is eating you but loving you.

ALLEN   Does it love you though?

COHEN   And consumption, because a lot of people eat the placenta, actually.

ALLEN   Cannibal's afterbirth.

COHEN   Middle-class cannibalism.

HILDYARD   *So* full of nutrients.

MCKAY   I think in terms of animalising, the thing I remember being struck by the most when my partner was pregnant was actually the technocratic control, the amount of measuring and watching and tracking and expectation to be at a particular place at a particular time, and forms and documents.

ALLEN   Does that feel more animal, then?

MCKAY   Well, it made me think of what meat animals in the main are subject to. A particular kind of algorithmic logic. In CAFOs, certainly, in the bigger farms. But even in small dairy farms, there will be lots of tracking of the best times to do milking or breeding – there are apps galore for this – so a kind of biopolitical control of the production. So there's the idea, I think, that when the baby comes along, you're going to look after it properly, and looking after it properly is keeping going with these kinds of processes of... Control's not quite the right word. Production of its life in particular kinds of ways. So there's a kind of animal connection there, not on the natural side, but on how culture deals with living beings.

TREAT ME LIKE A PIECE OF MEAT

STAFF   Before we met, I kept thinking that I wanted to talk about the pleasure of being meat oneself. I like hearing you guys talking about the relationship to pregnancy and the meat of a body being the food of the parasite, or whatever, but it also makes me think about the way the meat of the body can be a carrier, in both positive and negative ways. I'm thinking about, like, injecting hormones into the fat of your butt. The way that pollution, certain plastics, are held in the fat of the body. A kind of needing, a needing the meat of the body to be a mediating substance, but also one that is necessary and produces both positive and negative affect. It feels very liberating to get away from animals, maybe just because we've been talking about animals for so long, to try and think about the *other* meat. I'm also feeling that somehow trying to talk about meat is engendering a certain conservative impulse in the conversation, so maybe if we talk about our desires it'll complicate things.

MCKAY   So what kind of pleasure? I mean, there's obviously a rich language of erotics around meat, of carnal pleasures, literally. Perhaps that's not quite the sort of pleasure that you...

STAFF   No, I'm into that pleasure! I mean, my first thought is that, obviously, we normally say 'being treated like a piece of meat' with a negative connotation. But I find that quite often I want to be treated like a piece of meat. I mean, sunbathing can also make me feel like a piece of meat. Sometimes there's a pleasure to grabbing the flesh of your body or someone else's...

ALLEN   That comes back to your crisis idea, I think. If there's an extreme state in the body, or an alteration in the body, be that through health or something as minor as sunbathing, it's suddenly, like, oh god I'm changeable, the meat of me is changeable, I have control over my body. Which is so frightening, especially if you think about, like, how much we booze and cig and all the invisible changes that we make to the meats in our bodies.

HILDYARD   I think that's interesting.

ALLEN   And sexually, I guess, I don't know. Like, there are all these conversations about sub or dom, and BDSM communities, how the language of meat can infiltrate that world.

STAFF   I don't think that meat, being meat, becoming meat is necessarily implicit to sub/dom relationships, but there's something there I think in the relation between power and the substance of flesh. But I also don't think of this as an extreme state, in fact I think it's a quotidian part of having a body. I think that maybe, for me, the pleasure of being meat is about removing the – I don't know what the right word for it is – the cerebral, to some degree. Like, to be a piece of meat you get to remove a certain amount of control, or commentary.

ALLEN   Or to be given permission, almost, to just be meat. It's like I give you permission to stop thinking.

MCKAY   The objectification that's involved in fetishism is similar to what happens in the making of meat. You're trying to disaggregate a whole thing into very intensely invested-in bits of things.

ALLEN   Which then become powerful.

MCKAY   Yeah. But I suppose part of the pleasure aspect is being in the position to be able to play these things, perform them. So it's almost like you can be free of the requirement to think judiciously about the kinds of ideas that are floating around in your head, that's part of the play of the erotic, that essentially it becomes this kind of second order space.

STAFF   Or not to be liberated from it. It's for it to *not matter*. If I'm treated like a piece of meat, it doesn't matter what I think of that process. It doesn't matter if I'm thinking judiciously or not. It doesn't matter if I'm thinking at all, let alone *not* thinking. It's that it's beyond me entirely. I don't need permission for that. It's beyond that.

MCKAY   Well, it doesn't become that pleasurable if you're actually treated like a piece of meat, because that's the point at which someone is actually eating you. But it stays at some level of play, that not-conscious play.

ALLEN   It's about agency.

COHEN   And desire. I don't remember where I read this, but in almost every culture, in relationships, there is an instinct to say, 'Oh, I could eat you!' Which we say with children too.

I WOULDN'T EAT MY BROTHER

HILDYARD   I wonder, with the thrill of desire, whether it isn't precisely because we're not certain whether we're fundamentally out of control or fundamentally in control. That there is a thrill in the dangerous uncertainty – being somewhere between the two.

ALLEN   Yeah, so there's an element where you do have your consent to be treated like meat. You will always have to say, this is the way I want to be treated. There's always an active decision to become the meat. Maybe what I'm interested in here is where meat breaks down the humanistic logic, or our liberal impulses, to define consent, free will, bodily autonomy, agency.

MCKAY   This is bringing me back to your comment earlier, Patrick, about the relationship between eating and sex. This question around pleasure and disgust and the extent to which they're ethical… You might think that some part of the discussion around vegetarianism and veganism is to insist that the act of eating is ethical, while part of the kind of carnal-centric logic is not to agree that it is ethical, but to assert a different moral attitude to meat, to insist that eating is not really ethical. Might you say something similar about sex? If someone says 'Love me' or 'Desire me', you can't very well say 'Give me a rationale for why I should and then, as long as it's written down and I can believe it, then I will.' That's not how love or desire work. Is eating this kind of thing? Because there are certainly things that I wouldn't eat. But are these things that I could eat, but choose not to eat? I'm not going to eat a handful of dirt. But my son will eat a handful of dirt. So there are these questions around acculturation, and how deep into you that goes, to the point at which it's actually affecting your seemingly instinctive reactions to things. Maybe the reason I don't eat meat is very similar to the reason I wouldn't have sex with an animal, which is that animals are just not the kind of thing that I would do that with, based on the way I relate to them. So it isn't based on a moral reason. It's based on an entirely affective reason. It's the same reason that I wouldn't eat my brother either.

STAFF   Yeah. In the argument that I brought up with my boyfriend at the beginning, it would have been very easy for him to say, 'Well, I desire to eat the meat but I don't desire to fuck the animal.' And then I would have had to shut up, but the thing was he relented from a moral position, which meant I could keep arguing it with him.

ALLEN   And where does that desire come from? Is that a cultured desire? Are our desires defined by things that we come up against and are normalised?

COHEN   Yeah. In Belgium you walk past the butcher's and there would be a horse on the sign, because horse meat is totally normal.

ALLEN   Yeah, that comes back to the bestiality

thing, it's the exact same argument. If I can eat an animal, I can fuck an animal too, what's the difference? Other than what we've been cultured to think is OK.

HILDYARD   I talked to a scientist once who worked with prawns. He helped the Indonesian government farm trillions of prawns, by microbiome sequencing to identify diseases the prawns suffered. The scientist said that he believed in some radical sense that all species, prawns included, had a valuable lifeway, but that he still ate prawns. And he used this lovely phrase, because he's a German speaker, he said 'I'm not consequent'. At the time it sounded to me like a cute mistranslation, but I've often thought of it since. It seems to me that whatever position you take, whether you're vegan or you eat meat, you can't be consequent. Even if you're vegan and a purified clean eater, you're inevitably imbricated with many murky processes. No matter how you eat, really. If you're a meat eater, much more obviously, you can't be consequent unless you love causing pain and fear to other animals.

MEAT ABSTINENT

ALLEN   To link that back to the body as meat, the human body as meat, what do we think about the person who may be treating us like meat? Are they the butcher of us if we have given them permission to do this, are we taking away their meatiness by putting them above us?

HILDYARD   I like that you've raised the possibility of pleasure. It's under-acknowledged, I think, probably for quite sensible reasons – because people need protection from being consumed as meat.

COHEN   I don't know, I almost kind of envy it. I feel that growing up as a young woman, you're often told not to allow anyone to see you, talk to you or treat you this way, and the way that you talk about it, it sounds actually quite liberating.

HILDYARD   If people really didn't ever experience themselves as meat, would people just never have sex? Is experiencing your body as meat necessary to sex or not?

ALLEN   That's a really good question.

STAFF   I'm a firm believer that despite our best intentions, desire rarely conforms to political principle. And I think we easily get ourselves into trouble when we try to corral it, whether it's the things that people desire, whether it's to eat meat or whatever, or in relation to one's own desire.

I think it's interesting what we do with people who want bad things, you know? Including ourselves. I think about this a lot in my own life, whether it's a friend's desire to smoke or whatever, it can be stretched in many ways from the quotidian to far more complex situations. And I think the desire for meat sort of slots in there somewhere. I don't know really what to do with that. But it feels somehow integral to the conversation.

ALLEN   So many religions forbid certain meats, or require complete abstinence from meat, and they're also abstaining from sex. And you're supposed to just flagellate yourself constantly if you engage in anything perceived as pleasurable. It's funny how these things go together: meat, sex, desire. It's like the base part of us.

HILDYARD   This is the analogy a butcher used, when I asked him whether he worried about health vegetarianism. Well, he didn't use sex, but he said: Everybody knows smoking is bad for you. People don't stop smoking. Everybody knows drinking's bad for you, people don't stop drinking. There's a definite association between what we think of as vices.

MCKAY   It is entirely possible to point your desire towards any kind of object, I would think. But it's just that there's a secondary question of whether or not ideas that circulate in the non-sexual realm, like ideas that you have about meat and its rightness, or human–animal relations and the politics of them, whether or not they are sublimated into something else when moved into the erotic sphere.

HILDYARD   But you can't point your desire at anything if you don't have a body. I think that is where there is an affinity between meat and sexuality that is difficult to circumvent.

FLESH IS THE MEAT THAT DOESN'T GET EATEN

MCKAY   I suppose a distinction that might be useful here is between flesh and meat. Because to me, 'meat' describes something that is for eating. Flesh isn't quite the same. So flesh is stuff that dies, matter that lives and dies.

HILDYARD   That distinction concerns me in the sense that it seems to be following a distinction created by the meat industry: that the difference between meat and flesh is that meat is other animals. If you put a human liver and a pig's liver in front of me, I wouldn't be able to tell you which one was meat and which was flesh.

MCKAY   I suppose at that point, it's possible to turn human flesh into meat. But I would still try and maintain the distinction, that flesh is the meat that doesn't get eaten.

ALLEN   Do you think that distinction helps your thinking through animal-human relations?

MCKAY   I suppose it helps me with what Patrick said earlier on about being treated like a piece of meat. I think it's important not to ignore that there's certainly one main way to actually become meat in the world. And you're more likely to end up that way if you're an animal, even if it's not impossible otherwise – some humans do get eaten. There's a lot of cultural work going on around that process, which creates an image repertoire of meat that can then move across from animals' experience into other realms, like politics or the erotic. Here it's happening in the *like*, that when you say *like* a piece of meat, you maintain a distinction between you and the actual animal, or rather between partial and absolute objectification.

ALLEN   Like Daisy, I think, I agree with the idea that we should call meat 'flesh', so that there's a true indication of what it is.

HILDYARD   I wouldn't say that I would want to do away with that definition. It definitely exists in the world. But I also wouldn't want to depend on that definition as that of some deeper reality. I wouldn't say the cow's liver, the pig's liver, the goat's liver are one thing and the human liver is another, because it seems to me that that's a distinction made by powerful interests rather than a distinction made by –

MCKAY   Biology?

ALLEN   So it's more to do with understanding how we've been taught to think about these definitions.

STAFF   I think maybe if I were pushed on it, I would simply define meat as the extractable resource from that which is not human, with the caveat that of course the category of human is dependent on making many types of people not-human. So perhaps meat is simply that fleshy material which has been rendered non-human by the sovereign subject.

MCKAY   That 'resourciness' is the thing that makes it – the meatiness, when you get to the meat of the matter you're saying get to the energy, the source of the power, where the positive energy is.

THEY CAN EAT US, RIGHT?

COHEN   Meat has become quite a trashy thing. I keep thinking of this really gruesome exhibition that was running for a few years. Have you seen the posters in the tube for *Body Worlds*, that Gunther von Hagens exhibition? They're horrifying, the human body without the skin. But they also seem kind of cheap and vulgar, the sort of thing you don't even want to look at.

ALLEN   I was just thinking about how we position things as high and low. I really like horrifically gory horror films, for reasons that I cannot put my finger on. But I have thought about it a lot and I think that with those horror films, it's like I'm watching the truth, that we all have this inherent violence and cruelty in us. And when I watch a horror film like that – and I've been a vegetarian since I was 9 and vegan for four years – I sort of try and make it match up with my liberality. It's like, I want to be in touch with cruelty, however fictionalised and false it is, I want to see innards.

STAFF   Yeah, I think that's really interesting.

MCKAY   Do you mean slashers?

ALLEN   Yeah. Mark Kermode wrote this amazing PhD thesis on the ethics of horror. It's basically a defence of horror films and how they can reveal us to ourselves. And I wonder if horror films are positioned as low or base or not culturally relevant because they are showing us something that the rest of society works to obfuscate, which is the reality of being flesh, being meat. And that's where my interest sits with horror, because the violence itself is banal, we're so saturated with it.

HILDYARD   It is interesting in relation to your veganism though, isn't it. If you have meat-eating in the middle, then these two things on either side of it as extremes in which flesh is treated as untouchable, purified (through veganism) and touched or contaminated in the most brutal way (through horror narratives). I wonder how many vegans watch slasher films.

ALLEN   It comes down to the desire thing as well, I think. I morally abstain and ethically abstain, there are so many reasons why I don't eat meat. I think that as beings we can eat other animals, but I choose not to. There's no answer to this whatsoever, but the more I am vegan or vegetarian and abstain from eating animals, the more I see the reasons as to why, and the more I study human-animal relationships, the more I come to think we should be vegan. But I never will advocate for that. Does anyone else feel like that? Because I will never eat animals again, but I see how a relationship of consumption can make you actually closer to an animal. If you rear an animal... Because they can eat us, right?

MCKAY   Yeah, they don't make us eatable though, which is something significantly different about it. When an animal eats a human, every single time it is an event, but when humans eat animals it's not an event, it's the norm.

ALLEN   It's only an event because we've made it that way.

MCKAY   But that's where we are. Once you get to a point where it's normalised, what's happening is a kind of sedimentation of a power relationship that stops you seeing what another being might want to happen. And to me, in pretty much every animal I've encountered, I can read in it that it doesn't want me to do harm to it.

TOP PREDATOR

COHEN   Do you think eating meat is some kind of human assertion that we are somehow a superior species?

MCKAY   No, I don't think of it like that. Do you think that for a random person going into KFC that's what it is?

COHEN   I grew up in Jerusalem. And I've seen a lot of really, really tragic behaviours that are inspired or motivated by some idea of being 'Chosen'. And I wonder if there is a kind of license given by imagining that we are meant to do this. We're here to oppress the weaker, this is our role.

MCKAY   I think that's certainly available to tap into. I think that humans tell themselves stories about all kinds of stuff, to give ourselves the right to do whatever we do. That's where the ethics lie – we make them. And on the basis of that, we can also start telling ourselves that we shouldn't do it.

STAFF   Yeah, I kind of agree. In your question, Revital, of whether we believe ourselves to be a 'top predator' or something – it's a culturally and historically and context-specific production of a mass fantasy that everyone engages with, and one that says this violence is good and right and normal and needed, which as you suggest is the same logic as settler colonialism. But it is absolutely a logic into which we are all, in this room also, indoctrinated via our social, national or class positions.

COHEN   But also a story of feeling empowered by having power over an Other? Being cruel to others as a way of making yourself feel more powerful than perhaps your life makes you feel.

MCKAY   It's hard to work out if it's possible at all to tell yourself a story where humans don't exert that power somewhere. You mentioned colonialism, which shows that it's very easy to naturalise a story of the inherent need to subordinate others. It's what dominant groups have been doing for a great deal of time. It's why I'm always resistant to stories about what animals are. I think animals could be lots of different things. Being a cow is a different thing depending on where it happens to have the luck to be born. You know, you're going to be a different kind of being if you're born on a farm in Northumbria or if you live in parts of India, for example. But then every single cow, even the individual cows on the farm... I don't want to say, 'Well, we know what the cow is, the cow is this or that kind of thing.' Because we are making that story, we are telling it. We're not finding it somehow in the cow.

ALLEN   To get to the point where you're thinking about the animal's entire agency, you have to have thought this stuff through so much, it's very hard to do. I have been thinking about this stuff since I was 9 years old, and I turned it into an area of academic study for myself, and now write about it. I think it's more that people don't think it through, because they don't have the time, or because they are prioritising other kinds of thinking about life.

MCKAY   And that's happening all the time through meat, as well. Meat is a very strong attractor for cliché. So you just go well, OK, KFC, and here is a network of clichés that are classist, racist, all bubbling around it in terms of what it means to eat KFC. And that's just an example of exactly what you're talking about: not thinking through the complex lifeways of different people who choose to eat meat for different reasons, millions of different reasons for eating meat that aren't even the same for each person each time they eat it.

ALLEN   There's always an active choice to *not* eat meat, but perhaps there's not one if you do eat meat. By and large, there's an active choice to abstain and actively think.

STAFF   And without trying to sink the conversation...

ALLEN   Sink it!

STAFF   But I do think a sort of certain white liberal fantasy of human agency has suffused this entire conversation? We're talking as if there is agency within capitalism, which is truly a bourgeois fantasy. Even for me to say that the idea that we need to eat meat is essentially a fantasy – on the one hand, sure that's true, but on the other hand, I don't think really any of us get the choice to be outside of it. Really. And we certainly can't talk our way out of it.

MCKAY   Is aesthetic practice part of an attempt to get outside of it? So Rachael, you have said that you're interested in forms of language, perhaps poetic ones, that may give power to other beings or withhold it, so that's a suggestion in some way that the linguistic, at least, might be a space that offers some... wriggle room, if not an absolute exit from these kind of problematics. But it finds wriggle room within them.

ALLEN   There are poetry collections and poets who attempt to dismantle forms of writing, and sometimes these poets talk about animals... Like Ariana Reines's *The Cow*, which is one of the most significant books of poetry to me that dismantles and dissects everything we have been talking about, various bodies under capitalism and how they resist and survive – but the book is still sold and is a commodity. It talks self-reflexively about animal vellum, the history of writing on skin, but it's still a product. It's doing what it can to disentangle our ideas of the animal and meat and flesh, but still participates in a culture of being bought and sold. But maybe it's that slight chipping away of the things that we have control over that will eventually actualise material shifts, like it's semantics that will change the physical.

HILDYARD   I would visualise it differently and perhaps more positively. I would say that there is a space where there could be writing about human/ non-human relationships or interactions, which do exist everywhere and which are made invisible in most stories. The institution of marriage, for example, has probably had more written about it in Anglophone modern fiction than every single human/non-human relationship that has ever existed. And when you get a marriage in a novel, it's a novel about marriage. Whereas if you get a verminous insect in a book, it's never only about a verminous insect. Rather than using the metaphor of chipping away at some imagined wrong thing, I would say more simply that there's potential for new sights and inventions.

ALLEN   And from that it's whether you believe those things will actually effect material change or not?

HILDYARD   I think that's a question of form and skill. But narratives are just things that exist – I don't see them as parallel realities which occasionally break through into material reality. I mean that a copy of *Anna Karenina* is taking part in different kinds of interactions, like a sausage does, or a smartphone.

MCKAY   This relates to this discussion we had earlier on. Desire in some way seems to be saying that human relations to non-humans might be as opaque, strange, otherworldly, unknowable, but as necessary as something like love. If love then takes particular forms, like marriage, and those forms need to be thought about and worked over and worked through in art, because these are the ways that you actually think about how humans organise this protean thing – love or desire. And I think that the rest of this protean thing – life with other beings – is just miraculous. And it needs to be thought through – what it is to live and belong in the world with all these different creatures.

ALLEN   The whole role of this kind of conversation is trying to get towards a way to treat things better. Right? That seems to be the crux of it. But we don't know what anything requires, necessarily. We can only consider what is ethically suspect, and try to do what we can to acknowledge and alter that.

STAFF   I feel a lot more ambivalent about there being a positive knock-on effect of any of this. Actually, in the initial set of emails that we exchanged, I deliberately left out my 'status' as a meat-eater or not, which in a way was a deliberate choice to try to remove my stake of 'doing good' within the context of the conversation. I think it's so uninteresting. It makes me think about the film I have right now at the Serpentine (*On Venus*), which is a very colourful, psychedelic twelve-minute film that largely depicts animals being ripped apart and skinned and shredded. For me it was trying to question or think through, not only how much desire we can tolerate being mediated through an animal body, but also images of violence. And also maybe what is containable, and how much certain institutions can tolerate, or that mediate our own tolerance. And so trying to think about what can possibly be contained within the museum, which could be a book or a film or any of these things – how much desire but also trouble can really be contained within these spaces. And what can push at, or seek to really undo, the very liberal presumptions we have about what culture can do for us. I think for me, it was a moment of being able to really use images of violence mediated through animal bodies to put that into play, or just sort of forcibly twist that knife.

ALLEN   Did you anticipate any resistance?

STAFF   A lot of people say they can't watch the whole thing, which I anticipated. The museum was anxious about how to word it all and whether to put up warnings or things like that, which I antic-ipated. I mean, it's funny, because it's also in a way testing my own tolerance for these things. I took my cat to the vet recently and the vet was showing me how to pick her up by the scruff of her neck and it made me cry, because I honestly just didn't like him handling her so firmly, with such force, even though she was completely fine. But conversely, I'd spent hours and hours and hours meticulously going still by still through someone ripping the skin off a snake to find the precise moment of impact, or ecstasy. I think for me, again, it's about trying to set in motion a set of questions, but also demands about what we do with desire. I think that's what's at stake for me in a conversation about meat – what do we do with good desire and bad desire, the management or the control of other people's desires?

ALLEN   And give room to other people's desires which can sit outside of what's 'OK' or 'good'.

COHEN   And acknowledging them as part of being human. Did you change the colours before you edited the footage?

STAFF   No, I did what I think of as being an energetic assembly, trying to really get into the flow or the rhythm before I altered any of that. And then once I had that rhythm or energy, I went back through and colour-treated it all. So there's a lot of animals being skinned and cows on production lines and things, but it's constantly shifting, both with colour and speed but also, I suppose, legibility. It also spans between good, well-behaved violence – like there's clear butchery happening, but there's also footage of kids scooping tadpoles and half developed frogs out of ponds to look at. And then footage of people in Hyde Park relentlessly feeding the birds all day. And then there's also the extraction of horse urine for making synthetic oestrogen. There's also footage of bull semen being extracted from these big bull cocks. And then there's really straight-up graphic violence of people pulling animals apart that are still alive, scenes of illegal trade, illegal horse slaughter – most of it's them trying to get the skins off, fur, or whatever.

ALLEN   Did it affect you, going through all the footage?

STAFF   I don't think so. I'm not sure. Partly because I'd seen it all before, having done my years in the trenches, so to speak, as a vegan animal activist, and now feeling more agnostic about the nature of violence. But also, I suppose I knew I had to be disengaged and forensic.

HER LITTLE COLONY OF E. COLI

COHEN   For a show in Berlin a few years ago we had a batch of goldfish genetically engineered by a scientist to hatch without a reproductive system. And the whole process, which took about six years from starting to think about it until the fish hatching, was very thoughtful and not very emotional – but then once these fish were *there*, they felt like my babies. When they died one after another I was destroyed.

HILDYARD   Louise Mackenzie, who's an artist who works with E. Coli bacteria, told me that she felt some similar emotion when she took home her little colonies of E. Coli.

COHEN   It became such an emotional practice. They ended up living in our studio and their care dominated our lives for a few years.

HILDYARD   Perhaps that's a relevant com-parison, though, in the sense that the fish was a real being to you, somebody you knew, unlike the animals in the extreme footage. You could compare watching a horror film to sitting in a hospice with a relative who's dying. Sitting in the quiet hospice is going to be more distressing than watching a horror film, even though people are dying in more shocking ways in the film.

MCKAY   One of the things that we're talking about here is the capacity of the world to contam-inate your experience, so that you're changed. By which I mean that animals can contaminate your self-centredness. So that you move from thinking that your relationship to them doesn't matter, that you're hermetically sealed from them and what happens to them is irrelevant, to suddenly finding that barrier gets broken... I'm talking about a kind of ethical contamination, I suppose.

HILDYARD   But there are levels of contam-ination, aren't there. I mean, I think we've been talking about the duty to farm animals. But do we have a duty to wild animals that die every winter? We are capable of caring for them.

AFFECTIVE PLAYGROUND

STAFF   What I was going to say before was that I hadn't really considered until we got to this point in the conversation that meat might also function as a certain affective playground or affective testing ground to some degree. Just us talking about our work, for instance, I feel very much that it's about testing a tolerance of our relationship to violence. But when I saw your work about the goldfish, Revital, I was surprised at how upset I was by it.
COHEN   It's interesting that people are so upset by that, which perhaps means that something about it works. Rather than kill an animal, Tuur [Van Balen] and I created one, and then took really good care of it. I can see why it is upsetting, but when making work it's really important to me to remain somehow implicated while thinking of these processes, as they are so omnipresent and there is no real outside. So we had to test our tolerance and our ethics and beliefs quite radically. This work was made to ask these exact questions, while also thinking about how animals are produced outside of reproduction. What do these animals or this type of existence mean? Or, if we can define these fish as biological products rather than animals, whether this definition could possibly defy extinction, if sterilising can be seen as a ritual of transformation from animal to object? In this case their kind completely relies upon us, because they can't otherwise reproduce. We wanted to internalise within this animal's body a process that exists in almost all commercial breeding practices – the 'ritual' of sterilisation. Can we still call them animals, or are they some other biological being?
STAFF   Somehow it brings me back to watching horror films as a similar exercise, but also maybe the function of animals as a production of empathy for the Other. Pets are often a tool for teaching children, as much about feeding them as not hitting them, or kicking them, or even stroking them too roughly. I guess I'm coming back round in circles about modelling via animals, but thinking that there's a more affective quality at play than I maybe realised. That a set of emotions but also behaviours in relation to those feelings are modelled and exercised through human-animal relationships, and therefore meat.
MCKAY   But then what goes into framing that

modelling as OK or good? It would be so problematic to instrumentalise other humans as models or playgrounds, wouldn't it?
STAFF   I think we all already do it.
HILDYARD   One thing we haven't talked about is context for the artwork – we're talking as if aesthetics exist in a vacuum. And there's a much wider movement that has foundations in scientific discussions about species boundaries and symbiogenesis, and that seems to me to be relevant to any aesthetic work. If we're coming to understand the world in a different way, of course we'll need to represent it in a different way as well.

SUSHI EMBRYO

MCKAY   I think most of what's interesting to me is the way that meat still retains some kind of taboo force. Worries about hygiene, for example, might be one place where you get new kinds of taboos. I think that there is still a deep phobic investment in the idea of species as absolutely distinct, so that it would be somehow deeply wrong for there to be some horse in food that is not meant to be horse. Here, meat becomes a site for border control. And in some ways, it surprises me that that is still the case.
COHEN   I think more than anything that meat is widely seen as incredibly mundane. I wouldn't really see it as taboo, it's just basic. On a flight, for instance, meat will be the default. On our first visit to Professor Yamaha's lab in Hokkaido, after he showed us rooms, greenhouses and tanks full of various stages and species of chimera, he gave us a full demo of manually fertilising and genetically modifying a fish embryo. We sat through a presentation on his laptop, which oddly alternated between his scientific research papers on a few breeds of fish, alongside photos of the sushi that can be made out of them.
HILDYARD   I've been told that pregnant vegans are given anxious nutritional advice like, 'You need to eat four kilos of lentils every day, or something really bad is going to happen'. In terms of nutrition, that's just silly, pregnant people do not need meat or dairy, but this is still a medical norm, certainly in the NHS at the moment. So, that's both the mundanity of meat, the expectation that you'll be eating meat because it's normal to do so, but also its weird power, this kind of sense that you need to be consuming animal flesh, or you won't have this life force.

ALLEN   Yeah, no one's ever more an expert on protein than when you're faced with a vegan. And Carol J. Adams, who wrote the seminal text *The Sexual Politics of Meat*, talks about the normativeness of meat eating, and how when somebody is disparaged for not eating meat, it's because they might be lesser or something. And then she talks about how that disparagement also Others cultures and is racialised, because it means you're saying that entire subcontinents of people then are receiving less, are substandard, because they are refusing something that's seen to be the 'top' food group.

MCKAY   I've written in the past about the fact that someone used to say to me, 'Here's your "lesbian food"', when they were giving me my bit of – at that point – vegetarian food. But to that person, that made absolute sense, because of the slippage across those hierarchical normalisations.

COHEN   People feel judged when you say you're vegetarian, and they retaliate.

MCKAY   That one's interesting in the sense that it reveals that there's a certain performance of humanity going on in eating meat that's constantly anxious, as if perhaps one's humanity is not complete and needs constantly to be defended against the onslaught.

HILDYARD   I think what's tricky about that, and I completely agree with you, is that there is a concomitant narrative of veganism.

ALLEN   Whenever I say that I'm vegan it's almost like an admission. I feel guilty for aligning myself with a group where you supposedly have a greater moral fibre, because I don't think that's true.

HILDYARD   I think it's fair to say that you have a valid moral high ground.

ALLEN   I don't. There's a really significant vegan YouTuber called Gary Yourofsky and he always aligns the Holocaust with animal agriculture, which I think is horrific, and with this he has turned a large part of the Israeli army vegan. Because of this weird ethical emotional gymnastics he's done to make people relate to animals. I don't even know if I believe in morals. I've had room and time to consider this stuff, and education, which takes me miles away from someone like my mother who would never not eat meat and left school at 14 and worked 9,000 jobs and just doesn't want to consider it, but will weep at a cat advert. I have so much empathy for her and she has empathy for animals, but she'll cry at a cat advert and still eat the lamb.

HILDYARD   To me, direct comparisons between meat farming and the Holocaust, or slavery or colonialism (as we've mentioned several times) don't feel right – it doesn't feel respectful to the different sufferers. The comparisons are unhelpful when we're talking about meat farming because we can't just decolonise and allow all animals freedom – what we're talking about here isn't withdrawing from a lifeway and allowing it to flourish on its own terms. (My grandmother, who is a farmer, once sold a bull to a rancher in the USA who allowed the bull to roam freely outside, and in the first winter its balls froze off and then it died.) We've talked about the questions over whether forced life inside the conditions set by farmers is a life worth living and those questions – it seems to me – are finally unanswerable, but when I see the living animals – when the bull comes forward to have his nose scratched, or when the cows run out of the barn in April – I can't persuade myself for sure that their lives are not worth living, even if they're only alive in order to die. In most of the world, most animal farming is small-scale and humans gain from it in many ways, and there's no way that these relationships are not difficult or dirty and problematic, so I can see how the idea of doing away with multispecies work is attractively simple. It's much harder to transform our practical engagements than to get rid of them. But I think narratives like Yourofsky's could be a problem for humans because they play into the process of eradication of multispecies involvement, and this eradication on a bigger scale is – as much as anything – human self-harm.

SOY BOY VS. TOFU BOY

MCKAY   We've not talked about gender a lot. It's come up in much more interesting ways than talking about it directly, by these questions around pregnancy and stuff, but we've not talked about masculinity. But I mean, the world has enough of that.

ALLEN   Soy Boy. If you've drunk too much soy milk, if you're a vegan man, the oestrogen in soy milk, you're a soy boy. Go down the rabbit hole.

MCKAY   I was thinking myself about a great video game called *Super Meat Boy*. The character you play is basically like a piece of bloodied meat. And then PETA, the People for the Ethical Treatment of Animals, made a somewhat silly attempt to get coverage, which is basically their entire modus operandi, by inventing a game with 'Tofu Boy'. So then the game makers co-opted Tofu Boy, but Tofu Boy is basically useless as a game character.

I re-watched Carolee Schneeman's film *Meat Joy* (1964) last night. The film is famous for depicting a kind of bacchanalian happening, in which people roll about in a kind of orgy, many holding what I think are dead hens. And there was a thing that I'd never really noticed before, which I haven't seen discussed. There's one little bit where one of the performers, or characters, has this chicken and then starts properly cradling it, sort of rocking slightly, he's perhaps regressing. Because, you know, the schtick about *Meat Joy* is that it is a pure splurge of carnality. And then there are little moments in it that are just not like that, they are much more emotionally felt.

Sometimes there's not enough cross-contamination between vegan pro-animal discourses and ones that aren't necessarily at the radical utopian end. So that there might actually be listening in that space.

HILDYARD   I would guess that most people involved in the meat industry would be happy to do that if there was a viable movement that didn't ostracise them or preach from a distance.

MCKAY   I worked in a fish farm for quite a few years. This was after I was vegetarian, but that was just the only job that I could get. And one of the things that made me commit to being a vegetarian was the fact that I basically couldn't stop becoming hateful towards the animals in that place, because you're doing stuff to them and they don't like it. When you see videos of people harming animals in slaughterhouses and stuff, I can totally see how that happens from a certain kind of spiralling, slightly hysterical mindset that's to do with the hard work of the situation, especially if you're under really heinous working conditions. Because you start to feel like the whole world is against you. And these animals are right in front of you , they're your antagonists.

In the late nineteenth century, or early twentieth century, there were slaughterhouse tours. So our ideas about the politics of sight and invisibility are entirely flexible, and change through time depending on particular cultural pressures. In the white heat of modernity, people were quite happy to celebrate that new technological engagement with animals and want to show it and say, well, let's look at the fantastic way that we're doing this in a well-ordered, mechanised way rather than in this messy way in a backyard where you might make a mistake and stab a pig in the wrong place. I'm always dubious about the idea that if we just made it all visible everyone would chuck it. I think capital would just find new ways to sell us new stuff.

HILDYARD   My next door neighbour told me about the time he explained the origin of sausages to his 8-year-old son. The son is a sensitive boy and he loves animals, so my neighbour expected him to be horrified, but he wasn't bothered at all, he was just like, 'Oh. Cool.'

MCKAY   I think this conversation has consistently pulled away from a sort of positivist, moral set of claims about meat, and its rightness or wrongness, and rather towards the idea that it is essentially a set of deep, affective, and not necessarily rationally controlled investments. And that makes it really tricky to talk about, because it doesn't mean that there aren't power relations involved, and objectifications, and all these things going on. It's a very messy sort of space.

ZOSIA KUCZYŃSKA

POETRY

THE GIFT SHOP ELEGIES #6: ELEGY WITH POSTCARD FROM THE NATIONAL PORTRAIT GALLERY

I find desire ridiculous these days. Desire of course being different to need: for Jacques Lacan, the latter is a thing that can be met and satisfied like thirst; the former is a part of who we are – a lack that can't be othered or appeased.[1] I'm relieved to discover the women and men I want look nothing like my dad – but then again, the men take photographs and smile like buildings whose architecture is transformed in sunlight, are kind and talented and unconcerned with putting on those masculinities that poison their performers. Obviously, the things that I have lost have fused desire with need, and though they can be prised apart in time, for now, the need for other bodies is as difficult to separate from the desire that the dead might live as my dad's intestines were from the old scar tissue cobwebbing his abdomen.

When I found you lying in the field –

I should say at this point I am writing about a rabbit I stumbled across at the Skylarks Nature Reserve, not the hare stuffed in Sam Taylor-Johnson's photograph in which she stands in a single-breasted suit, alive and wielding a 'traditional symbol of lust and passion'[2] by the paws. I should also say I'm imagining the rabbit as the body of a man, which is problematic on many levels, because I am addressing or trying to address my fear of living bodies through the bodies of the dead; dead bodies through the bodies of the living. I never dared to go and look at Dad when he was dead in hospital. I knew that he was there inside his coffin because how often had I sat beside his bed? How could I not know where the head and hands and feet lay in relation to my heart? But when I saw the rabbit... Oh, I stared.

When I found you lying in the field, your one Knave's eye a blooming
& your arms & legs stretched out like a bounding bridge
& your stomach drawn in as though a hand had pulled you back & under
into the arms of a body over your shoulder

it seemed you were part of the experiment –

1 See Denis Donoghue, *The Arts Without Mystery* (London: British Broadcasting Corporation, 1983), p. 72.
2 ‹www.npg.org.uk/collections/search/portrait/mw58423/Sam-Taylor-Johnson-Sam-Taylor-Wood-Self-portrait-in-Single-breasted-Suit-with-Hare›

the Anglo-Saxon huts, their wattle & daub, the raven & hammer,
the moat & mound at the edge of which you had been laid
imperfectly but with irresistible significance.

Experimental archaeology is practical: you recreate the past by way of testing
out hypotheses. Dad always joked he wanted to be scattered among the Rollright
Stones – a *Doctor Who* location where they filmed 'The Stones of Blood' (a serial
from the 1970s). The Rollright Stones have stood five thousand years and more;
four thousand years ago at least, cremations were in evidence, and when we scat-
ter him in 2017 from a plastic urn, Dad sounds like chicken feed. And though
it seemed appropriate as hell to feel such reverence, irreverence – the specula-
tive pull of ritual, the humdrum glamour of location shooting – I also felt not
unlike Sergeant Howie, the virginal policeman who was burned to death in the
eponymous *Wicker Man*. When he exhumes the remains of Rowan Morrison, a
missing girl on a pagan island ruled by a windswept Christopher Lee, he only
finds the carcass of a hare inside the coffin; he's furious; the locals wind him up
and say it makes a lovely transmutation.

I laid wildflowers on you then, incapable of suspicion
of foul play or assumption of natural causes,
unsure, without touching your mattedness, of the basis of my fear
that want might go fulfilled – whether desire
for the miraculous or need for cathartic confirmation:
you might have been cold; then again, you might have been warm.

The following night, as he sleeps on the whereabouts of Rowan's body, Britt
Ekland sings to Howie from the room next door; she slaps the walls; he grips
his upper arms and sweats and sweats and sweats.

THE GIFT SHOP ELEGIES #7: ELEGY WITH POSTCARDS FROM THE BIRMINGHAM MUSEUM AND ART GALLERY

Anne Carson talks at length about desire, its being a want that cannot be ful-filled, and claims that Sappho writes a triangle of lover and beloved and the thing that stands between the two, not in the way we'd talk about a love triangle now, but rather in the sense that the obstacle is a necessary, stabilising part of eros.[3] And I think the same holds true for the bereaved – triangulated grief in which betwixt the living and the dead is the obstacle of... what? For atheists, there is no distant shore, no river Styx, no place we'll meet again in future time. The theist balances the here against the great there-after; dying stands between. The atheist must stabilise their grief in time alone – there are times when people live and times when they do not, and the self is stretched in three directions: past, present, future – remembrance, attendance, expectation.[4] Between the self expecting that 'he'll be no more' and the pined-for self remembering that 'he was once alive', there stands the self that knows that 'he is dead' – a triangle of selves that makes bereavement possible and brings no comfort to the elegist.

Three dreamers, one of whom is not asleep.
Reading left to right, the future wakes;
reading right to left, the past won't rest.

Time distends the sofa and I dream
extensions of myself – awake, asleep –
in the hope of finding, somewhere in my past
or future, you beside me, though I know

the language of my system of belief
reads one way only, and my future self
will never share this sofa with you now.

To be an atheist and be bereaved is to be immune to consolation: he is not – or his living consciousness is not – in a better somewhere else or anywhere. You have to be polite when people say 'he's looking down on you' or similar, despite its minimising of your loss, which will forever be an unlined cloud. Insisting on

3 Anne Carson, *Eros the Bittersweet* (London: Dalkey Archive Press, 2015).
4 See Paul Ricoeur, *Time and Narrative*, 3 vols, tr. Kathleen McLaughlin and David Pellauer (Chicago, IL: University of Chicago Press, 1984–1988), I (1984), pp. 16-21 and St. Augustine, *Confessions*, tr. Henry Chadwick (Oxford: Oxford University Press, 1998), pp. 233-43.

being inconsolable, however, runs the risk of petulance – of being the supermarket kid who cries because they have to wait until the coins are in the checkout till before the prize inside the Kinder Egg can be revealed. Or, if you want a classical metaphor with the same transactional overtones, here's Louis MacNeice and his early 1960s 'Charon': 'If you want to die, you will have to pay for it.'[5] The problem is that I don't want to die.

> A teddy bear made from a woollen army blanket.
> Blunt instrument of comfort.
> Hammerhead wrongness of the natural world:
> an adult who cries for the comfort of childish things;
> a child who finds comfort in relics from a bed of nightmares.

In season 7 episode 13 of *Charmed* – which follows the adventures of three sister witches in the early noughties – the world has been remodelled overnight into a world beyond conflict between evil and good, but which can be maintained only by an absence of free will, which manifests itself as seeing death as positive so that, when those who cause conflict are killed, nobody notices. The means by which so-called Utopia is ultimately overthrown by the Charmed Ones turns out to be acknowledgement of grief: two sisters of the three have lost their partners, but when asked how they feel, they only smile and say aloud, 'He's in a better place'; it's this that alerts us to the wrongness of the situation, and it's only when they stop believing that they should be happy and are made to feel their loss that the spell is broken.

> Who would wish to sleep like one consoled
> if they could remember the price of consolation?

---

5 Louis MacNeice, 'Charon', *Collected Poems*, ed. by Peter McDonald (London: Faber and Faber, 2007), p. 593.

SECOND PERSON SINGULAR

David Gilmour records a setting of the famous sonnet
– the one about comparing thee – afloat upon a river.
It starts with an octave leap, then down a semitone-and-tone:
eight and six; octave, sestet – clever, but not Shakespeare.
The tune is like *Twinkle Twinkle Little Star* but slightly jumbled
and with an insistent shift to the relative minor, though not as often
as I remember when I play it back inside my head.
There's no guitar and the reverb is excessive, but I listen
obsessively all day; at the end of the day, I don't remember
the middle of the sonnet or the melody in order.
And *thee* is nondescript and impersonal and intimate,
and language is transcendent only up to a given point.
An ageing rocker is singing on a boat upon a river
and thou art gone as unused grammar in the mouths of lovers.

LISA OPPENHEIM

Lisa Oppenheim's practice is an ongoing experiment with the medium of photography. Working on to found images, unearthing technical processes, and re-exposing and redeveloping images, she makes visible the medium's chemical magic and explores its capacity to record.

For the series *Smoke* (2012), Oppenheim collected photographs from public archives, encyclopaedias, museums and Flickr, showing smoke rising out of volcanoes or bombed cities, enveloping riots or factories. She then made new prints using firelight, rather than a typical darkroom enlarger, to expose the images. In *Burning of the Imperial Refinery Oil City PA 1876/2012* (2012) – included in *The White Review* – the smoke captured in a photograph from 1876 has been re-developed using match light, so that fire is both the subject and material of her print.

For *Landscape Portraits* (2015-16), Oppenheim created camera-less photographs by placing silver gelatin paper directly on to the veneers of trees. In the images included below, the rings and patterns of sassafras, cherry tree and walnut were transferred directly on to the paper, creating photograms that echo fingerprints.

In her new series *The American Colony* (2019), Oppenheim delved into the photographic archive of the American Colony in Jerusalem. Founded in 1881 by a small group of Christians who left Chicago to settle in Ottoman Palestine, the Colony established a hotel, hospital, and eventually a Photo Department in what is now East Jerusalem. Members of the department set about documenting local archaeological sites, desert flora and fauna and urban life, often in stereoscopic photographs – then in fashion – where two images of the same subject are set side by side to give the illusion of depth. *Olive Tree and Wall to Stop Locusts, 1915/2019* (2019), included below, records the aftermath of a locust plague which devastated farms around Jerusalem in 1915. Oppenheim has cropped sections of the photograph, which shows a zinc wall built to repel larvae, so that the stereoscopic split becomes part of the composition, thus evoking the wall that now runs through this region, the Israeli Separation Barrier. In other works, stereoscopic photographs of flowers have been re-exposed on the same print to create spectral double images.

PLATES

XIV

XV   XVI

XVII XVIII

XIX

XX   XXI

SANKI SAITŌ
tr. RYAN CHOI

THREE DEMONS: SERIES V

Piano
plays   your

sacred
winter

trees and days —

Tears —   *rain*

  on   *young*   *parents' graves.*

End of waltz —   gourds outdoors —

outshine   the   mildew-
ridden   home —

Sick   of spring,   even

sicker of jet-   black tadpoles —

On
the beach slope —

sun-

burnt
mushroom

archipelago —

Town — the deepest
                    winter

days,   bundles

of
          fists   on the move —

Falling silent —   a crowd

          scrambles   toward the sunset —

          Silence —   elevators climb

                    through   the night,
                    lightning   streaks —

                                        Summer — daydream:
                                        warships

                              bob
                              in the orphan's

          gaze.

From   sky to earth —

          rose   petals drift   through drought —

Feast

          of rice balls: rotted   twigs, wedged

          in the hat   rack —

Lucid —
       moonrise,

       hatching

       locust eggs —

Violet — twin
       gales,

       rumpling   the boat-
                 pond skin.

Cooped in

    a white   mosquito

net,
fatigue   dense

    as iron   bricks —

Sucking on

pine pollen, the

      teacher
      cracks walnuts —

Morning frost — we

      soar

above   clouds: snow

      flits

beneath —

Mirror cakes —
sitting,

    broken   in the   dark —

    Wild   geese   winging

             north,   hauling
             commodious   sacks —

                      Winter —

                        ambling
                        cows bore

                        into the dirt

                        flecks on

             the icy   path —

             Machine
             guns   *between their brows* —

             blood

          flowers   *bloom.*

Sense   of relief:

        pure   salt

     crystals   on   soybeans —

Sun   wanes: the dead

     goldfish

     plop into   the bowl —

Table —
    in the pine

    grove, an
    omelette

        for my solitude —

Soldiers —

    zipping by on   *pitch-*   *black trains.*

        Spring — playtime:

          grinding toy

    trolleys
    against   the hillside —

Skylarks —

    in the down-
    pour deliver

themselves   one

    by one —

Chickens

    in the spring, stagger
    through the

    windstorm —

        Voices — in

          the iron fort,
          lure the buzzing

      mosquitoes in —

Afraid — of red

    mushrooms   that are unafraid

    of me —

After   thunder, after

    rain —   wooden

    clogs clatter   in search of stars —

                  Vashikov — the Russian

                  growls,
                  swipes at   dangling

                        pomegranates —

Autumn harvest —

in the dirt,
you dig   up your

own   shadows —

        Winter garden —
     index

     finger   nicked: a girl

     bleeds —

                  Airport — MPs

                    on patrol,

                    our   *bitter farewell.*

THEY'RE REALLY CLOSE TO MY BODY

A HAGIOGRAPHY OF NINE INCH NAILS AND THEIR RESIDENT MYSTIC ROBIN FINCK

JOHANNA HEDVA

'We possess nothing in this world other than the power to say "I".
This is what we must yield up to God.'
– Simone Weil

'God break down the door
You won't find the answers here
Not the ones you came looking for.'
– Nine Inch Nails

1.

I was 10 years old when *The Downward Spiral* by Nine Inch Nails was released in 1994, and I listened to it more than any other record for the next six years, when everything I knew about myself was disintegrating and becoming unknowable. It lives in my blood memory, the soundtrack to the most formative part of my life. When I think of that time, my memories resonate with those songs, I can't imagine myself without them, who I would have been. Since then, twenty-five years, I regularly go through periods where the only thing I listen to for weeks, months at a time is Nine Inch Nails, and this locates me, returns me to myself. When you love a band for more than half your life, something happens as their songs come to live in you, they echo through how you remember the past, and fortify how you are legible to yourself in the present.

NIN was the first band that got me in trouble with grown-ups – for this, they have a special place in my heart that no other band will ever touch. For Christmas vacation in 1996, when I was 12, I brought the *Broken* EP with me when I went to stay with my Catholic grandparents. *Broken* was packaged in a cardboard 'digipak', so my grandmother, rather than struggle with a plastic jewel case, could open it like a book. The lyrics were printed on the inside, though I was singing them aloud all the time too. I think Grandma had the biggest problem with my favourite lyric – 'Gotta listen to your big-time, hard-line, bad-luck, fist fuck' – but there was enough offensive sentiment on that record to compel her to gather my family for an intervention. They asked me how I could listen to this violent, raging, blasphemous music. My answer, 'Because I like it,' still seems to be the best response to such a question.

The 'Closer' video also got me in trouble. It was rarely played on MTV, and since these were the days before YouTubing could satiate fan cravings, I lived in constant, nervous hope that I'd be lucky enough to catch one of its late-night airings, maybe even be able to record it on VHS. One night I did get lucky, but I was at a sleepover birthday party, with giggling girls in pyjama shorts. We were 13, maybe 14 years old. The TV was playing in the background. That electronic beat came on – *dum, fft! dum, fft!* – animating, via air through tubes, the raw pig heart nailed to the Cherner chair. I squealed, turned up the volume, and sat six inches from the screen. I sang along, knew every word. 'I wanna fuck you like an animal / I wanna feel you from the inside / I wanna fuck you like an animal / My whole existence is flawed / You get me closer to God.' I clapped when Trent Reznor, his aquiline profile in silhouette, licked that strange, vintage microphone that looked at once phallic and mammillary. When the shots of him bound and blindfolded came on during the second chorus, I remember swooning and sighing, as if I were watching a boy band. No one joined me. They all hung back. I can imagine this scene now, how they saw me, a person lonely and young and singing to herself, leaning in to that bizarre world on the screen, with its spinning eggs and crucified monkey and apple-mouthed pig and split-open nautilus, the world that summoned something powerful and fundamental in me and told me that, although I felt like it, I was not world-less. Even if the world I'd lived in so far, the very world of this generic, bland, teenaged living room, had been deserted and companionless for me, the world of that video promised that, somewhere, there were people who saw visions like mine, full of nihilism and perversions but also twisted beauty, a kind of gracefulness in all the shit. The birthday girl's parents called my parents, expressing concern, and banned me from coming over again.

I saved up to buy the VHS tour documentary for *The Self Destruct Tour*, called *Closure*, which was released in 1997, when I was 13. It was the first VHS tape I ever owned, and what it contained, what it revealed, about this band felt like I'd discovered the Gnostic Gospels. The grainy image storms with brown light and shadows, and the music they play, on a stage draped in shrouds and scrolls of loose cassette tape, is brutal and desperate. The band destroy their instruments, each other, and them-selves. Keyboards are stomped on until the keys look like ribs that have been cracked off their spines. Multiple band members get injured: Trent throws a microphone stand that lands on the drummer's head, and, with blood pouring into his eyes, the guy keeps playing. The crowd doesn't just mosh, it tears itself apart, punching each other, crowd-surfing, and clawing their way toward the stage. They grab for Trent while bouncers fight them off. Trent sneers back, 'Whoever threw that, fuck you.' It looked like the most exciting live show imaginable. I'd dream of it sitting in class, while the teacher droned on about the quadratic equation. I'd wonder what it felt like to be in that crowd, that room drenched in fury and sweat, with those songs, that music, the most explosive noise I'd ever heard. Around this time, I started playing in bands, and I got to learn for myself how good it feels to turn your amps all the way up and scream until your throat breaks. It instilled a belief in me that I still have to this day: that any spiritual ailment can be cured by playing music at maximum volume in a small, dark room.

The behind-the-scenes shots in *Closure* are even more infamous than the concert footage. They show the band destroying dressing rooms by heaving couches against walls, staggering around hungover in clothes whose rank funk you can practically smell off the screen. They snigger at Midwest gas stations where they shove oranges up their shirts to look like tits, and howl with laughter during a prank call to a sex worker, where they ask her to 'Tell me you wanna fuck my nine inch nail'. I remember that there was a lot of ass and genitals on display, most of it male. Jim Rose's Circus, a BDSM freak show, was one of the opening acts, and we watch one of the performers backstage try to lift an armchair that's hooked to his limp dick. Marilyn Manson, another opening act, is young and lean and impish, sitting next to a pair of strippers with a look of inebriated glee on his lipstick-smeared face. Buzz Osborne of Melvins is persuaded by a drunken mob of band members to throw a lamp at an EXIT sign that is dripping with beer (this lives on in Tumblr gifsets entitled 'Buzz, et. al., versus EXIT sign'). NIN begin the tour playing small theatres, and end, two years later, in arenas. Lou Reed comes back-stage after a show and says, 'It was so smart, it was just so fucking smart.' There is the terrific version of 'Hurt' sung with David Bowie and the notorious, mud-covered Woodstock '94 performance. This was the tour where they wore black leather and latex covered in cornstarch, and Trent was in short-shorts with garters, dripping in sweat and blood. He careens

around the stage, jerking off his microphone stand, and knocking over his bandmates by roping his mic cable around their feet, or sometimes just outright tackling them.

Some of the most exhilarating scenes – not only in *Closure* but in most of their live videos from the tours of the 1990s – show how Trent particularly enjoys attacking the lead guitarist, Robin Finck. Trent gropes him, leaps on him, twists him to the ground, shoves him off the stage into the surging crowd, and if it's not a tackle, it's an erotically menacing embrace of an arm around Robin's head, bending his neck back and stroking his forehead, or pushing up against him from behind. On YouTube, there are several fan-made compilations, with titles like 'Trent Reznor vs. Robin Finck (Part 1)', that give a sense. There is also a sequence on *Closure*'s 'bonus materials' where a nearly-naked Marilyn Manson appears onstage and shoves Trent to the ground while kissing him. Along with the 'Closer' video, these scenes constructed a world where sex converged with rage, encapsulating the turgid passions of puberty in a way that no other band at the time did. Gruff, melancholic Pearl Jam could not get close to the feeling that being inside the belly of the beast of lust is warm and wet but also suffocating. More than anything else in his repertoire, Trent has had to account for these boiling, carnal eruptions in interviews. ('I don't walk around throwing mic stands when I'm eating dinner,' he pointed out in an interview with *MuchMusic*.) In 1995, at age 11, I remember reading a particularly lurid article in the magazine *Details*, which bloomed in my fantasies for years after. The interviewer asks Trent the five words he associates with sex. Trent replies, 'Taste, sweat, lick, come, bite,' and is then asked if he's into masochism and whether he associates sex with pain. He says yes. As I would experience in the next few years – making out awkwardly in closets and cars, bumping teeth and wincing at too-long fingernails, not to mention being confronted with the banal brutality of young desire – not only were sex and pain linked, but they felt like the same thing. Masochism was not a choice or a kink. It was how sex felt all the time. All you could do was submit. This was especially compounded for someone, as I was, assigned female at birth. Growing up, I was told not just by adults, but by so many depictions of erotic love in movies and TV, that if a boy called you names, insulted you, ignored you, and even (or *especially*) when he hit you, it was because he liked you. To be wanted was to suffer. And *to* want was to be monstrous.

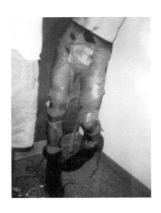

The lyrics of Nine Inch Nails, so simple and vulnerable in their angst, in their need, in their defeat, offered articulation and insight into this rough new world. They were embarrassing as hell to sing along to – so bald and filthy! *so* corny! – but that's exactly what made them meaningful. They explained the stuff that embarrassed you, gave it shape, cause, and expression, and validated it as true. In that same interview from 1995, Trent says, 'Every day I'm saying the most personal thing I could ever say... But one of the prices is that there's an open raw nerve that I'm letting everybody look at. There's a hole in the back of my pants with a bare asshole showing, and you can see right in there. And sometimes I wish I hadn't.' Here, he could be describing having to endure one day of high school when you've got a crush on someone who doesn't know you exist and you've just gathered your courage to say hi. NIN was the perfect band, especially for a goth, for an adolescence of gender confusion and the violence of craving. Lain over the harsh, wrathful quality of the music, you could scream and thrash and flail around to the huge sounds, but still be talking about how small you felt. I remember so many days of shuffling through the hallway at school, chewing my own tongue, my body crawling with thirst, and my only relief would come when I got home after school and cranked NIN up on my Walkman. It was transcendent in a basic way that I've never experienced since. As an adult I listen to a lot of hardcore, metal, and noise – bands that make angry, desolating music about being angry and desolated – but I keep returning to NIN precisely because of those naked lyrics about want. Let's be real: you can't sing along to Merzbow.

Along with satisfying the untamed needs born in that vortex of sex and rage, one of the reasons I'm so unabashedly a NIN fan, and have been for so long, is because they've never humiliated me as they've gone through the years, like nearly every other mainstream band I loved growing up in the 1990s. I can declare my love for them without having to suffer the scorn that so many of those bands now deserve for selling out in various, pathetic ways. Indeed, it's recently felt as though all these years of cult devotion are being validated in a populist way, as NIN re-emerged in the late 2010s as a singular bastion of uncompromising artistic vision, the last men standing. *Billboard* recently declared us to be in the midst of a 'Reznorssance'. After winning the Oscar for Best Score for *The Social Network*, and going on to score *Waves*, *Watchmen*, and the new Pixar film *Soul*, a meme went around stating that 'From now on all good movies will be scored by NIN.' The band appeared, as 'The' Nine Inch Nails, in the new *Twin Peaks*, and they looked and sounded fucking amazing. Miley Cyrus sang a warped version of 'Head Like a Hole' on *Black Mirror*, turning it into a capitalist nightmare of so-called feminist empowerment, which Reznor celebrated by releasing a T-shirt with the hilariously uncanny lyrics: 'Head like a hole! I'm on a roll! Riding so high! Achieving my goals!' At the end of the episode, Miley sang the real lyrics, which were as clarifying and articulate in 2019 as they were in 1989. The many years where the band's popularity receded from mainstream success are now seen as evidence of their integrity. NIN has always foregrounded politics, not only before it became cool and trendy to do so, but at a time when it was likely to harm one's career. During the record-industry crisis brought on by the internet – the one that made many artists turn into ass-holes whining about their bank accounts – Reznor released a new record, not as a pay-what-you-want download, but for free, saying, 'This one is on me.' When NIN won the Webby award for it, Trent's entire speech was, 'Wait. We didn't charge anything.' After the 2016 US election, he declared that if you voted for Trump, he didn't want you at a NIN concert, and during NIN's world tour of 2017-18, while playing outside of the States, Trent consistently apologised for his country. 'Please, forgive us,' he said. This during the same year the Smashing Pumpkins staged a 'reunion tour' where Billy Corgan monologued every night that he didn't care who you voted for, what mattered most was that you were here – or, in other words, that you liked his band.

Beyond politics, something elemental about what NIN did for me as a kid has remained central to who I am as an adult. My precious VHS of *Closure* and the band it depicted represented everything I wanted, and still want, the world to be: chaotic, feverish, ungovernable. It had the power (maybe not literally, although it was thrilling to think so) to blow up the walls around me, the ones that kept me inside those bland generic rooms, lorded over by lifeless adults who insisted I obey rules that had no meaning beyond control. Watching *Closure* as an adult cracks me up with its childishness, how adolescent all those boys are, snickering at their dicks out and their rowdy tantrums. But I'd be lying if I didn't admit to some nostalgia.

Adulthood has sobered me on the actual political impact of rebelliousness. I know that flipping off cop cars doesn't actually *do* anything to dismantle oppression, but it sure as fuck still *feels* good. It will always thrill me to shout 'Fuck you!' to teachers, parents, bosses. To spit on the door of a bank, to crush a cigarette into the face on a politician's sign. What a feeling of liberation to go to my high-school campus on a weekend and piss on the office door of the chemistry teacher who was giving me a D-. When I see young goths and punks sitting in piles of each other outside drugstores, smoking their clove cigarettes in their Dr. Martens and writing lyrics on their fragile skin in ballpoint pen, I will always smile and nod and want to lean over and tell them to try to stay romantic about all that acrimony for as long as they can, because the romance of it is what will help the most.

NIN is the purest expression of fury in music that I've experienced, and I love them most for how they femme-ed it, made it queer. It wasn't just that they wore lipstick while they broke themselves. It was the excruciating nakedness of the lyrics paired with the visceral embodiment of their performance. Though their performances proposed the body as something to hope to transcend, they only revealed and articulated this hope as false. Such transcendence was not, in fact, possible: the body was not something from which you could escape, you'll always have to drag it along behind you. Rather than this feeling like a punishment, however, a live NIN show was a testament to the fact that this embodiment could still feel enraptured, generative, even mystical.

This is because NIN is the band who most corroborate the fact that there can be a mysticism of fury. There are different kinds of mysticism, but all are primarily defined in terms of ecstasy, which comes from the Greek *ekstasis*, *ek* meaning 'out' and *stasis* meaning 'stand'. Ecstasy is the standing outside of oneself, an experience that requires a total transformation of self, one that also transforms where (and through what) it can stand. We usually understand ecstasy as being conjoined with joy, affording an escape by catapulting you in sweet relief outside of your confining, earthly body of pain and frustration. But ecstasy can also be understood in terms of fury, rooted within, and because of, the bounds of your own skin. From this place, and only ever bound to it, implosive rather than explosive, fury mutates those bonds. Think of being throttled with rage: how your body shimmers with it, how you are changed. Think of the Furies, the ancient goddesses of vengeance and justice (which is where we get the word; the Romans invented it to translate the Greek name Erinyes), who are prescribed by their transformations: when an injustice occurs, they morph into human-shaped birds with blood shooting out of their eyes. They torment the perpetrator, shrieking at him, until he is brought to justice, and then they shape-shift again, this time into mourning old women, cloaked and heavy with despair at the fact that they've had to metamorphosise at all. Crucially, the centripetal collapse of fury, its core and border within the body itself, can be understood both as feminine and subordinate, because the oppressed – women, slaves, the disabled – have historically been equated with the body, reducible to and by it. Rage at such bondage is both liberation and limitation. Like the Furies, what fury produces is catharsis, a totalising change, but the thing that is altered is not the external world itself, but the bodies of those who are most affected by that world's perfidy.

Fury can never be asked for more than what it is at its most pure – and the same could be said of joy. Both are primordial, basic materials, the raw stuff of life. Depending on your worldview, either one or the other is what's required to first kindle anything at all. Obviously, I'm of the mind that fury is the OG ingredient. To begin anything we need a spark, a flame, a big bang, a fist punching through a wall. Although joy extends outward (to stand outside of one's self), fury expands what is interior. It tunnels into the deepest redoubt of your being, excavating a violent, primordial place made of need and want. A definition of fury could be that it is the near-unbearable reckoning with how you didn't get what you needed or wanted. This, necessarily, must take place at your tender, wounded pith, which means that the transformation fury offers, though it uncovers an infinite space within yourself, stops at the edges of your own skin. NIN's fury, especially onstage, reaches this limit quickly. It produces a storm of ferocity, throwing the band members against themselves and the crowd, hurling the music forward in rapture and rupture. But if this storm was all their performance contained, the band would not be as powerfully purgative as they are. If they began and ended at fury only, the transcendent capacity delivered at a NIN show would stay grounded within the material perimeter of the body, circumscribing how lonely it is to live there, that place, that thing, which is all, in the end, that one has. But it doesn't stop at this – because NIN has, as its touring guitarist, an actual ecstatic mystic on their stage: Robin Finck.

2.

Robin Finck. He is the biggest reason I am a NIN fan, but he is also something more, someone I've followed for 25 years, who has shown me the way to places I never thought existed, let alone imagined that I'd one day go to. It's not enough to say that he is my favourite guitar player, or one of the first rock stars who I wanted to be. What he's revealed to me has felt less like a veneration and closer to a kind of communion with another world. First it was how he looked, which was unlike anything I'd ever seen before, not entirely man, or woman, and which revealed the way to a world beyond gender and the regime it imposes on the body – making his kind of ecstasy the sort that stands *outside*. As a dreamy queer kid on the brink of puberty, such a guide was life-changing and life-saving. But then, it was so much more: it was how he played his instrument, which is signatory for its refusal to conform to the context in which he exists, and his performance while playing, whose fundamental characteristic is of someone with bottomless presence who is also entirely gone from this world. He is the strangest guitarist I can think of, not because his style of playing is the strangest, but because of the choices he makes for the kinds of stages he plays on. What he does – or perhaps it's more accurate to say, what he refuses to do – produces a kind of radical negation of presence. Such a negation deviates from the world of rock, which is almost ontologically about the exaltation of the performers' presence. Robin never does what you think he will, what you'd expect from someone in his place. Robin's also the strangest celebrity I can think of: he's played on some of the biggest stages in the world with NIN, and for a decade as Slash's replacement in Guns N' Roses, but his career is a demonstration of the refusal of celebrity. He's given only a handful of interviews in twenty-five years – the first on-camera interview focusing on only him just appeared in 2018 – and when he does speak, he is extremely self-effacing. When asked to introduce himself in a feature on NIN, he said, 'I'm Robin Finck, one of the guitarists in Nine Inch Nails.' This, from *the* guitarist in Nine Inch Nails. (There have been other guitarists in Nine Inch Nails

when Robin didn't play with them, but, no matter how good they are, I consider them interlopers next to Robin Finck.) I've heard from a fan who waited for him outside the venue for hours after a concert that when he appeared, he introduced himself to her. 'Hi, I'm Robin,' he said. 'Yes,' she said. 'I know very well who you are.' It took many years for all of this to synthesise into something that made sense, and only now in my mid-30s, after watching him for more than two decades, do I understand that he has been a role model for me, not in terms of how to be a musician, or a performer, or an artist, or even a person. Rather, Robin Finck showed me how to be a mystic.

Despite its reliance on ecstasy, I can't explain what exactly mysticism *is* – no one can, that's the point. Mysticism is a state, an experience, where language can't go, and this ineffability is precisely what defines it. Another way of saying this is: if you can define it in words, it's not mysticism. The root of the words 'mysticism' and 'mystery', *myst*, comes from a Latin word for 'secret rite, worship, or secret thing', which originated in a Greek word that meant 'to close, shut', as in, closing one's lips in secrecy, or shutting one's eyes so as not to see. The secret, unknowable-ness of it is the only way to define it. What this means is that mystics as such are ultimately unknowable. The closest we can get to them is some sort of reading and writing that cannot be hermeneutical, cannot be oriented toward definition. An explanation of mysticism will only ever fail, so a circumscription of that failure, an account of the unknowing, must be the point.

It took me a year into writing this essay to understand that I am actually writing a *hagiography*: a writing of the lives of the saints. 'Hagio' is a Greek word that means sacred, holy, and devoted to the gods. Hagiography was, during the Middle Ages and into the Medieval period, the primary literary genre of Western civilisation, because it was the kind produced by the Christian Church. For several centuries, the only literate people were priests, and so they wrote for each other the stories they deemed worthy of being written, and the ones they wanted to read. Before I was able to articulate that I was following this lineage, I explained why I was writing this essay by saying that I'm just a really, really big fan. But fandom, which is perhaps one of the primary literary genres of *our* current time, is different to hagiography in that, for the latter, your subject might as well be dead. In fact, for hagiography it's better if your subject *is* dead, because it requires idealisation, a certain amount of romance and fantasy. It asks both writer and reader to devote their time to that which is no longer alive, proposing that through the hagiography the subject can live on, an eternal life. It also insists, since the text's subject is dead, on making an account of someone who can no longer account for themselves. Amy Hollywood, in *Sensible Ecstasy*, writes how the task of the hagiographer is to interpret not only the life, but the very body, of that which is beyond interpretation. This is especially true with women saints, and has significant political consequences: to write their lives, literate male priests attempted to clarify behaviours that they found incomprehensible. The result of this was that so many Medieval women saints were said, by their hagiographers, to do bizarre things as expressions of their mysticism: some can fly, some weep until they Biblically flood the village, St. Catherina of Siena was said to have worn Christ's foreskin as her wedding ring when they married. The list goes on. If one cannot hope to know the unknowable, then hagiography is perhaps a coming-to-terms with this. People cope with unknowability and that which cannot be known in different ways; sometimes I think mysticism is simply the experience of living for, because of, and within this coping.

Crucially, hagiography is a solitary genre, both to read and to write, but it is necessarily and fathomlessly solitary for the writer. To write a hagiography is to bear the knowledge of just how small you are, a small thing reaching out to a vast, unknowable heaven. My hagiography began as an email to a friend: I'd invited them to a NIN show, and they said they'd of course love to join, but they never got into NIN, what was it that I liked about them? I started typing bits of answer, as if I were a priest hunched over my scroll, writing by candlelight, to say, let me show you what has given my life purpose. After my email swelled past 2,000 words, I thought, maybe I ought to move this to a Word document and take it seriously as a piece of writing. This felt strange; I've never before been compelled to write from a place of enthusiasm. It was hard to justify, I'm so used to needing critique – or fury! – to be my reason. Eventually, I turned in a 7,000-word version to my agent, who, a little bewildered (all year, I'd been turning down paying gigs in order to write this thing that no one had asked for), told me I'd probably need to cut it by several thousand words for publication. I took all of her other edits, but not the one about the length; instead, I added 8,000 more words. It wasn't that I was obsessed with Robin Finck: it was that I was obsessed with *writing* about Robin Finck, which kept seeming like an impossible task. As my essay's word count still climbed, I understood that a part of me was surrendering to something I couldn't explain at all, and although an essay, etymologically, is an attempt at some sort of explanation, I realised that as I got close to definitions, I simultaneously got close to paradoxes, that as I made my way towards the shore of perceptibility, I was also becoming drenched in the incommunicable. This, then, was how I realised that I was writing about mysticism.

For me, the way mysticism feels in practice has to do with a paradox: it's where you can feel the edges of your body as they are being annihilated by, and into, something greater than you. In order to encounter anything, you first need a body to experience it. The enigma comes at this place of simultaneous existence and obliteration: to feel something being destroyed, you first have to feel its intactness. How else will you feel your edges burning away? Don't they have to remain, somehow, as edges? But how? It's so illegible a feeling, and yet it still happens inside your skin, or very, very close to it. It opens up an alien world, and yet that world seems to still be located in your body. It troubles the understanding of ecstasy as something that forces you outside of yourself – in a way, it asks if the transformation that mysticism produces is happening to you, or the world, or both. Or, something else that neither of those two are – yet.

Music, perhaps more than any other art, produces this simultaneous feeling of something happening very close to you, alongside, or within, while feeling something much bigger than yourself, which you can't see or touch, overwhelm and engulf you. At least this is where I've experienced mysticism, when playing my own music and being in the audience of others. There are plenty of musicians I like who seem like mystics in more obvious ways than Robin Finck, but it's precisely because he doesn't seem like one – that paradox – that pronounces it for me. From a hagiographical point of view, Robin Finck is not dead, but – with his unknowable-ness, with how he mystifies me – he might as well be.

Like most frontmen and lead guitarists, Trent Reznor is a god, but Robin Finck is a demon. Reznor is plenty diabolical, but Finck has a serpentine energy, Medusa hair, and it feels plausible that, at some point in his life, he made a deal with the devil for the superhuman ability to excel at a wordless, subterranean language. On stage, he moves as if no one's watching him, as if he's conferring with an oracular force that feels as interior and intimate as it does radically extrinsic. I can't say this about any other lead guitarist of Robin's stature. He's definitely classifiable as a rock guitar god – a category whose tautology is its ostentatious flamboyance – but because he refuses to perform the choreography attendant to this category, something important is revealed about how he positions himself on these rock-star stages, what he takes from them, what he gives. Despite this rejection of the spotlight, or maybe because of it, he is one of the most captivating performers I've ever seen, and this is saying something, since he's sharing the stage with Trent Reznor. My friend, who knew nothing about NIN, grabbed me about halfway through the show to shout, 'I can*not stop* watching the guitar player!' At that moment, Robin's head and shoulders were bent over as if in a pillory, and he was trembling, almost motionless, like a Butoh performer. When he performs, I mainly feel as if I *shouldn't* be watching him, that I'm invading his privacy, bearing witness to a secret act that just happens to be taking place on a stage in front of 20,000 people.

He most resembles one of those inflatable, dancing tube-bodies in front of car dealerships, whose limbs unfurl and elongate, keeping a time that seems like breathing. He convulses hypnotically, as if in a trance, lifting his arms up and away. He often falls. He is very awkward. When he steps in time, he lifts his knees high, like a marionette puppet. He'll hook his neck around his microphone stand and rock back and forth with it, or grind against his amp, not in a sexual way, but as if it's a door he wants to go through. At the end of playing the bar, his spine often curls over, guitar touching the ground, like he's exhaling his whole being. He does a lot of crouching at the side of the stage, hidden behind the speakers. He's the only one other than Trent who leaves his designated area, climbing up the platform where the amps are, lurching back and forth in front of the drums, though this never has the practised sweep that Trent's has. Robin looks more like Frankenstein lumbering around. When not in a swoony reverie, his expression is set to a haunted, grimacing frown. Sometimes he'll stop playing his instrument altogether, stand eerily still, and peer out into the audience, as though looking beyond but also through them, into some other depth. In bzarektah36's description of a YouTube video where this is featured, we are warned: 'Be on the lookout for Robin's death stare.' The entranced inelegance of his movement is interrupted by the moments when he explodes with violence, though he never harms anyone else as Trent does, and this makes it seem less like violence and more like a part of himself is breaking open. There are fan videos online of Robin smashing, breaking or throwing his guitar, knocking over microphone stands, and leaving the stage in the middle of the song if something doesn't sound right. But perhaps because his entire affect is of someone not entirely in or of this world, you get the sense that when he exits the stage, he is exiting this plane of reality, going to a place no one can follow. In many songs, when it's not his turn to play, he disappears from his spot on stage left completely, reappearing only when it is – often, magically, from stage right. I don't know where he goes.

3.

I first saw him in the 'March of the Pigs' video, from 1994, when I was 10. I somehow managed to download it – over dial-up! – and would watch and rewatch the 200-pixels-wide file because it felt like it contained clues for how to live. This first encounter with Robin Finck changed my world. It was how he looked, how he moved, and what that seemed to mean – or, maybe it's more accurate to say, the meaning it resisted. He was different from anything I'd ever seen, and also different from the video itself, a tension that dilated the world of what NIN promised. Standing next to the other guitarist, Danny Lohner, who had the goatee and unmistakable aggression of a straight white boy, Robin looked alien, femme, a future gender. His face was childlike and open, Caravaggio beautiful, with pouty lips, shaved eyebrows, and big, moony eyes. He seemed possessed, swinging his feet around in graceless arcs and grimacing in time to the harsh sounds. He didn't have a recognisable gender, but it was more than that: maybe he wasn't even human. 'You can *do* that?!' I remember thinking, which was another way of saying, 'You can *be* that?'

About every great rock band ever, it has been said, as a high compliment, that girls want to fuck the singer and boys want to be the lead guitarist. Categorically, I've always been in the boys' camp – I never wanted to fuck Trent Reznor, I wanted to be Robin Finck. I could understand the sex appeal of these frontmen, but it absolutely diminished when compared to what the guitarists represented. Frontmen embody a kind of divine charisma, strutting across the stage and mesmerising the crowd with their god-like powers, like preachers who can open up the kingdom of heaven for you. They are the ones front and centre, their hearts on their sleeve, spreading their arms up and out and singing the lines that will lift everyone into the sky. How clichéd, but still, how you want to go there. Off to the side are the guitarists. They don't smile at the crowd, or talk, or sing, and if they do, it's backup, turned down in the mix. They hold their instrument close, intertwining their bodies around it. They seem to have gained access to a place hidden from our world, ferrymen on the river Styx.

The *fuck vs. be* configuration of rock-star fandom has never made much sense to me. Rock music elementally is about how wanting to fuck someone converges dangerously and deliciously with wanting to be someone. The maxim is meant to explain how much desire has accumulated around the band, not only in terms of how we lust after them, but in terms of something that cuts closer to how we desire ourselves. Audiences, as much as they are fans of particular figures, want to see themselves reflected back through those figures. All good rock stars have a bewitching power that goes straight through the sternum and touches something quivering and central in the gut. It's the feeling that you can find yourself, or who you want to be, in one of the musicians onstage. In psychoanalysis, this would be called projection, the transfer of your desires on to another person. But a more ancient way of explaining it is through the spiritual idea of communion, which has to do with an unspeakable sense of connection with something that both lives in your body and beyond it.

Watching a rock star onstage, using their body and face to express something interior now made into flesh and sound, can show you all kinds of things: where the edges of your body are, and how they can be dissolved; how you can feel connected to other bodies around you, and also to something you can't see or touch, but which you can hear and feel. It can help you understand *what* you feel, by affording you the sense of recognition: you can hear your feelings and thoughts emerge from someone else. But it also shows you what is *possible* to feel, by letting you see what someone else has done with those same feelings. This is what connects you to that thing that is both in your own body and beyond it. Because connection has to do with desire, all of this can point toward how you *want* to feel, which is to say, how to get to the self you want to become. You can do that. You can be that.

But upon first seeing Robin in the 'Pigs' video, he confused me: he was as delicate and lissom and ethereal as he was scraggy and agitated and wild. There was his long, lithe, snaky body and narrow hips, and his soft, feminine face. There was his grimace, that mesmerised look of being taken over, and the wrecked sound of his guitar. He seemed at once lost, out of place, and exactly, perfectly fitted to where he was. Although the camera, in one charged take, fixates on Trent, who pummels around the sound stage and rubs the crotch of his oxblood-red leather pants, it is Robin who is a personification of the song itself, which goes from its thrashing 7/8 time signature and hammering screams – 'Bite! Chew! Suck! Away the tender parts!' – to a major-key piano breakdown where the melody lilts and the vocals entreat, 'And doesn't it make you feel better?' Robin stands behind Trent and the camera only catches him in the frame sometimes. He curves his neck and tosses his hair and plays his guitar as if he's in a different room, and even world, to the rest of the band. This air of displacement, of existing somewhere else while you are also right here, which has continued to mark his stage presence, reached into me as an explanation for the strange dislocation I'd felt in my body and its place in the world so far. I'd never felt comfortable in my own skin, not because of the skin itself, but because of what the world said it signified. When I looked at myself, I saw one thing – I was a dragon, I had snakes for hair! – but when the world looked back, it insisted that it saw another, something that was supposed to be docile, pretty, manageable. You're a girl, it said. A *what*? I said.

The confusion Robin instigated felt somehow familiar, and at some point, it made me wonder if I was looking at something queer. 'Queer' was a term I'd heard about but not known exactly what it meant – it was thrown around by kids my age as well as adults, along with 'gay', as both an insult about a deviant form of desire and a marker of something consummately strange. When I saw this person, embodied it seemed in multiple worlds, some made of the recognisable world around me, some from nowhere I'd known before, I understood how the word 'queer' means things that are not articulable, that cannot be contained according to conventional laws of meaning. It made me realise not only that 'queer' could describe me too, but that I *wanted* it to. It activated that experience of communion. There was a reverberation of recognition that told me the quivering thing in my gut was not alone – this is what I could be, what I was – but also that there was a place beyond what I knew so far about myself, outside it, and maybe it was populated with others who felt the same way, and this was how to get there.

On the surface, Robin was an exemplary figure of the 1990s era of rock-star gender-fuckery, especially the goth section of it, when Kurt Cobain wore dresses, Marilyn Manson looked like a woman, and PJ Harvey's voice sounded like a man's. It was fabulous. All that mesh and black lipstick was our generation's Bowie-inspired glam moment, and Robin embodied it perfectly. Robin's squirming presence during the muddy Woodstock performance is the one people remember next to Trent's. (One of the first sentences of his entry on the NIN Wiki reads, 'His appearance, particularly during *The Downward Spiral* era... has arguably made him one of the most iconic members of NIN other than Trent Reznor.') At the time, being 10 years old, my identification with his look as something queer had less to do with sexuality, per se, and more to do with the way a body looked and moved, and how it did those things by either conforming to or breaking the rules. Encountering Robin Finck was a concurrence with someone whose embodiment was capacious enough to contain many seemingly disparate parts, and it appeared that, despite this (or maybe, perhaps, *because* of it?), he lived in his skin comfortably, which was the first time I'd ever seen that such a state could be possible for someone who looked the way I wanted to. But even as a child, before I'd started to think about mysticism and what, exactly, it was, something about seeing Robin Finck had more in it that pointed me towards a standing outside of myself, which was an order of magnitude bigger than the usual celebrity worship and the feeling of being a fan. The feeling of my own body compelled me toward thinking about mysticism because, for the mystic, the body has to be simultaneously felt and exploded. The feeling that dominated me, and still does, is that I wanted to live outside of my body, without and beyond it. I didn't know how to do this, or if it was even possible, but watching Robin Finck, slipping out of the roles that the world tried to put him in, showed me a way.

Despite being in two of the biggest rock bands of all time, very few people, even fans of those bands, can tell you who Robin Finck is. Trust me, I've asked. He's perhaps of the same species as Blixa Bargeld, whose own band is the magnificent Einstürzende Neubauten, but who's most well known for playing guitar and singing backup with Nick Cave and The Bad Seeds in the 1980s. Blixa has currency among Bad Seeds fans as much for his bulging, insectoid eyes and ur-punk mullet hair as for his brutal scream and guitar sound – but what makes him so beloved is the very fact of his sidekick status. Similarly, because Robin Finck has stood to the left of Trent Reznor and Axl Rose, some of the greatest frontmen of all time, he attracts the attention of those who prefer to look towards the liminal rather than at what's at the centre.

Born in 1971 in New Jersey and raised in Georgia, most of Robin Finck's biography is unknown. He's given few interviews and, when he does do press events with NIN, he sits silently at the edge of the band. He is especially committed to maintaining his anonymity, even for public work. In my research for this article, I encountered more stories of him intentionally removing his name from projects than projects themselves. When I interviewed Kelly Kalman, who runs the Facebook fan page Finck Yourself (which currently has 305 likes), she told me that she started the page specifically to keep track of him, but it's been slow going. The only public performance he did in 2019 was as one of a dozen performers at a charity ball for an animal shelter in Sonoma County. Following his hashtags on the internet, Kelly learned when tickets went on sale and bought two, travelling across the country for the concert. She said she had no idea that it would be as intimate as it was until the event organisers emailed her to ask what she'd like for dinner. It was set up in a tent outside a farm for 300 people; she said the stage was about as large as a king-sized mattress. Sitting at her table, she was literally bumped into by Robin Finck as he walked past. She described how he recognised her (she's the same fan who waits for him outside venues), how his eyes darkened. He gently led her and her friend outside, and said he was happy to take photos and sign autographs there but that, once inside, they had to promise that they wouldn't draw attention to him in any way. 'I'm here to support my family,' he explained. (The performance was directed by his wife.) Kelly said her stomach dropped then, worrying she'd overstepped some boundary, despite it being a public performance for which she'd bought tickets. In general, she said, she worries about being creepy, since following him demands a certain persistence, as there is hardly any trace of him in the world.

In 1989, he briefly attended the Berklee College of Music, and we can confirm this because a photo of his student ID card exists on a fan's Tumblr. In the 1990s, between NIN and GNR, he toured as a guitarist with Cirque du Soleil, where he met Bianca Sapetto, a choreographer, acrobat and trapeze artist, who became his wife. They have two children together, and have collaborated on projects like LedZAerial, where he plays in a Led Zeppelin cover band while she and other performers dance suspended from the ceiling. For most of his career he has worked as a touring musician, and since NIN and GNR don't tour often, he is out of the spotlight for years at a time. The only music of his own that he's released was a collaboration in 2015 with a Portuguese electronic artist named Wordclock, for the instrumental soundtrack of a horror video game called *NOCT*. Occasionally he's released a collaborative track, and by occasionally, I mean a total of three times, and these have been for the trailers of video games or films. He has appeared on several NIN and GNR records, but not all of them, and only on certain tracks. Kelly pointed out that Robin refuses credit for his work on the GNR album, *Chinese Democracy*, which is notable because Axl Rose, who Kelly says is 'the man who loves to take credit for everything', insists on citing Robin's contribution.

For a short time he maintained a web presence by answering fan questions via his website's message board in terse, enigmatic sentences. When asked, 'Robin, do you think time will end?' he replied, 'with every blink'. When he has had accounts on social media, they've been similarly short and baffling, as in 2010 when he tweeted 126 times to say things like, 'A course amid the smoke and silt, is there if look for finding wilt.' At the start of NIN's *Cold and Black and Infinite* tour of 2018, he began an Instagram account, but mainly posts collages of the sky with no captions; if he posts a selfie, he edits it to make his face look deformed. In 2018, he gave his first of two video interviews ever, one of them a rig rundown with *Premier Guitar*, where his long silences and awkward rhythm with the interviewer compelled YouTube comments like, 'Oof...brutal! I'd rather hear gunshots coming from my Grandma's bedroom then continue watching this,' and 'I had a root canal on Wednesday and that was easier to get through.' (When asked what he likes about a particular guitar, the silence hangs until he can muster, 'I just like the way it feels.') Some comments defended him, with suggestions like, 'This is a great unintentional ASMR video!' and 'David Lynch directed this rig rundown. Love it!'

Until 2018, the *Closure* documentary from 1997 was the longest screen time he's ever had. In it we get only a glimpse, but in that glimpse, his archetype was established. He wears black nail polish, a leather slave collar, and fingerless metallic silver gloves. This look, more than any other, comprises the Patronus of my gender identity as a teenager. In a black unitard thing with booty shorts and ripped stockings, he could be mistaken for a tall, broad-shouldered woman, though once or twice he wears a codpiece made of glittering chain mail. (Before NIN, he had a brief stint in a band called Impotent Sea Snakes, which performed in drag; Robin's persona with them was 'Queenie'.) He's 23, 24. He's quiet and aloof, not one who throws couches. He has shaved eyebrows and paints white Kabuki-style slashes in their place, and we watch him carefully draw lines on his nostrils with black eyeliner and put a dot at his third eye, for reasons we shall never know. He opens his make-up box and compact, saying proudly to the camera, 'See how fast I can do that?' He has a reedy, gentle, almost girlish voice, which clashes with the shredded-sounding screams that come out of him onstage. In almost every backstage shot of him, he's doing his make-up in the background or briefly pushing his face into the camera (if I were that pretty I would too), and his ass, in those booty shorts, is one of the ones on display. As always, he rarely speaks. Another fan-made compilation is 'Robin Finck Talking', only two-and-a-half minutes long. An article once strutted the title, 'CONFIRMED: Robin Finck Has a Speaking Voice.'

And of course, there is that hair, that *Robin Finck hair*. The first suggestion Google offers when you type in 'Robin Finck' is 'hair'. Shaved to the scalp on the sides of the skull to accentuate the long wisps of sideburns, the creation's focal point is the mullet-y back-patch of dreads that go past his shoulders. In the 'Pigs' video, *Closure* documentary, and Woodstock show, a kind of half-ponytail sprouts from the crown of his head. It looks like a rotting palm tree. It could be said to be a precursor to Ariana Grande's signature half-ponytail, in the way that the dire wolf is the prehistoric mother to the Chihuahua. Over the years, Robin's mullet-dreads would be topped with various arrangements: a Mohawk-shaped stripe, a widow's-peaky spike, and, sometimes, incongruously soft bangs. On the *Fragility* tour he is shaved bald or Mohawked, the sideburns fluffy curls at his ears, with make-up reminiscent of Kembra Pfahler's The Voluptuous Horror of Karen Black. When Robin toured with GNR, his hair was remarkable too. First, in 2002, he wore a monk-like tonsure, the front half of the crown shaved, with the hair long and loose in the back, as if he'd dipped his bald head into half a wig. In 2006 and 2007, he grew out his mane and beard to look like a homeless beach bum (completing the look with a shirt made of garbage bags). Around 2013, with NIN again, the dreads left, replaced by a rat-tail-looking swatch, but the long sideburns, shaved sides and top-spikes are still there, and in any live video you watch of NIN since then, someone in the YouTube comments section is going apeshit for Robin's hair (YouTube user LetsGetHighonMorris regrets: 'Too bad I'm not man enough to wear my hair like he does.').

In one of *Closure*'s most memorable scenes, Robin shaves his trade-mark hair. Trent helps, leaning over him and asking, 'You wanna leave the little sideburns?' As they head to the stage, Robin tosses on a long black wig, and calls 'Trent!', then hurries to follow him. It's a moment that feels slightly erotic, but more companionably intimate, with a whiff of care. In a film that rejoices in self-destructive delirium, here we have a moment of trust. Anyone getting their head shaved to the skin by someone else is in a vulnerable position, but there's something deeper here about what Robin incites people to do, to feel. Trent and the camera, and us by extension, are all helping this young man achieve the odd vision for how he wants to look, though what that exactly is, we can't say.

Any witch will tell you that hair is everything, the container of your power. If your hair is right, your confidence, your command and your sense of self are secured and definite and indestructible. Your hair is who you are – and, as any queer kid will tell you, if it's not yet, you can get it cut to be that way. Getting your hair cut is a sacred ceremony, and when it goes wrong, the results are disastrous. I once wound up in the hospital with suicidal depression after a particularly atrocious haircut, and I'm only half-joking. Rock stars live and die by their hair. In *Just Kids*, Patti Smith acknowledges that the minute she got her iconic cut, the world started to notice her and her career began. It's certain that Robin Finck wouldn't be where he is today without that hair. There's never been a sustained review of Robin as a musician, but in nearly every article where he is mentioned, this one included, the writer will remark on his hair. Robin's hair seems to signify everything notable about him: his strangeness and out-of-place-ness, something only he can pull off.

Offstage (and sometimes on) Robin has a penchant for wearing feather jewellery, chokers, shawls and clogs, and this also makes NIN that much more voluminous for his inclusion in a band of guys dressed in black jeans and T-shirts. In every candid and behind-the-scenes photo and video I've ever found of him, he's wearing clogs with notable socks (pink stripes are a favourite). It appears he has several well-loved pairs of clogs, including white ones. My friends must be quite tired by now of me sending them photos of Robin in his clogs, and I've heard Trent give him shit for it, in videos of soundchecks. 'Robin's out here... he's got clogs, he's got red socks,' Trent laments. During performances, Robin replaces his clogs with sneakers, which is sensible, it's easy to sprain an ankle by jumping around in clogs.

These fashion choices may seem superficial things to dote on, but they substantiate for me why Robin's presence is so amplifying to NIN, and so noteworthy in the world of rock stars. It's not just his queer – in all senses of the word – comportment, but how indecipherable he is. The most common word I've seen used to describe him is 'weirdo', and that's by *fans*. His only mention in the fan-made NIN Drinking Game, to be played during concerts or while watching live footage, is to drink 'when Robin does something weird'. Robin himself remarked upon this in the only interview of substance he's given about his background, which was with *Ultimate Guitar* in 2014. When discussing his audition with NIN in 1992, he said, 'My kneejerk reaction was, "Nine Inch Nails? Isn't that a lot of black hair and synthesisers? I'm really not sure where I'd fit in."'

This inexplicability of how he managed to have a place in the world of mainstream rock, and the way he occupies that place, is why I care about him so much. I don't pay much attention to mainstream rock, other than to know that almost all of it is not for me. And I sometimes hesitate to call Robin Finck my favourite guitarist over Japanese musician Keiji Haino, because Haino-San's music is the kind I listen to on a daily basis and go to see live and try to make in my own work, and Robin's is not. (And if we're talking hair, I'm definitely going for Haino-San's.) But despite the fact that Haino-San is an unearthly, shamanistic creature who conjures new universes of the strangest sounds I've ever heard (in 2018, NPR called him the 'dark wizard of the avant-garde'), I find Robin the more perplexing of the two. Haino-San is the premier experimental guitarist and, in my opinion, has the best hair of any musician of all time. He is also absolutely otherworldly – but he is legible as being of this otherworldly world. When I say that Keiji Haino is a mystic, it's obvious. Of course he is.

Calling Robin a mystic, however, is not at all explicit, and it's taken me years to realise that this was the role he played in my life, that by watching him slip in and out of legibility, I was not necessarily watching an individual, but what was coming *through* that individual. Sometimes he seems made of flesh and bone, within grasp, sometimes he's on another planet. Here he is onstage with NIN as Trent blasts around the stage and breaks shit, but Robin is off crouching in a corner with his head down. Here he is listed as performing at a public, ticketed show, but he is disturbed when a fan actually comes to see him there. Here he is playing the beloved guitar solo in 'Sweet Child O' Mine', but he's doing it while wearing a white satin Pagliacci suit and standing motionless, looking with a blank face, not at the sea of screaming fans before him, but off into

another dimension. This incongruity is more intense in GNR than NIN.
Where GNR glories in its hyper-masculine instrument-stroking, Robin
seems to glory in nursing an oddly beating heart to aural life. In every
video I've seen of Robin onstage next to Axl Rose, I think, who let this
poetic, sonic-seamstress freak on to the same stage as a bunch of goons?

4.

The thing about playing the guitar is that it *is* a body, in and of itself, and
so you have to meet and understand it with your own. As with any lover,
it requires that you invent and share a language together, which only the
two of you speak. To play it, you have to hold it close, carry it on your
shoulder, use your whole body, both hands, you feel it vibrate through
your bones, the skin of it rubs against yours. It has its own smell that
mixes with your sweat, and you have to wipe it off when you're done.

Robin has said that he plays an instrument 'you can carry', and this
is key to understanding his role in a band like NIN, whose catalogue is
constructed out of synthesiser-based sounds, the 'only constant' of which,
Trent's said, 'has been [the archetypal synthesiser] Moog'. In one of those
two interviews of 2018, Robin explained why he chose the guitar, 'I just
like the push and pull of it. That's one thing I like about the guitar, is this,
is this thing here.' He moves his left hand up and his right hand down.
'There's not a lot of instruments where you have a push and pull, with
such a nuanced articulation, of both hands hitting the same string, but in
all these different distances, but at the same time... It's all right here, it's
the strings, and it's the chords, and – they're really *close* to my *body*.'

The reason why guitarists seem more likely than singers to have made
deals with the devil is because the devil and the power he possesses, what
he's selling, can't be contained in an ordinary human body part like the
throat, and it can't be something as democratic as words, these common
things used by so many people to communicate boring shit like what you
need to buy from the store. And yet, for all its transcendent power, sound
is material. It needs matter to exist, it needs ears and a brain and a heart
to hear it, flesh to resonate through, a body to hold it. In the case of the
guitar, though, this flesh has been possessed by something else. Singers
inevitably lose their mojo because the throat ages, but guitarists, as if
propelled by a kind of sorcery, get better with time (just look at Keith
Richards). If you play the guitar, you've consented to let this magical,
unworldly force burrow into your soul, claim it, coil up in your gut, that
place that quivers, it lives there now. It changes you, from the inside out.
As Robin says:

> It's a super power. It's an invisible cape. It's a magic trick. It's a
> tenuous operation of unfathomable nuance. It's an ever-evolving
> stream of happy accidents. It's a culture made up of weirdos
> and rule breakers and geniuses of design and beach freaks and
> brainiacs and cavemen and crooked little flowers. And it's been
> a huge part of my identity for as long as I can remember.

This is why it's so disquieting to watch a guitarist destroy his guitar; it's
like watching someone break his own arm.

I prefer the live versions of many NIN songs just for Robin's guitar.
Unlike the albums, it gets to snarl and growl, and in the mix, the guitar
is pushed forward, loud, abrasive, the highs right on the edge of making

you wince. NIN songs build for a while, with a heavy groove, a bass line that anchors as it throbs, layered soundscapes of noise, and Trent's singing, always more melodic than you expect. By the time the guitar comes in you're a little hypnotised, lulled into submission and singing along. The guitar cracks the song open. But it doesn't wail with masturbatory rock-guitar-god moves. The way Robin plays, how he encounters this other body with his own, can be heard in his choices. There are hardly any guitar solos, in a traditional sense, in Nine Inch Nails. (This is borne in the songwriting: Trent has remarked that it matters more to him that his songs make people feel seen rather than incite a few nerds to go, 'Cool guitar solo.') Instead, the guitar cycles through orchestral chord progressions, bent, strident, or one riff, repeated over and over, which Robin plays with more upstrokes than down.

When I talk about Robin to other guitarists, I get my whole point across by describing him as 'the motherfucker who upstrokes his way through *Wish*.' That song – thrashing, belligerent, with my favourite 'fist fuck' lyric, and one of the most hostile riffs there is – is the last place you'd think an upstroke would work, but Robin bobs his hand through it with the pluck of a polka. Josh Homme, of Queens of the Stone Age, has described upstrokes as 'like yanking a feather out of a chicken', noting that 'you can't upstroke your way to toughness'. Upstrokes are not common in rock, because downstrokes feel so good to play. They're like stepping down hard on the gas pedal, or punctuating a sentence with an exclamation mark. (Punk is an entire genre played in downstrokes; while funk flourishes with ups, mainly because they fit so well in the pocket of the downbeat, those little breaths between the kick.) If you've never played guitar, I don't know how well I can communicate the feeling of playing down. It's orgiastic, it stomps and punches, as gratifying (I would imagine, and, O, how I love to imagine it!) as breaking the windshield of a cop car with a baseball bat. But where downstrokes are a declaration, upstrokes are an inquiry, which makes them more interesting because they complicate, rather than simplify, what you're playing. If you think of each bar as a sentence made up of words, strung together by a series of commas, and gathering momentum as the sequence starts to coalesce into an idea, upstrokes are like a colon, setting up the thought of the downstroke to be conclusive: *bam*, *this* is what *that* means. Or, they can be a question mark, opening the sentence upward, a petition to the heavens. They ask – what goes up – and then they wait for the answer, needing the next stroke to bring it – must come down. It's like an inhale waiting for its release.

Robin is a master of the upstroke in a field of players who tend toward the down, and this disregard for what is considered acceptably tough in rock music is a hallmark of his playing. He often starts the riff up, making the whole thing feel catapulted upward by its own velocity, as though he's stepped on a landmine (like the verse riff in 'Head Down'). Even when the other musicians, including Trent, play the same riff alongside Robin with only downstrokes, Robin goes up, slapping at the strings, flicking his hand away and sideways and around his head. He often wields his whole right arm like a violin bow, tapping the strings and letting them reverberate while his left hand does hammers-on and pull-offs (a good example of this is the solo he plays in the live versions of 'Closer'). I guess it makes sense, if you already live in the underworld, to make moves that pull you skyward.

It's not just upstrokes that make his playing what it is, though: it's the entire universe he conjures with his right hand. The left hand is often the star for guitarists, how their value is measured. Bring up any YouTube video of a 'best guitar solo' and watch the camera pull a tight focus on the left as its fingers dance around the fretboard, and not stray once to the right, as though the player were one-handed. But a guitarist is only as good as his right hand, because that is where the notes being played by the left find their voice. You're playing an E chord with your left, but is your right hand chugga-chugga-ing because you're in a speed metal band, or is it oompa-oompa-ing because you're in a bluegrass band? Are you screaming the phrase 'I want to die', or are you moaning it, mewling it, weeping? Are you saying 'I love you' as a plea or as a threat?

I can't think of another rock guitar god of Robin's calibre who smuggles in such weird shit with his right hand. It's like he's carrying a little bomb of subversive sound, letting it explode within the verse-chorus structure of a pop song. He has cited more textural guitar players as influences, with, as he puts it, 'lots of right-hand funny business', and says that he's 'always liked guitar players that play in phrases, maybe like a horn player who needs to take a breath.' Similar to wearing clogs in an aggressive industrial rock band, playing lead guitar in terms of texture and breath situates him askance. Yep, he's a weirdo. This could make him one of those arrogant noise boys, flagrantly displaying his skill with weird chord voicings, and drawing attention to himself via obnoxious clamours from a colossal pedal board. But I've never heard him cited by, or claim, this crew, and I don't think he really fits there, simply because he doesn't permit himself to go on too long. On the other end of the spectrum, conventional rock fans complain online that he is 'untalented' because he 'cannot phrase licks properly'. In a way, these complaints can be forgiven, because he doesn't, say, arpeggiate his way into bombastic lead guitar land with gasconading wailing. This makes it impossible to locate him in one place – he's neither all the way in the land of avant-garde guitar-noisemaker, nor is he reigning over the territory of the rock guitar god. He has the dexterity and range to take him to both those places, but he doesn't linger in either one. He's here, he's there, but then, he's not, he's somewhere else.

There are plenty of adroit, eclectic guitarists out there, but what's different about Robin is the stages he plays on. It's not hard to find a trickster guitarist playing in a math rock band at your local art bar. It is hard to find one, however, on a stage in front of 80,000 people, playing in a band not known for being weird. Those kinds of stages are the places where you find guitarists whose rock licks and screaming solos communicate just a couple of ideas, and almost all of them have to do with ego. When I interviewed Kelly Kalman (who runs the Facebook fan page), I asked her if she could explain her devotion to Robin. She said, when people ask, she accounts for herself by playing a four-minute live video she took of him on the 2018 tour, playing the song 'The Background World'. This is remarkable because practically nothing happens in this video. Robin plays just a few sustained notes and hardly moves, only swaying a little. His eyes are closed and his mouth is open; sometimes he winces. He even plays a wrong note. Kelly said, 'He's expressing a different part of his ability than speed. It's not, "Look at this sick solo this guy can do, no one can do that." Maybe someone else *can* do this, but no one does.'

You can also tell a lot about a musician's personality, or, if you will, his soul, by how he moves as he plays his instrument – the meeting of these two bodies together produces a specific sound, their shared language, as well as a specific way of being embodied within the sound. Watching how a musician moves is similar to witnessing what gets displayed when a person dances: you can guess how he fucks, how he rages, how he cries and laughs, how he sees himself and his place in the world, what he's like when he needs something. A good guitarist will move his whole self, not just his body, while playing. Or, let his whole self be moved. Think of Jimi Hendrix's knee-bends while he strangles the neck with hammers and pulls, almost as if standing were too strong a stance to take in the presence of such sound. Think of Prince, at the end of the bar, shooting his thumb all the way down the E string, as though he were resetting the fretboard in a kind of ablution before attacking it again. If someone moves as if they think no one's watching, especially someone onstage in front of tens of thousands of adoring fans, something integral gets revealed about how they envision themselves in relationship to the world. It's about what they think they deserve from it, and what, if anything, they think they ought to give it. Watching Robin play, he doesn't bend the guitar to his will or use it as a means to showcase his talent. Instead, he makes his whole body writhe with it, like they are breathing into each other's mouths. At, for, the guitar, he keeps vigil. A guitarist who's consented to be possessed by the guitar is, in a way, consenting to let his entire body become the throat for the guitar's voice. This is why his body's movement is so important in carrying the sound, because it lets the guitar sing.

As guitar nerds know, the best guitarists are identifiable by their guitar tone, which is as specific and individuated as a singer's voice. And speaking of guitar tones, oh mama (when Robin finally did that *Rig Rundown* interview, in 2018, it propelled me to spend hundreds of nerd hours in Reddit forum holes, not to mention hundreds of dollars, in order to mod my Tele to sound like his, but that story is for another hagiography). Robin's tone is created by technical wizardry but shaped with an ear for the visceral; he often removes pickups from his guitars, playing only through the bridge pickup, which, rather than thinning the sound to be emaciated, hones and sharpens it, like a shaved spike of metal. He gets his guitar to sound like a rusty zipper being opened and closed ('Discipline'), or a big-toothed saw scraping to life (the verse of 'Letting You'), or a deranged voice howling through a wire (take your pick, but the live version of '31 Ghosts IV' is a good one). And when he wahs, my god – it's like what comes through satellites in sci-fi movies when the aliens attempt communication. The distorted fuzz that Robin gets from his guitar tone feels less garage rock and more corroded, like the signal is being pumped through an old computer, spitting out digital decay. It's partly the Les Paul, his main model, which always sounds a bit shimmery, with bright high- and mid-tones, but lots of guitarists play this guitar and none of them sound as damaged, as gone, as Robin.

In 2009, NIN played *The Downward Spiral* in its entirety to a flabbergasted crowd at NYC's Webster Hall, two shows of the first song to the last, the only time they've ever done this (you can watch it on YouTube, or download it from the fan site ThisOneIsOnUs). People shout at each other: 'Oh my GOD!' 'I'm amazed! I'm *amazed*!' 'I've died and gone to hell!' The version of 'Ruiner' at these shows, rarely played live, has one of the closest instances we get to an epic guitar solo, albeit a defiantly NIN guitar solo. After the second blasting chorus, all the sound diminishes except for the bass. Then Robin's guitar comes in like a drill and makes a ragged, tearing sound. He has the stage for a full minute. His body twitches like an eel, and he stretches each note out for what always feels like a few beats too long. Online wimps would gripe about the improper lick-phrasing, no doubt. He swings his feet around in stomps and kicks, just like he did fifteen years before in the 'Pigs' video, though they seem to be off time, swinging during silences. Toward the end, he lets the distortion deflate, muting the strings with his right hand while his left goes up the neck – a deft, if unusual, choice, which punctuates how this was not really a rock guitar solo, but something that, instead of dominating with his own control, he let slither away.

It has long been said by musicians that you can tell a good one by what he doesn't play, by the notes he chooses to leave out. It reveals his understanding of the song as a structure, and how his decisions not only hold it up but give it space to breathe, let it live its own life without him. It also shows how self-confident he is as a player, knowing that he doesn't have to blow his load over everything to leave a mark. Of all the rock gods, Robin is the only one I can think of who lets one or two notes do for him what the rest of the guys use dozens for.

Look at the video of GNR guitarist Richard Fortus and Robin playing an instrumental cover of Christina Aguilera's 'Beautiful'. Fortus starts with a cascade of noodling. He's a fine player, and I have nothing against him, but when Robin starts playing, you can see what is soul, and what is not. It has to do with Robin's timing, his choices about what *not* to play. Remember that he thinks of the breaths between phrases, like a horn player, so he doesn't fill all the space with wiggly notes, showing off how quickly he can go through scales. He lets one note sing, really sing, and there are as many soundless pauses as there are notes. At around two minutes, he starts to play rhythm so Fortus can have his turn to solo. Listen to the difference. The spacing becomes rapid and crowded, which indicates rock-guitar expertise, and draws the focus to Fortus as a player, but pulls the focus away from the song. It's like Fortus has something to prove about himself that doesn't include the song, whereas Robin is content to let the song be bigger than he is, which it is.

5.

Because he seems driven to let himself be annihilated so as to make space for something bigger, I think of the Medieval women mystics (many of whom, notably, were *auto*hagiographers), like Marguerite Porete, Julian of Norwich, and Hildegard von Bingen, who spoke of letting themselves become nothing so as to let God in. I think of Anne Carson's essay 'Decreation', where she quotes Simone Weil: 'We possess nothing in this world other than the power to say "I". This is what we must yield up to God.' Mysticism is different from spirituality and most religious practices in its insistence on this radical yielding. Religions, the institutions of them, are structured as hierarchies, with a divine force being worshipped and served by its disciples. Mysticism, on the other hand, is the total inverse of hierarchy: it's structured by nothingness, and, if there is a hierarchy, it's the idea that the first thing that needs to be obliterated is your self. But this kind of obliteration is not a harmful one. What happens during mysticism, as Anne Carson's essay suggests, is *decreation*, rather than destruction. It has to do with love, the most daring kind of it: 'For when an ecstatic is asked the question, *What is it that love dares the self to do?* she will answer: *Love dares the self to leave itself behind.*'

This yielding is what I see when I watch Robin perform. It's not just that he yields the centre of the stage to the frontmen, and it's not just that he plays fewer notes so as to yield to the song. It's that, in his hermeticism, his demeanour onstage and in the press, and his choices about what and when and where to play, he seems to yield his entire self toward the goal of making music with what he can, and no more. The humbleness of him is so absolute it feels an order of magnitude bigger than someone being modest. (I've heard some compare him to Jonny Greenwood, another famously reclusive, brilliant guitarist standing to the side of the stage. But Greenwood's prolific career as co-songwriter of Radiohead, not to mention all his solo film scores, and the ample adoration he enjoys among fans, put him in an arena of visibility, and choices made in favour of that visibility, that Robin is definitely not in.) A note of this yielding of the self can be found in Robin Finck's few public statements, as when he wrote on his website, 'i'm not interested in saving music. i'm here to serve music.' When asked what kind of music he enjoys, Robin replied: 'an open window. two hawks circling out there up there somewhere. the white blue sky. ana's piano in my kitchen. early mornings. the rush of a freeway in the distance.'

While writing this essay, my agent urged me to contact Robin for an interview. But that's not what I want from him, or what this essay is about. (I did email his manager, asking for his birth time, to cast his natal chart, but, obviously, never heard back.) So much of fandom is about belonging to a community of fans, but meeting Kelly was the first time in my life I'd ever met another Robin Finck fan. No, this is a hagiography, a profoundly solitary genre: I am trying to account for someone who is unaccountable. He showed me how to get to a world where language made of words can't go; I can only report back about how he first guided me toward the gate. I can't explain what happens once you pass through the gate, and I doubt Robin could either; here I am, coping with the unknowable. When I considered which questions I'd ask if I were given the chance, I first thought I should ask about how he gets to this other place. 'Where do you go?' I thought would be a good one. But then I realised that no one who's been to that other place is able to answer such a question. If there were an answer, it would be something like, 'Nowhere.' A better question might be, 'How do you stay? What ways do you manage to inhabit this material plane, with the rest of us?' Although I imagine the answer to this would be, 'I don't know.' After our interview, I sent Kelly a draft of this essay, and she highlighted this point, writing: 'There's not much to ask him – because that's like asking somebody to interview music. What would you say to music if you could? I can't think of a thing; I just have to let music be what it is, and that is what Robin is.'

When I suggested that he might be from another dimension, she agreed instantly, and told me how she'd once asked a friend of hers, who is a spiritual medium, to read him. The friend said, 'I don't mean that his body is extraterrestrial, although it is quite unusual, but his soul energy.' (I told Kelly that I explain it by the fact that Robin shares a very specific astrological signature with Simone Weil.) Kelly pointed out that every Robin Finck fan she's met ('there are few of us but we're all like this'), including me, has no sexual interest in him. She said this after I'd explained my mysticism argument, and it reminded me that mysticism, despite its deep enmeshment with the body, is often thought of as asexual. But then, I think of the queerness of communion: the desire to eat your god.

I worry that by writing this, I'm going to anger Robin, or make him uncomfortable. I'm certain I will never meet him, never hear from him. That's not why I'm doing this. As a hagiographer, my task, my work, is one of devotion. Here I am, a small thing, hunched over my text, hours and hours and hours, trying to cope with the unknowability of someone who has meant this much to me. I think of another Simone Weil quote: 'We cannot take a step toward the heavens. God crosses the universe and comes to us.' I hope my labour, this text, this time I've spent, is a small gesture of care to him, and for something so much bigger than me, music itself. I've only ever wanted to be a humble servant to a craft: Robin, more than any other guide, has shown me how. I think of how Kelly works as a nurse. In astrology, nurses are ruled by the house of care, which is also the house of devotion and service, and includes nuns. Also known as the house of ritual and work, some astrologers, including myself, explain it as the house of magic – the ritual labour that one must do every day in order to make the most powerful magic there is, staying alive.

Sometimes I think there's no difference between mysticism and magic. Both have to do with that paradoxical convergence of materiality and immateriality, when one transforms into the other, and yet, somehow, both stay intact. That disintegration I felt as a teenager, when NIN first rescued me, it transformed me totally, but my body didn't disappear, my materiality didn't cease to exist. It had just changed form. As death does to life. As communion does with your god. This is how magic works and how mysticism works. It's also how music works. Without logic or language, it takes you somewhere not here, not on earth, maybe above it, maybe below, a place, or a state, where the rules and bounds of your materiality no longer hold. It defies gravity, and time, and space, and words. It gets you out of your head, your body, your self, and lets you feel, if only for a moment, somewhere, someone, some*thing* else. But despite whatever transcendence it offers, it still happens here, in your bedroom, your kitchen, your little life, within the bounds of your skin, and it changes those material conditions. It lives in your body, but then it also becomes your body. This is why it helps so much. It's got enough magic to bring you through the gate to that other dimension, but more than that, it's what makes being here bearable because it is ultimately your companion in this world. Take me away, for where I'm going and how I will get there, but also, for where I live, for where I always am, here, right here. Give me something I can use to feel the scintillating spark of what it means to be changed.

EXTREMITY

HSU YU-CHEN
tr. JEREMY TIANG

Let perfection rest with perfection
I will go far away

You have been squatting in this dark corner for quite a while now.

The crystal fragments in front of you glimmer in the faint light, like constellations. Everything else is pitch dark. You can't see anything. Your eyes might as well be shut.

So cold. You are completely naked, hugging your knees, which are pulled right up against your chest, fingers brushing like jellyfish tentacles over your arms, mottled with goosebumps like Braille. The orange towel slipped from around your waist when you sat against this wall, the knot loosened by your belly, and now lies spread beneath you like a picnic mat. The wall pressing against your bare back is made of wood, as is the floor, both varnished so they feel thickly slick. You're stiff from being in the same position too long, but you don't stand up.

The large air-conditioner pumps cold air at regular intervals into the borderless room. From time to time, someone walks through the darkness with a jittering sound, a cloud passing through and momentarily obscuring the stars. Time dissolves in the darkness like a sugar cube into black coffee. The stars no longer revolve around a nucleus but are still. There is no movement in this night.

Without setting off on an expedition, you attempt to reach another place. Your naked body remains in this icy land as you attempt to move ahead.

What's the farthest you can reach? Your body trembles like a kettle reaching the boil, its lid rattling from the steam – that's your teeth chattering. Steps come closer then recede. Bats navigate through this dark, dank cave with the aid of sonar. You hear a heavy footfall and imagine a sturdy body, huge feet like a lion's paws, sniffing the air, following behind a more delicate tread. The footsteps stop. Faint sounds drift through the space like a secret code, the frantic rasp of skin rubbing against skin. Moist and sticky, an open mouth smears the other person's chest, arms, shoulder blades with its fluids. They have found their meal, and are settling down to eat. You can clearly hear every bite and swallow. A short distance from you, two stars collide and are destroyed on impact.

Where are those prickles of light coming from? You stand, and like a sleepwalker, feel your way along, moving your nude body towards the dream sky. Faint breaths slowly become frenzied moans, *pak pak pak*, which you understand is the violent collision of back against bum, a crisp, resounding rhythm, the taut skin of a drum.

A distant glow solidifies in your field of vision into angular, pointed shapes, sharp fragments from a shattered mirror. You slowly reach your hand out to touch. It's a window, carved up into a honeycomb design, each tiny pane covered with an opaque sticker. There are tiny rips in the material, slices of glass that haven't been fully covered, and through these seeps bright, abundant sunlight.

*

There are no seasons in the icy room.

The cold wind has been blowing for years, gusting in through the overhead vent, a square within a square, fluorescent light within a silvery frame, neatly segmented like the eye of a housefly. The electric switch points up. In this place, it's forever daylight.

A large, bright office with desks and chairs in neat rows. Between them walk blockish suits with blockish shirts and ties, but no one can find their way out of the maze, so they go back and forth all day long. The desks are chaotic with documents, but from a distance they present a scene of busy orderliness. There are no windows. Along the outer wall are doors that look like someone drew them in with marker pen, each leading to a hermetically sealed meeting room. The sky is tucked away in an inaccessible corner, and whether the weather is sunny or grey outside this skyscraper has no effect on the steady temperature indoors. Ripples across the surface as one of the doors opens, and out trickles a line of ants, smartly dressed and clutching their laptops. You're an insignificant figure in that swarm, an indigo-patterned tie choking the collar of your white shirt, dangling limply in a platonic display of haplessness.

The ants split up, each with their own task. No one can tell that your crotch is bursting with the urge to pee, particularly as you're walking away from the toilets, an ant who doesn't know his duty and can't sniff out the right direction, so just wanders through the busy hordes empty-handed. Holding yourself upright, you return to your workstation and pull the chair out. Like gears clicking into place, the entire office apparatus rumbles into action. The ventilation shaft above you blows down on to your forehead, sweaty from the effort of holding it in, and the chill makes your muscles tauten. You stretch out your legs, the soles of your leather shoes gently scraping the floor. The slightest relaxation would set loose a gush of warm piss. Across from you, a colleague's tiny desk poinsettia, appropriate to the season, has dry, cracked leaves, though it may have just enough life to make it through the festive period. You grab your newly-purchased black woollen V-neck sweater from the back of your chair, and pull it on. Your meeting duties are done for the day. Now you can slow down and look at all those unopened Outlook emails, subject lines bold and black on your desktop.

'Hey, if you want to come tonight but haven't signed up yet, let me know ASAP.' That's all in the subject line – the email itself is blank. It's from your colleague across the corridor. Sandwiched between a dozen work messages, it darts right into your eyes. You stare at the words for a very long time, as if their meaning isn't as simple as it looks. There's a get-together on Christmas Eve: carolling and a Secret Santa. This email didn't go out to the entire company. You ought to be grateful to have passed the test. Those distracted eyes didn't, while scanning the rows of names, flick you out like a speck of dirt. You read all your other messages, and know that in the hour or two left till the end of the day, you won't be doing any more work. You left your enthusiasm back at the meeting-room podium, a burden to be picked up again the next time you're there. The mouse drifts across the screen and clicks open a complicated spreadsheet you've been meaning to take a closer look at – a screensaver for your blank stare.

You're aware of nothing else but the figures going back and forth from the loo. The people who left the conference room at the same time as you, their bladders similarly straining with pee, have now found relief, and are trickling back from the bathroom with expressions of rosy satisfaction. You're the only one who's clinging on to your warm effluvia like a treasure, holding it all in. The discomfort flows upward from your nerve endings, approaching pain, and then a moment later something akin to pleasure. This is nothing. You could take much more. Your cowardly nature, which doesn't dare let go of its dignity, will force you to put up with anything.

In the restroom is the only opening you know of to the outside world. The ventilation window is a segment of neatly sliced-up grey sky, signalling imminent rain. When you finally enter, it's as you expected: completely empty. Next to the sinks and mirrors are the white porcelain crescents of three urinals, their gaping oval mouths across from the wooden doors of three cubicles. The farthest one is being used to store cleaning equipment. You go into the middle cubicle, and lock yourself into the tiny cube. The space isn't sealed – there are gaps above and below the door – but this is enough to give you a breathing space.

No need to explain why this is the highest happiness known to man.

You grab a wad of toilet paper and wipe the seat, then lay two folded lengths in a rough square along the rim. The neatness of the arrangement is satisfying. You undo the button at your waist. Inside your trousers, the bottom half of your shirt is a wrinkled mess, in stark contrast to the smooth white expanse above. You push the trousers down past your knees, and settle your bony buttocks on to the loo-roll seat.

Before you can seek release, you hear footsteps, with the jangling accompaniment of a pocketful of loose change. You are bubbling on the brink, but this guy is brisk: he strides in, takes his position, and right away piss is tinkling against the shiny urinal. Instinctively, you give way. Your shiny shoes stealthily retreat round either side of the toilet bowl, still swaddled in the fabric of your trousers. You clench, and it feels as if the piss swirling around inside you has reached up to your brain. You're not in the mood for a duet, at least not with you lurking in the dark. Two tiles away from the door – a safe distance. There's no way anyone could see you. From outside, you're often able to guess who's inside from the splayed feet beneath a cubicle door. Right now, no one could know you're here. No one could wonder: what's wrong with this person, just standing at the urinal? Or, why has he locked himself in this little cube? There are no answers to these questions.

A cataract flows. You're a burglar hiding in a closet, surprised by the houseowner. Your eyes roam silently around the tiny space. To your right is an uncovered bin, half-full of used toilet paper, white smeared with shit stains from your colleagues' anuses, flower petals festering with filth. Why do you have to share your delicious private moments with such foul objects? You look directly ahead, at the back of the cubicle door, where the firm has stuck one of the inspirational stories with which they seem determined to cover every surface: a frontline soldier lost a leg to a bomb, and returned in absolute agony, only to have his commanding officer say to him: At least from now on, you'll only have to polish one shoe.

Can such agony be so lightly passed over? The rifleman outside has put away his gun, and you hear a tap running. In your dark theatre box, it's all you can do to stop yourself applauding his outstanding performance. Another sticker above the inspirational story reminds you to flush.

The last line of the story is its moral: at the darkest moments in life, you need to think positively, in order for there to be hope.

*

Somewhere in the east of Taipei, a shopping mall built around a giant bookstore.

Your leather shoes tap along crisply, keeping time with the heart-warming Christmas carols. This is something from a musical: you in a dapper suit, hair as neat as you sculpted it this morning, striding through the shopping paradise in tap shoes. Before putting yet more unnecessary expenditure on your credit card, you and your imaginary companion turn to the camera, grinning broadly. Behind you, the chorus is in two rows, designer bags flapping from their arms as they dance energetically.

What a perfect world. If you could choose how everyone perceived you, you'd pick this: you strolling slowly through this space. In the gift department, you see liquid crystal clocks more expensive than time itself, action figures more lifelike than human beings, and electronic photo frames able to contain much more than anyone's memory. Exquisite things scattered around, waiting to be assembled into a complete, beautiful life.

You're skipping the work gathering, having found the perfect excuse: a family dinner up north. No one dares to come out and say that festive family gatherings are meaningless. While your co-workers head to Ximending, you alone have swum against the tide and ended up here. Last night, even before picking a Secret Santa gift, you'd decided not to come. All day you claimed to be unsure whether or not to go, but that was play-acting. As if there was ever a chance you'd show up. Is this a sign of faith in yourself? Believing there'll be a better option than karaoke singing with a bunch of colleagues you don't know particularly well? That you'll be able, without fear, to get through this holy, silent night?

You stop before a glass display case and gaze at a tiny humanoid robot, no larger than the palm of your hand, gleaming silver all over, a sapphire glow faintly visible at its joints. The price tag says 15,000. Next to it is a robot fish made of the same material, eyes feistily lit up in red, tail made of metal rings so you can use it as a keychain. It costs 10,000. The back wall of the display case is a dull mirror. You stare at your bony face. Your cheeks are so hollow, they probably wouldn't puff out even if you pumped gas into your mouth. Your eyes are bottomless pits. Next to your reflection, others from your tribe are walking slowly past. As they brush past, you can practically smell the anxiety coming off them, exactly the same as yours: should you find a cock tonight to stuff the gaping emptiness inside yourself?

Fortunately, you're not there yet. Looking at them, you feel more confident. These pathetic dregs will, this Friday night, open their slutty legs and once again allow a stranger's dick, long or short, girthy or slim, straight or curved, quick or slow, to thrust in and out of them. You raise your head to prove you're different from these terrified shadows who scuttle along with their eyes fixed to the ground. Turning, you lift your tap shoes, and trot past them like a happy mule.

What a cause for celebration and pride: you've chosen what you want. Now you look for a classy restaurant for dinner, then enjoy a sophisticated latte before frittering away the rest of the evening listening to random tracks at the music department's listening booths and flipping through every book in which you have even the slightest interest. Finally, you catch the last subway home. This leisurely evening belongs to you alone. Much better than listening to your office mates crack their voices stubbornly reaching for high notes, then receiving a crappy gift you'd want to toss out right away.

What would those idiots get you? At a guess, probably some stuffed toy, maybe a plush teddy bear, all glassy eyes and soft lines, the ideal prop for faking warm emotions. Or maybe essential oils to clog your nose, the sort of present only a moron with BO could come up with. None of those fools could imagine what you want.

And yet, what you want is what everyone wants: for your broken self to be whole again.

Just because you didn't go to the gathering doesn't mean you're all on your lonesome. Merry Christmas – you got yourself a present yesterday, and you've been wearing it all day long, showing off how much you adore yourself. This is your trophy from last night's wandering: black, the most elegant colour, with a V-neck to make you look like an intellectual. At moments like this, with the figure you cut in this tender city, if not for the reminder of your reflection in the mirror, you might actually have a chance to be whole again.

You're as pure as a backward child. Like everyone else, you just want to be good.

*

From a distance, you see the light emanating from him. He's a fixed point, a lighthouse shining through grey drizzle.

The shop is still open. Are you here too early, or is he knocking off late? This is unexpected. Good or bad luck? If you'd known, would you have stayed away? Even at this distance, his blurry silhouette no bigger than a grain of rice, it's enough to scrape off a layer of your skin. He speaks a secret language that forces something deep inside you, like a clam held over a flame, to surrender and spring open. Such an unfortunate moment, as understanding leads to breaking faith with yourself. Sure enough, your willpower is no more than a sandcastle on the beach, and he is a tsunami rolling easily over you.

You can't look directly at him. Trying hard to stay calm, you clutch your briefcase and shopping bag in one hand, a white folding umbrella in the other. Your back is a little hunched and you look tired, the picture of an office worker after overtime. That shouldn't arouse suspicion. On the other side of the road, you attempt to walk casually ahead, but instead march as clumsily as a new army recruit. As you draw closer, you notice out of the corner of your eye that he has his back to you, and only then do you dare turn your head to gaze greedily at him.

It's Christmas night in this residential district, and the shops on both sides of the road are shut, the Christmas trees at their entrances no longer twinkling with lights, inflatable Santa Clauses abandoned to face the cold winds alone. The fun-lovers are still out partying, and the alleyway is utterly silent. Against the backdrop of this darkened street, the spotlight falls on his motor garage. His work ethic clearly takes precedence over the holiday.

At this moment, he's on the pavement outside the shop, crouching by a motorcycle on its side, probing energetically at its undercarriage with some tool you don't know the name of. As usual, his short hair is sticking up hedgehog-like, or perhaps more like wild grass. He is wearing his usual indigo short-sleeved shirt with the collar flipped up, the form-fitting chest, shoulders and arms covered in decorative patches in all colours. Underneath, he wears a long-sleeved grey thermal T-shirt that clings to his muscular arms, then trousers of the same indigo material. From head to toe, he's splotched with filthy black oil stains, which makes him look to you like a brave warrior, a manly Sagittarius.

When he has his back to you, like now, you can see his broad shoulders taper down to a narrow waist, a hunter's physique. On this dark, rainy night, he's cutting apart the prey that found its way to him, celebrating the holiday in his own style. There's something very alluring about the way he's squatting, spine curved as he leans forward, stretching the fabric of his race-car driver's shirt taut, emphasising his deltoids and the curves of his broad back, like the gold figure on a fighter's sturdy shield. His trousers encase firm, full buttocks, and are low-waisted enough to reveal his tailbone and the unmistakeable crack. A sliver of warmth in his ice-cold armour, stirring up the enemy. There've been times when you've been so bold as to walk right by him, peering eagerly into his trousers for the enemy's final secret. Several times, you came close to conquest. In tonight's skirmish, though, you don't dare venture on to the minefield. How cruel, that you have to pretend nothing is happening as you walk on. The most thrilling show in the world is being performed right there beside you, yet you're unable to stop and find a good vantage point from which to watch, never mind stepping any closer to study it in detail.

Your gaze is parched with thirst, freighted with so much desire it actually feels weighed down, sinking heavily on to the back muscles of the race-car driver across the road. All of a sudden, he stands and turns around, staring directly at you. Your eyes meet, and in less than a second you've been defeated and look away. Even with the width of the street between you, every bit of information has been transmitted. The harsh, perfect lines of that exquisite face; the deep cruelty of those cold eyes. Before him, you desperately long to not exist. In that moment, you want nothing more than to destroy yourself completely.

Mission failed. Once again, your ravenous nature has been exposed, you hungry ghost. When a hunter fixes his sights on a low-life like you, the food chain determines which of you must surely be eliminated. Your heart thumps violently. Your whole body is stiff, and the energy has drained from it. It's all you can do to keep yourself under control and walk the plank calmly, step after small step. When did this start? When he discovered this slave of lust, this fly hovering around him, whether or not your eyes lingered, he was alert enough to stop his work and stand up, retaliating with his scalding gaze on your shoulders, your back, every moist scrap of skin you put in his way. You're a new recruit who can't even march straight, forced to parade awkwardly and nervously before the eyes of your commanding officer. You know you're guilty, so you lower your head and accept this punishment.

The appearance you've carefully cultivated gradually cracks apart, and a barely visible trail forms behind you, brittle shards of your face flaking off. This man knows exactly what you have beneath your designer clothes, and certainly is aware that you're not just an innocent passer-by on your way home. On this dark, wet night, he's seen all the way through you.

You reach the end of the block without looking back once. Rain spatters against the face that has now lost its glossy surface, and slithers down bare flesh. You can't let your suit jacket get wet – you'll need it the next time you pretend to be a normal person – and so you open your white umbrella and turn into your darkened alleyway.

*

And so you know this evening won't pass so easily.

You shut the metal gate and enter your dim rented flat. Shopping bags, leeched of their bright colours, lie strewn on the bed, containing various care-fully chosen CDs, a translated detective thriller, and postcards advertising all manner of cultural events. The sophisticated night you'd planned now feels ridiculous. You turn on your computer and a low hum fills the room. This isn't the first time you've disappointed yourself. Let's be honest, at this point that's pretty much your calling card.

What stupidity to imagine you could somehow get through this unscathed, to so blithely refuse the warmth of a gathering. Your co-workers' singing might be cacophonous, but better that than a cavernous silence. Of course you now regret actively segregating yourself from the festivities. The ceramic floor tiles are freezing – you can actually see cold rising from them like smoke, turning your solitary figure into a column of ice.

Should you just give up, and go in search of the sort of fetid dick who'd fuck anything, even a mousehole? Let it coarsely, violently wreck your stinking hole? On nights when you lose control, trying desperately to outrun your rational self, you take refuge in the coldest corner of a dark sauna, listening all night to the repeated couplings and frantic breath around you. An unlit stage, but with actors experienced enough to hit their marks anyway. Too dark to make out each other's faces, which only increases the thrill. Perhaps this is what you want, skin-deep sensations arousing deeper desires within you. You'll never leave the darkened stage to find out what horrific deficiencies these men have when seen in the light.

The dimly lit corridor makes you fearful. Leftovers like yourself wait on either side, pretending indifference, as others pick over the remaining bodies, hoping for some lost soul to choose you in a moment's carelessness that they'd surely regret. Several times, you accepted an invitation to enter a little room with a fellow straggler who, like you, had run out of patience with the minuscule odds, but no matter how you fondled each other, the little creatures between your legs remained wrinkled and shrunken, pursed lips refusing to stir. Less fun than you'd have on your own! In those dark rooms, where beautiful bodies couple. You might lock yourself into a cubicle next to one such pair, pressing your ear to the wooden walls that allow sound to pass clean through, stroking yourself in rhythm to them.

Your computer has finished turning itself on. You click on a video file: dazzling sun on a white beach, where a blond and blue-eyed muscle boi, rock hard and enormous, is inserting himself into another magnificent body. Your window is ajar, and you can hear the rain outside. Has this put a dampener on the partygoers' mood? Still in your dress shirt and suit trousers, you open a drawer and grope around inside, then get up to fetch a glass of water, which you gulp down with the pill in your hand. The inevitable ending to your day.

Nothing to hide here. As the two males continue to bellow lustily, you open another tab and enter as many filthy words as you can think of into the search engine, setting off on an endless journey into an imaginary kingdom, seeking clues about yourself. This leads you to a dazzling array of porn sites, and the sort of erotic stories you understand, where the sex is nastier than it would be in reality. For yourself, you'd rather read about yearning, about people who'd do the most degrading things for the sake of lust, just like you.

The pleasurable sensation comes from deep within you, fine horses galloping from a distant land. You accept the command, and shut your eyes, fingers adrift over the keyboard, a pianist silently contemplating the first note to be sounded.

The most awful performance is about to take the stage. In a daze, you leave your seat and reach into a glass jar of random junk, fishing out a vial of medicinal brown fluid. Next, you head for the kitchen cupboard where you keep the rubber dildo you bought online. Its proportions are modelled on a porn actor, 25 centimetres long and 5 around. More lethal than a truncheon. Maybe police officers ought to go around with one of these, the better to conk criminals over the head. The intellectual evening you'd planned ends supine, and the cultural events whose postcards you picked up will go unseen. You strip off your trousers and underwear, lying back on the ice-cold white tiles in just your white shirt. What a ludicrous sight, you sliding a condom on to the dildo, scared this porn actor might get you pregnant. Everything in readiness. The disembodied dick, now wearing its cap, gets to work. You bring the poppers to your nose and sniff hard. A steam train enters the coal mine, carriage after carriage at exactly the same speed, swallowed one by one by the dark, narrow cave.

But you know the limit lies far beyond – your body can contain far more than you imagine. You pluck out your shitstained perfect lover. Goodbye, you filthy devil. Heartlessly, you rise to your feet, and walking unsteadily, head to the fridge. These healthy stem vegetables are ripe now, mature enough to understand that this world contains people who'd like to taste them in an entirely different way. A hardworking farmer, you harvest them one by one, laying them out in a neat row on the stark white polar surface. How should you think of yourself now? A fruit and veg expert? These poor, frostbitten specimens are finally thawed by the warmth of your body.

How much time has passed? You have no idea, desire has covered your eyes. As various objects, long and narrow or otherwise, are shoved inside you, a question bubbles up inside you and will not be resisted: where does this pleasure lie? Maybe you should just go outside and whore yourself out, putting an end to this long voyage. But you're too dazed to answer. A clumsy machine, you thrust over and over into the small opening between your legs, reaching to its very extremity.

Finally, exhausted, you have to stop this mechanical action. This factory, which only produces waste, has been working overtime and needs to rest. Clean yourself up. Slumped on the icy ground, you carefully mop up the specks of blood and filth with a snow white Kleenex. Heading back to the computer, you click open your secret folder and are back on the street. A slideshow of him. Summer, plenty of light, him in a tight white singlet chatting happily with a customer. Cold with a north wind blowing, but his arm muscles still bulge as he leans over a lucky motorcycle, vigorously fitting a rear-view mirror. You on the other side of the lens, foolish as any mortal gazing at the unimaginable physique of a god above. You remember the moment, how bold you were, pretending to send a text message but actually committing this unspeakable act of disobedience, capturing the image of a god come to earth in a variety of poses. Such a thrill that your long-numbed senses jerk to life with a shuddering convulsion.

You have a drawer of treasures, keepsakes he has bestowed upon you. Time to take them out for a breath of air. With utmost tenderness, you lay them out like a display of antiquities: soda cans, clumps of tissue paper, scrawled notes, condoms washed clean, and a small box of hair, long or short, straight or curly. Items abandoned by him, manifestations of his utterly mundane existence. You read the note like a poem that has touched your very core. White paper lined with red, the old-fashioned sort you only get during national service. Such simple romance in these words: 'Just let me know if it's all right, how I am to you. You should know how I feel. I love you, I love you so much...' These must be his most private emotions. So private he couldn't bring himself to send this, so it got discarded. Unbelievable.

Amid the solid mass of your lust is a shard of hatred so strong it could destroy the other man. How can other people be so complete? And how cruel, that your broken self has to see this proof. There he is on your computer screen, straight-backed, brow lightly furrowed, eyes looking directly at the camera, witnessing you once again irredeemably transgressing.

*

Which is why it's no accident, when you show up once more in this street scene.

Deepest, darkest night offers the only chance you have to enter his life. Silvery shutters gleam across the entrance of the motorcycle repair shop. Not a soul to be seen along this entire terrace. Time for the least popular actor to take the stage. The lights refuse to come on, no backdrop except the grubby, oil-stained metal pipes littering the ground. Dressed all in black, you stand before his space, heart colliding violently against the inside of your chest, heightening the sensation of the poppers. The rain slowly calms. Such pure light from the streetlamps. You glance across the street. What did you look like through his eyes? A disgusting, limping grey rat? Or a loathsome scuttling cockroach, lousy with germs? Either way, you deserve to be exterminated.

The ground is dark with a thick layer of grime. In the middle of the sidewalk is a black plastic slab, where motorcycles recline to be diagnosed by the sexy race-car driver doctor, running his nimble fingers over their undercarriage, releasing the bellyful of oil that's been troubling them, then plugging them full of his precious fluids, guaranteed to cure all ills and make you feel good all over.

You stand on the slab trembling, teeth chattering. Could it be that at this very moment he's lurking in some dark corner, arms crossed, quietly enjoying this all-out performance? His living quarters are the other side of these metal shutters, and he might be woken at any moment by your strange cries. Then he'd craftily wait and watch for this sinner to finish his nasty business, ready to leap out and deliver you to the law.

Never mind how risky this could be, you still choose to lie down on that filthy black patch.

Several years' worth of grease clings to your clothes and hair. At long last, you're in the same position as those motorcycles you envied, only the doctor is missing. Lucky there aren't any other bikes around, or they'd all be mocking you: the doctor doesn't want to touch you! But it's just you. The awning overhead is covered in spider webs, so dilapidated it could have been neglected for a thousand years. An icy wind blows. On behalf of the doctor, you run your hands over your black-clothed body, and without a hint of originality, they eventually descend into your trousers.

*

The long night must come to an end.

You're back home, taking great gulps of air. You're not empty-handed either – you're lugging a trash bag into your frosty apartment. Experience tells you this small bag must be from his personal quarters, not the shop. He must have left it outside the shop, ready for collection along with the business refuse.

Throbbing with excitement, you strip naked, carefully folding the oil-stained garments, ready for the next time you set off on one of your high-tide full-moon expeditions. Your bare, bony bottom goes to the floor, but you're too agitated to feel the cold. You're a scrawny, pale child, reaching out with both hands for some warm food, ready for your sustenance. You've been waiting so long for this, hoping for traces of his lovemaking. Such a thrill. It crosses your mind that this is probably more of a turn-on than if something were to actually happen between you and him.

You open the plastic bag. There are a few crumpled newspapers, which you discard. Nothing else, not even dirt, just more papers, like a riddle with no answer. Just as you're about to give up and curse your bad luck at only getting his recycling, you come upon the object he wanted you to have.

A palm-sized card cake-box, its pink surface embossed in gold with the name and address of a bakery. The top is caved in from the weight of the news-papers, and a red ribbon is still tied around it, the bow a limp butterfly pinned to the cross. A clumsily wrapped Christmas gift. You keep looking, but there's nothing else in the bag. With both hands, you hold up your gift. The shit stench wafts up and assaults your nose.

In the end, you haven't been abandoned. On this festive occasion, without the need for an exchange, someone has given you a present dedicated to your most intimate needs. You imagine him, such a stud in his racing outfit, standing in the distance, the tension finally gone from his face, replaced with a crooked smile and a teasing look in his eyes, as he beckons to you...

The drumbeat in your heart comes to an abrupt halt.

All of a sudden, you have no idea what you're feeling at this moment.

Is it shame? If this man ever saw your remains, and knew what you get up to in the dark, he'd want you severely punished. You can barely sit still. He wouldn't need to do a thing. If you had a knife, you'd stick it right into your guts.

At the same time, the excitement of this forbidden fruit rises slowly from the cold surface. After all, weren't you longing for a relic of that perfect physique? And isn't this something from his body? Can't it bring you as much happiness as a sex token? Should you smear what he has given you over your face, and greedily stick out your tongue? Or would it be more intimate to stuff it entirely within the bottomless cavity inside yourself?

What should you do at this moment? Completely naked, you stare at the unopened box, still as a stone sculpture in an abandoned park. Time ticks by, moment by moment. It's so cold. The chill sweeps over your unprotected skin, inch by inch. You understand very clearly that none of this has the slightest connection to him. You wouldn't shed a single tear if he died. The whole affair is just about you.

You don't know how much time has passed before you raise your stiff neck and look out of the window. The rain has stopped, and the edge of the sky is beginning to turn fish-belly white. A new day has arrived. Naked on the icy floor, you finally begin to feel exhausted, a dazed sensation, the soft desire for sleep.

INTERVIEW   SAMARA SCOTT

In the autumn of 2019 I visited Samara Scott in her studio in an industrial zone of Barcelona. The shutters raised on a scene of frenetic activity. Her shelves were filled with unruly boxes of detritus, and stacked in the corners were piles of fabric samples. Made from old clothes and latex, they looked like test-runs for a DIY *Fifth Element* costume party.

Born in London in 1985, Scott is a collector and collagist of cheap and used materials. Her practice is object-based, but her interest in ambience and surface – and her machismo, high-octane mode of self-expression – places her in conversation with abstract painting. For her show *Silks* at Eastside Projects in 2015, she cut cavities into the concrete floor and filled them with liquid concoctions, producing otherworldly pools from bath salts, dog chews, betting biros and Irn Bru. In 2016, she transformed a fountain in Battersea Park with liquid dyes, strips of tarpaulin and chrome bitumen paint, creating a sci-fi breach in the aesthetic of the 1950s architecture – an effect that belied the simple materials from which it was made. For *Belt and Road*, a solo exhibition at Tramway in Glasgow in 2018, Scott covered the entire ceiling in a semi-opaque plastic skin, filling the reverse with plastic trash and synthetic foodstuffs. The work cast an atmospheric spell, turning the gallery into a cathedral for an era of hyper-consumption.

Scott's art is undeniably seductive; it is also corrupted. Spend time with her work and the glamour soon gives way to something sordid. Perishable materials are left to rot, and the sheer mass of plastic speaks of suffocation and toxicity. Like the moment prior to puking alco-pops into the gutter, or passing out from the fumes of a cheap perfume, the high feels moments from the headache.

Over the course of an afternoon we discussed swimming, contamination, hedonism, Impressionism, whether and how materials speak, and collaborating with fashion houses. A few weeks later Scott broke her ankle. She sent me a photograph of a reproduction of Monet's *Water Lilies* on the wall of her hospital ward, an artwork we had discussed. The photo triggered a second, brief exchange on her relationship with modern painting.
ROSANNA MCLAUGHLIN

THE WHITE REVIEW   For years now you've been making bodies of polluted liquid, in which beauty goes hand in glove with toxicity. Dirty swims are an apt metaphor for your work, especially as you've swum in all kinds of places. Is it true you swam in the lake at Burgess Park in South London?

SAMARA SCOTT   It feels so intimate to talk about, and showy somehow, but I'm pretty addicted to getting inside all types of water. I've always been crazy about swimming but over the last years it's become chronic, compulsive. I scare myself – I think I'd almost swim anywhere. Even super-polluted places have this irresistibility. I find myself compelled into these menacing bodies of water which beckon me, almost drag me in, drag me under. I've swam in cruddy soiled Burgess Pond in the middle of the night in winter, and in an August heatwave when the lake was a lime-coloured, gelatinous liquor. It's unexpectedly creepily shallow.

TWR   That is a gnarly swim. The lake has got a particular smell to it: dead fish, pondweed, rotten bread, duck shit…

SS   There's all the stoner fishermen around, too. I love those silty oily smells. The smell of stagnant water is so ominous – chlorinated water, too. Fountains smell like that. Drugged-up liquids. I've also swum in the fountains at Buckingham Palace and Canary Wharf. I had a heady, throbbing summer swim in the Thames at Vauxhall last year, with motionless cranes overhead from the development sites. In the water there was a black swan and a white swan, faded slithers of Twix and Dorito packets were floating past, and the silver glinting material was creating all these euphoric refractions. The gutter-y-ness made the potent sensuality of that moment – the thing I'm always chasing.

TWR   If Ophelia is floating down the river, the flowers are plastic bags, and her body is a composite of soft drinks and body glitter.

SS   I have a kind of allergy to things that are too slick and clean. I find it fictional, deceptive, like a face-lift. It means you don't see what we're actually producing and using. Painkillers and make-up over the grazes. Bruises, stains, scars – we have to take responsibility for that information. I remember gliding through those smooth, untarnished Scandinavian cities years ago, and coming back to London afterwards and admiring the scummy markets – the squashed fruit and cigarette butts and broken glass, stuff streaming from living. I have a Robert Rauschenberg feeling about messy cities, the presence of the streets, the way they show the leakiness of the world, the leakiness of our living bodies. There is no such thing as pure water, there never was. Tap water comes from a reservoir that sops up everyone's hormones, it's full of piss that's been swilled round and condensed. It's inescapable that we inhale each other's vapours and exhaust fumes, swim in urine, sweat, hormones, anti-depressants, birth-control, anti-freeze and all the injectables undergirding us. Plastic ancient lifeforms, pumped out of the deep ocean and turned into something colourful and pink-tinted, turned into dog-poo bags in order to take away something that's been labelled 'bad'. I'd rather see the innards, smell the odours, feel the dirt, feel the shame.

TWR   For your exhibition *Belt and Road* at Tramway in 2018, you installed a false ceiling in the gallery, which turned the entire space into a colour field. Looking closer, you could make out some of the materials placed on top of the ceiling that were used to build the composition: brooms, plastic bottles, tarpaulin, chopsticks, weeds, fake nails, carpet tiles, onion rings, phone chargers, lighters, air vents, noodles… How did you construct it?

SS   I almost called that work *The Doldrums* – I wanted it to be a weather system, a mood. It took over three weeks to install. In preparation I constructed a ceiling in my studio, so I could rig it up, take a look at it, and then wind it back down, endlessly testing and reshuffling compositions. I arrived at Tramway schooled in these strange techniques: how to spread broken glass and mayonnaise, how to spray pizza sauce and beach sand with a leaf blower. All the materials were sourced in Glasgow from the big wholesale food stores or gleaned from street-cruising motorway underpasses.

The ceiling at Tramway is made up of stretched polytunnel plastic on a series of metal frames. I did a course to obtain a licence to drive a cherry picker, and I made the thing one small square at a time, taking up a kit of materials in the casket, placing them, coming back down to take a look, endlessly re-parking and re-positioning this tiny aerial studio, so I could hover over different sections of plastic canvas terrain. I had to wear a restraining belt to stop me from falling when I was leaning out. Parts I couldn't reach with my hands, so I used sticks. I also used a rake and brushes. I often end up making strange, amateur, cowboy tools.

TWR   In many of your works there is a tension between the point at which you recognise what the objects included in it are, and the point at which the experience of the work becomes abstract. Looking up at *Belt and Road*, if I let my eyes relax, the experience was reminiscent of a Helen Frankenthaler painting – all expression and colour. But if I focused, the composition broke down into a collection of trash, some of which was visible through the plastic sheeting. Are you after a particular sweet spot between abstraction and recognition?

SS   I like the delay. You know that butterfly feeling in your body when you want to look at something but you can't see it, the way you feel swirls in your stomach when something is coated, when you want to peel a sticker off a surface? Or even frosted windows – that frustration of wanting to know what's on the other side of something but not being able to get around there. Within the laminated sky of *Belt and Road* there were tighter, sugary spots: something sexy, something disgusting, something high-end, something slothful, something polished, something clumsy. I wanted there to be warm patches – bits where palpable visual references surge through that field, that mood.

TWR   Your description of desire and delay makes me think of a lesson I learned about roses when I was a kid. I wanted to run my fingers over the petals, dig my nails in, yet doing so spoiled them. It made them tawdry. It left me looking at the damage I had done rather than the thing I found beautiful. This is one reason why not touching art, but wanting to, can be powerful: it maintains the suspension between desire and destruction.

SS   I once found a huge bunch of seemingly perfect red roses upturned in a bin in Barcelona. I buried my face in this rejected 50 euros of cool, velvet softness that reeked of splashed beer... Working in delay means stretching out desire, so you don't get everything at once, so the gratification of viewing isn't automatic. The works are nearly always these suspended reliefs dealing in wanting. But desire is no light thing. I wanted *Belt and Road* to have an emotional weather to it, to maintain a kind of lightness but with a bite of sour gunge. Like Monet's *Water Lilies*.

TWR   What do Monet's *Water Lilies* mean to you – as a sculptor who works with colour fields, as an artist who constructs ponds and swamps?

SS   I'm into Monet. I was taught to think he was the symbol of the money-grabbing Impressionist painter, you know? That he just churned out all these woozy, cosmetic-y, dainty paintings. That's what I learned at art school: he was a symbol for everything shallow and light, he made work to be sunk into pretty interiors. Even his name sounds like 'money'. He knew how to perform and he understood what people wanted. But he understood ambience, which is something I've actually got a lot of time for. I'm also excited by how his oeuvre has turned numb, how it's trickled down into this trashy, keyring, dishcloth narrative.

TWR   Many European painters turned their backs on Impressionism for the jaggedness of Cubism, the promise of a kind of knife-throwing machismo with the power to cut the world up into pieces. 'Decoration' became a dirty word, and anyone who drew from Impressionism was vulnerable to being called out as bourgeois. Today Monet has become synonymous with gift-shop reproductions, but IRL his paintings really *move*. He used a technique called 'Melange Optique' – placing colours side by side rather than mixing them on the palette – which reminds me of the way you rub objects up against each other. It leaves your eye to blend them, making the colours tremble on the surface.

SS   This kind of friction, this abrasive grappling for attention between component parts, is a way to produce energy in a work. Gavin Wade, the director of Eastside Projects, once told me he likes the word 'cleave', because it can mean both to take something apart and also to put something together. I find Monet's paintings delicious in their queasiness. They make you sea-sick, you don't know what way is up and what way is down. It's that excess. Eye gorge, disorientation, over-stimulation, druggy potpourri. It's seeing too much. Clingy friction, bickering surfaces. It's the way they tremor between soft, wet and hard. On a surface level I find them extremely stimulating. Isobel Harbison once described my work as 'plasmatic spunk' – I can relate that to Monet too. And then there are those thick, gak-y bits.

TWR   What's 'gak'? I see you have boxes on your shelves labelled with that word.

SS   My work is an archive of what I call gak. It's a kind of debris. When I brush up dusty remains from the studio floor, I know that I can revive them to make good material affects. So I keep the stuff in little bags. That's gak. But it could be made of all manner of things: orange peel, cigarette butts, other gutter totems. Yesterday I found a beautiful sim chip with a blue casing, maybe I'll find wax leg-strips that have an iridescent purple sheen or a hair bobble that looks like cherries. Or chewing gum, and it'll speak to me because I'll want to ask: why is it encased in this particular mint shell, why is it this shade of creamy blue? Or why is this shampoo scented coconut and papaya? Or an air freshener shaped a particular, curvaceous way?

TWR   A kind of childish, everyday alchemy is active in the way you combine materials. It reminds me of making potions as a kid, mixing shampoos and shaving foam, using the colours, textures and smells of available products.
SS   I like this idea of sorcery, of the work being these weird, witchy potions. I was thinking about that when I made those puddles for *Silks* at Eastside Projects in 2015: this cauldron vibe, this Lidl elixir, these glitchy stews. Maybe it's important to reveal how we are tricked by objects and effects, to show that the world is full of of these tricks. It's possible to unravel each object to its source, to inspect the conditioning and associations behind it, the semiotics. I also keep a box of gak from pockets, the furry cysts that come out of the wash and build up in nests in the seams of your clothes.

TWR   Speaking of clothes, you recently collaborated with the fashion house Mugler on a series of coats.
SS   Mugler's archive is incredible. It's full of sculptural, futuristic materials that mutate the body. It's super digital, there are all these sexy, slimy surfaces, and tonnes of latex – clothes designed in proximity to the fetish underworld of Paris in the 1980s. I've been working with latex on and off for years and it's a fascinating material with a complex past. Pure latex is 'milk' bled straight from rubber trees; it's erotic before you do anything with it. Now it's synonymous with modern lifestyles – car tyres and condoms, things that enable us to glide free from the inconveniences of human bodies – but it's also bound up in a toxic colonial history of land exploitation.
      When Mugler asked me to make clothes with them it was irresistible. I ended up making these latex garments. It can feel lonely in the studio, and I wanted to find more ways of working with other people. My studio practice can have an uncontrollable volatility: everything dribbles into everything. I can't contain or organise anything. I considered

it an opportunity to see how this incoherence might be shaped by another party. For me there aren't these neat distinctions between mediums, and I'd wanted for ages to have a space away from my own private throbbing, and the churning-ness of the work.

TWR   How did you find the switch from studio to catwalk?
SS   I always wondered what that Paris fashion world would be like off-screen. It's *steaming* with passionate cliché – a thrilling montage of carrot sticks, cocaine and bitchiness. I was a tourist. Just to be there among that for a pocket of time, to lurch through a portal into a weird vector of culture and then be ejected automatically at the end, was incredible. It felt hedonistic and teenage.

TWR   Some of the coats you made, which were shown on the catwalk in Paris in 2019 at Mugler SS19, were sculptural: see-through containers filled with objects. How were they produced?
SS   We developed this shell from clear plastic with an adhesive layer, which basically meant I could stick stuff to the inside surface. I get fanatical about colour, and I wanted to make a beige trench coat that's a bit like Burberry but which is actually made from cigarette butts and sand from Barcelona beach, and a particularly elegant shade of beige bin bag I found.

TWR   From a distance, the coats appear as a sophisticated blend of colour and texture. Up close, when you see what's inside them, they have a kind of bin juice glamour.
SS   They're like stained windows. People often ask me if my work is sculpture or painting, but really it's to do with questions of how we record, process and remember things. It's about the construction of flat imagery from objects. Like Monet. He made hundreds of those gushy waterlily paintings – he also designed and built the original garden in Giverny where the ponds and flowers were. He had to get planning permission in order to irrigate part of the Seine. I always imagined him going out and painting some bourgeois neighbour's gaudy garden, but he actually constructed the entire scenography himself. He sent off for seeds that got shipped from Asia to Paris, and created the specific scientific conditions required to make the famous ponds. He built this completely fictional set-up, this dreamland, like Disney. It's arrestingly post-modern.

TWR   He wasn't only observing and responding to phenomena, as we might expect of a landscape painter. He was also operating as a sculptor, an installation artist, a set designer, a gardener, a lifestyle influencer. In this regard you share an affinity, in that you stage atmospheric effects, and you draw from a large range of visual sources and object categories. Has your material base changed over the years?

SS   It grows. I think it's got saggier. I used to be more interested in collecting materials affiliated with glamour or luxury – objects heavy with want, like a shit carpet, but a *white* carpet – and then perverting or hijacking them. Now the things I'm drawn to have already been spat out. I'm archiving the bruises, the emotional ambiences. I find materials everywhere. It sounds like a cliché , but things call to me. It's sonic. I look at an object and I can't help thinking, how might it behave in a certain situation?

TWR   Your description reminds me of the protagonist in the novel *Confessions of the Fox* (2018) by Jordy Rosenberg. He's a thief, and objects speak to him – they call to him asking to be saved, to have a life beyond the market. Perhaps there's a politics to listening to what objects have to say, beyond the sales pitch they've been wrapped in.

SS   My response to objects happens on a metabolic level. I feel it in my skin, it's hyper tactile. The things I use can be really sad. In fact I feel more and more tragedy, I feel scared for material objects and I want them to talk. Often they are blaring, groaning. Sometimes I have to crunch past them, ignoring their sonic lamentations. I'm using the cigarette butt that's been smoked, the stuff that's already blemished, worn, dumped.

TWR   The materials you work with belong to the bottom rung, and because of this they have the capacity to be highly emotive.

SS   What I feel about so-called 'everyday' materials is less chronic guilt. If I've got an old shirt I can cut it up, I've got freedom because the object has already sort of given up. And if it's already dead, I might be able to swing it back to life, perhaps, but I can't destroy it. The pressure I would feel going to an art shop and buying materials. What the fuck am I supposed to do with that stuff? I've always felt comically impotent with a paintbrush or a stick of charcoal, like I'm imitating Leonardo DiCaprio in *Titanic*. With objects I can point at things better.

They are spillages of the present. They are words that can be rearranged.

TWR   We have spoken in the past about the difficulties of identifying your work with an environmental politics – because your work is as much about desiring excess as it is critiquing it. Nevertheless, it feels wrong to consider your practice apathetic.

SS   I could never think of my role as an artist as a preacher or a shepherd – it would be arrogant to think my work could teach a lesson. This is why I feel allergic to the idea of the work being called 'environmental art'. It's not that the work isn't engaging in the state of things, but it's also a portrait of desire and longing, materially and emotionally. How do you square the realities of life with what you wish it was? I read that since 1992 there is 70 per cent more toxicity in the world's oceans, and that's not even including the plastic content. In the face of this kind of information it's so easy to feel entirely overwhelmed. The sense of trying to gather everything together in my work, of including moments of optimism but also feeling this horror when all the materials clunk together, is an expression of this disorientation and corruption. This is why the register of my work is often delirious, neurotic, feverish.

TWR   Recently you were in hospital with a broken ankle. You sent me a photograph of a reproduction of Monet's *Water Lilies* on the wall of the ward.

SS   It was so small, yet I could still recognise it behind the blurry, plastic sheet used in the frame instead of glass. It was postcard size and entirely without texture. All that was left was a shadowy powder.

TWR   Are you interested in the afterlife of modern painting? When it's passed through the market and come out the other end as a cheap and ubiquitous product?

SS   Perhaps it's something more like biography. The further an artwork has travelled the more complex its story. It's amazing to me how far an artwork, or an object, can travel while still retaining the memory of its origin. That spiral, that fracture, that skid away from the original, is where my work exists.

R. M.,
October 2019

WORKS

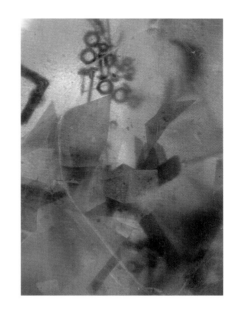

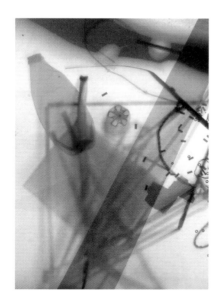

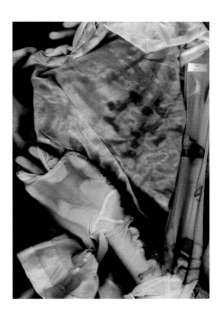

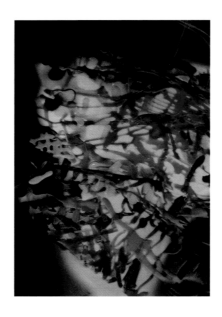

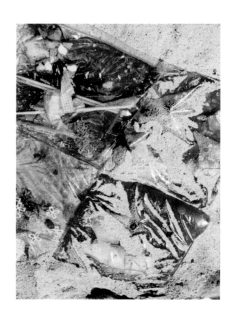

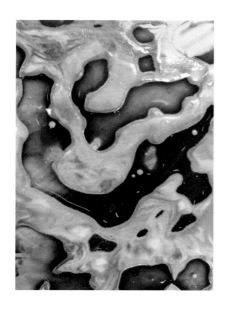
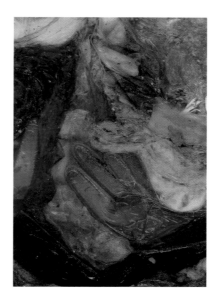

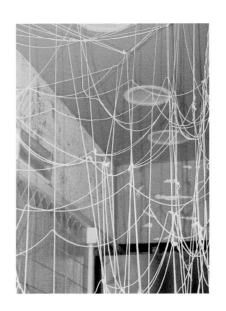

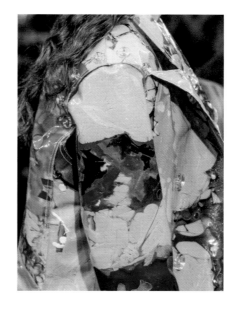

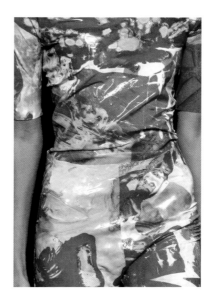

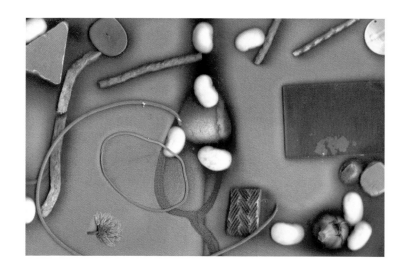

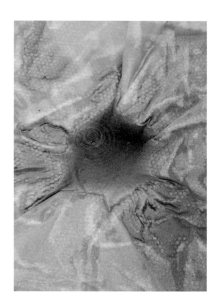

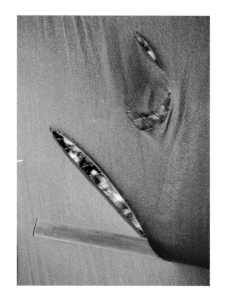

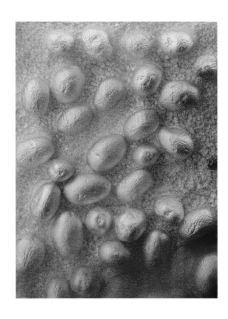

VERACRUZ WITH A ZEE FOR ZETA

FERNANDA MELCHOR
tr. SOPHIE HUGHES

¶ Tired of all the chitchat from your relatives – recently landed in town on a visit – you take the car and head for the beach. It's a glorious day: the sun beams down from high in the sky, but the breeze is still cool and carries the scent of distant lands.

You park up by the seafront and light a cigarette without getting out of the car. The water is almost motionless, and as pale as the sky. The waves break listlessly on the beach; tiny waves, which at times seem to be made not of water but silver, of liquid mercury, of that stuff Robert Patrick is made of in *Terminator 2*.

The beach isn't empty. In fact, it seems a lot busier than usual for a Wednesday morning. A group of thirty or forty young men walk along the shore. They're wearing rolled-up jeans and hold their shirts in their hands. Their chests are tan and smooth, and their hair is gelled, either spiked up or slicked back. It catches your attention that the group appears to be heading toward a specific spot by the water's edge; they even ignore the lurking beach rat cajoling them to take a seat at the tables with beach umbrellas set up on the raked sand. The group's movements, the way they wear their clothes, remind you of the tourists who flock to the beach to paddle in the sea and take photos. But these kids look more like construction workers on their day off than tourists.

A beat-up white van comes to a halt 20 feet from your car. Four men dressed like rappers – sportswear, tattoos, sunglasses – get out and catch up with the group on the beach. You can't make out what they say, but it looks like the new arrivals tell the others to form a line. It looks like they're going to take a group photo because they all shuffle in with their backs to the sea, and the ones in front even crouch down. But no one has a camera.

You light another cigarette while the ringleaders and the other guys walk off the sand and up on to the esplanade. Some of them congregate next to the white van and one of the men giving orders – in a pale green basketball jersey – rails at them and then sends them packing. The van door slides open to reveal more people inside. It looks like they're assigning jobs to the boys, who approach the vehicle in pairs and then walk away with small Manila envelopes in their hands. You spot a girl (there are three or four among this new crowd): she walks toward your car counting crisp green banknotes, which can only be 200 bills. Her plump lips mouth numbers while her fingers expertly flick through the banknotes. A yellow Mitsubishi pulls up next to her. The girl – cinnamon skin, Mexican pink top, diamante sandals and dark glasses that cover half her face – opens the passenger-side door – reggaeton blaring – and climbs in. Moments later, a black BMW 325i pulls up and three scrawny boys get in – the youngest can't be older than 15. Next, a pickup, whose model you don't recognise: it's white, brand new, and has tinted windows.

At this point you clock two guys loitering next to your car. They're not looking at you, but you notice that they've positioned themselves in your blind spot. You take out your cell and call your friend Agustín, the first name in your contacts. You chat about this and that while you smoke another cigarette. When the ringleaders from the van start looking at you suspiciously you make some wisecrack and laugh, to relax your face and avoid giving yourself away.

You get out of there the minute one of the men lifts up his shirt to reveal a gun grip poking out from the waistband of his shorts.

❡ You never found out his real name. You were too scared to ask. The friends who recommended him called him Ángel del Mal, Angel of Evil; one of them even wrote the nickname on the card he gave you with the code for the guy's two-way radio and his cell number. That ridiculous name made you cringe so you just called him Ángel.

The first time you contacted him over radio you arranged to meet in a small park two blocks from your house. You didn't want him to know where you lived. It was 8 at night and the park was unlit. The cool October breeze filtered through the branches of the almond trees; the faintest of breezes that smelled of woodlands and dispelled the sultry city air, and which, come night-time, made the dogs on the block howl inconsolably.

Ángel del Mal rocked up in a dark car: the latest model but nothing flashy. He told you to get in and then drove around the park while showing you a grocery bag stuffed with little packets; each one contained a gram of cocaine. You bought four off him that first time. Your wife had felt like some marijuana but Ángel didn't have any on him. He explained that he didn't like dealing dope: it took up too much room, it stank, and it was so cheap he barely broke even. You liked his frankness, his Pedro Infante moustache, his faint Norteño accent, his unassuming clothes that made him look like a shoe-store manager. You had him down as about 40, ex-military.

You started calling him once or twice a week. It was a relief not having to skulk around at neighbourhood stores and deal with the street pushers; they were always after a tip, always side-eyeing your car jealously, resentfully. Over time you built up the courage to make conversation with Ángel, and even to ask him some questions. You knew it wasn't wise to show that much interest but you really wanted to know if he worked for Los Zetas, although you didn't call them that because you were used to not speaking their name out loud, just like everyone else you knew: instead, you called them 'the last letter guys', as in, zee for Zeta. Ángel kept talking for the entire transaction. While neither confirming nor denying it, he managed to get across that the merchandise he sold all over the city and that you and your friends snorted brazenly at parties came from that very criminal group. He led you to believe that he was just one of many authorised dealers and that, if he occasionally charged more than the official cost per wrap, it was only because he was saving his clients the trouble of leaving their homes. This admission made you nervous; you stuck your hand out hurriedly, opened the door to get out of the car, and almost fainted when you spotted the police car trailing you with its headlights off. You pictured yourself in some squalid police cell, your wife forced to pawn your possessions to pay a five-figure fine, your friends furious because you never showed up with the blow. But Ángel, perfectly calm, with the hint of a smile on his face, told you not to worry when getting out of the car: immunity from the police came included in the price.

'If they fuck with me, they fuck with my bosses, and they're not that stupid,' he said.

Another night, back in his car, you asked him if there were more dealers around like him. His face grew long as he told you about a kid who used to do home deliveries of coke and who always took a girl along with him, to throw the military off the scent at the checkpoints constantly popping up across the city. Ángel explained that the kid had begun to 'do a number' on Los Zetas: in order to maximise his earnings he started buying drugs off the *chapulines*, members of the other cartels who dealt on the fringes of the city, until eventually the bosses caught wind of his betrayal and ordered Ángel del Mal to 'sell him out', to talk to the kid over the radio and tease from him the information of where he was hiding. The *sicarios* killed both the kid and the girl who was with him; Ángel was there.

'They made me section him,' he said, twisting his moustache nervously. The word kept bouncing around in your head, but it wasn't until you got back in the house and bolted the door, the goods safely stashed in one of the compartments of your wallet, that you understood what your dealer had meant by that half-medical, half-bureaucratic term: namely that the bosses had forced him to carve up his ex-colleague's body to prove his loyalty.

The coke you bought that day tasted like poison but you finished the lot, down to the last speck stuck to the 20-peso bill you used to snort it. After all, you needed something to pair with the two bottles of 12-year-old whiskey your friends had brought: there was no way you'd get through both of them neat.

A couple of months later, Ángel stopped answering his radio and you had no choice but to go back to the street pushers.

¶ It was a Saturday like any other. The wholesaler where you worked as a cashier was teeming with shoppers and their kids. Your day began as usual: with a motivational team meeting at which your manager forced all the staff ('members' was the company's preferred term, to save on employee benefits) to chant chants as we jumped up and down with our arms around each other. Your smile should be as wide as the one on your employee badge, your supervisor would say, but you seldom managed to hold it for more than an hour, which lost you points and pesos come payday.

Everything was humming along as normal. Your feet weren't aching too much yet. Shoppers filed through your register: women buying frozen gateaux and gigantic cans of food; men who came for cigarettes, microwave dinners and liquor. Then, at around noon, a convoy of forklifts appeared in your line hauling a pair of fridges, three sinks, five microwaves, piles upon piles of clothing, and boxes of liquor and candy. You were used to running big orders for restaurants and hotels so you didn't bat an eyelid when the total came to just over 10,000 dollars. A middle-aged man emerged from behind the last cart, accompanied by six gangsterish youths. You smiled at the customer, said good morning, and asked him how he'd like to pay. Without a word he handed you a credit card, which the machine declined.

You apologised to the customer and explained that your terminal was showing that the card had been cancelled. Completely unfazed, the man pulled out a second card from his back pocket. It was a blank piece of plastic, with no words or numbers or logos of any bank on it. You turned it over in your hand and looked at the magnetic strip while every hair on your body stood on end. Stretching your smile even wider, you apologised again to the customer: you couldn't run that card.

'Run the goddamn card. Run it now,' the man said, through gritted teeth.

'Run the card, asshole. Don't make a scene,' one of his henchmen cut in.

Unsure what to do, you followed company policy and called your supervisor. The guys were glowering but there was no way it was going to be you who refused to give them what they wanted. Your supervisor took fifteen minutes to arrive; the store was crawling. You handed him the card; he looked at both sides and also refused to run it.

Without so much as raising his voice, the man told you and your supervisor that if you didn't charge him using that card you'd both end up dead in the parking lot with a face full of holes and your brains blown out.

Your supervisor immediately ran the card through the machine. The men walked off calmly with their goods.

The next day you handed in your resignation. You needed the job but you didn't know if those guys would come back. Later you found out your supervisor had done the same.

¶ Your thing, your thing had always been the clubs. Even your *quinceañera*, back in the late 90s, had been at the coolest spot in town. Your dad had gone and booked the Naval Casino and he envisioned you in a puffball dress, releasing white doves into the air, surrounded by teenyboppers in tuxes. You'd locked yourself in your room for two whole days screaming that you'd rather kill yourself than have your friends show up to see you waltzing with some douche from the Naval Academy. Only then did he finally agree to rent out the club and forget about the three-tier cake.

You know all the nightspots in Veracruz, or at least all the ones worth knowing. You don't really care if it's pop, reggaeton, lounge or salsa blasting from the speakers. For you it's always been about hanging with the crowd: being around people you love and admire; just letting loose, not getting bogged down in boring conversations, dancing and drinking and laughing till dawn.

Your favourite was a retro-style club, all velvet chairs and chandeliers hanging from the ceiling. And you liked it because it was the most expensive in town, the newest, the most exclusive. Only beautiful, well-dressed people could get in; you could be a blue-eyed blonde speaking French, but if you rocked up in shorts and sandals, *ciao*, you weren't getting past the door. It was so, so hip that sometimes you felt embarrassed to have to wear the same top twice when you knew there were girls there in 30,000-peso designer dresses. But once inside you'd find your crew and all your complexes would melt away like the crushed ice in your colourful cocktail.

That's why that group of brown kids with dumbass haircuts dressed in sports tops and fat chains stood out like sore thumbs when they started showing up at the club on weekends. They looked so out of place that the whole room would throw glances at them and at first nobody understood why the club's owner fell over himself to keep them happy, always offering them the best tables, the ones not even your friends were able to reserve. It made a lot of people really pissed, and not because those guys were dark-skinned (some of your friends were too, and they had even more money than you *güeros*): no, the weird thing was that those guys never danced or looked like they were having a good time. They'd spend the whole night just gawking at each other and drinking like fish, all in complete silence. Sometimes they might have a few girls with them; common, trashy-looking girls, even with the enormous jewels dripping from them.

A friend explained to you that those guys were narcos and you took his word for it: they looked like the ones on TV, sitting handcuffed at tables piled high with submachine guns. Your friend told you never to address or even look at them because in another club in town a group fitting their description had been known to take a shine to some girl and just take her, even if that meant having to get rid of the husband or her other admirers first. This you couldn't believe; it seemed like the plot of some shitty movie, but then your mom told you that it really had happened to the daughter of a lady who'd written an email to a friend of hers. Your mom drove you nuts with her well-intentioned warnings and advice every time you got ready to go out, and you ended up promising her you wouldn't go back to the club. But you did. Bars and house parties bored you shitless.

The last time you set foot in that club was a Saturday night. The place was buzzing when suddenly the lights went on and the music stopped. A group of armed guys had come in, walked up to one of the tables, and hauled a young kid out to the street. You could see everything they did to him because the club had big windows facing on to Boulevard Ávila Camacho, the avenue that ran right along the coast. Three vans were blocking the traffic; five men were taking turns pummelling the kid; blood was pouring from his face as they smashed it in with the butts of their guns and then, once he was out cold, they picked him up and tossed him inside one of the vans.

Inside the club, you could see the shock on everyone's face; everyone apart from the narcos at the table by the dance floor. You thought about that poor kid, such a cute-looking guy. People were muttering to each other and someone near your table began shouting into a two-way radio saying something about the police.

One of the narcos, an imposing guy with a crew cut, got up from his seat and shouted, to no one in particular, 'Nothing's happened here.'

'Or what, did someone see something?' he asked with his hands on his hips.

There was a stampede toward the exit. People left without even settling their bills. You were crying. You were really scared and you couldn't believe that the city where you were born was turning into one of those horrible places up at the border where you can't go out anywhere because of the constant shootouts.

¶ You're woken by the sound of machine-gun fire outside your house. You jump out of bed and fly down the hall to your son's room: he's lying in bed, awake and frightened. Your husband looks out of the living room window and shouts at you to get down on the floor. He says there are soldiers outside, armed soldiers who are using your car as a barricade, who are aiming at an overturned truck at the end of the street.

You don't dare open the front door until well into the morning. Some reporters ring the doorbell but you don't answer it.

That whole month you don't get a single night's sleep: every time you close your eyes your ears ring with the cracking of gunshots.

¶ It's been a long time since you walked through that neighbourhood. There are a lot more houses now than you remember, nicer than back then, painted in cheerful colours and decked out with white window frames and electric gates. There isn't a trace of the vacant lot where you used to play baseball and hunt lizards with your friends, but the elementary school where you went for six years still stands on the same site; it's still painted white, too, although it looks smaller than you remember.

The main entrance isn't a cast-iron gate any more but a heavy white aluminium door. Behind it you can hear children shrieking and giggling: it must be recess.

You feel a sudden urge to go in and up to the main office to say hello to that short, squeaky-voiced resource officer who used to tug your ears sweetly whenever you spoke too much in class; or to your fifth-grade teacher, the one who gave you Rius and *Mafalda* to read and who lent you her copy of *La noche de Tlatelolco*; and to the dark-skinned woman with thick-lensed glasses who showed you and your friends how to play baseball without gloves, the way they did in the small jungle village where she came from. You're about to ring the bell when you remember the time; you'd better hurry if you want to get to the office punctually. You stand before the white door for a moment more and then promise yourself that you'll come back another time to say hello to your old teachers. Turning to leave, you notice a vase that's been placed on the curbside next to a small tree that didn't exist back in your day. You go over to take a better look. The flowers inside it are withered but can't be that old. Strewn across the ground around the vase lie the broken pieces of a plaster cross. You bend down to look more closely at the fragments; they have gold writing on them. You piece them back together on the pavement to form a name and date: 'Miriam M. Barra. 1974-2010'. A metal crucifix nailed to the tree trunk catches your eye. You do the corresponding maths: Miriam was 36 years old on the day of her death, which took place on that very corner; probably in a traffic accident, you suppose. You walk away whistling the song from the radio you woke to that morning.

Two days pass. You can't get the name Miriam M. Barra out of your head. In the office you grow bored waiting on instructions that never come, so to kill time you decide to search the name online, but the search doesn't bring up anything interesting. You decide to try using the street names. You type 'Invernadero corner of Marte': the first hit is from an online newspaper and it says, 'Discovered mutilated'. The photograph accompanying the article shows a group of policemen dressed in black picking up a bloody mass wrapped in sheets, almost directly in front of the school's white door. All the articles concur that the body belongs to Nayeli Reyes Santos, an employee of the federal judicial branch, kidnapped four days before the discovery. There are endless images: photos of Nayeli still alive (sleek blonde hair, cheeky smile, sharp, defined features) and of her severed body (legs cut off at the thigh, bruised arms detached from the torso, barely covered by a striped T-shirt) and a cardboard sign: 'this is wot u get if u disrepek or rat out the company. Yours Z', that someone had driven into her chest with a knife, right down to the handle. Subsequent articles reported that a relation of Nayeli had identified the body, which was then returned, two days later, before the wake was even over: the parents of the 32-year-old lawyer had opened the casket to find that the body they were mourning had dark curly hair and tattoos that didn't belong to Nayeli.

You're overcome with sadness. There's no article reporting the eventual identification of Miriam M. Barra, 36 years of age, or the reappearance, either dead or alive, of the employee from the federal judicial branch. You remember something an artist friend who'd worked with an embalmer once told you: you don't get female bodies in medical schools because nine times out of ten they end up being retrieved from the dissection hall, which isn't always the case with the men. You think about the pain Miriam's family must have gone through, about the flowers, wilting in the heat but still relatively fresh in the vase. Who'd had the nerve to smash the little plaster cross bearing her name? The killers themselves, perhaps? School kids? Had it been a regrettable accident or was it the deliberate act of some neighbour wanting to wipe all memory of what had happened?

Your eyes well up. You dry them angrily: you're not a little girl any more; you can't go around crying over people you don't even know. You're reminded of the time your fifth-grade teacher gave you that video of soldiers shooting at students, there in the Plaza de las Tres Culturas, and you also remember that you had trouble falling asleep that night because in your head you could still hear the kids' screams, their songs and furious chants. You tossed and turned beneath your Garfield sheets long into the night; it felt to you as if you were as guilty as the soldiers, or the monkey-faced president who'd appeared in the video flailing his arms and who the students had laid into just hours before they'd fallen, riddled with bullets, to the ground.

¶ You've been lying on a hospital stretcher in the Instituto Mexicano del Seguro Social Emergency Room for eight days now. Your aunt is looking after you. Every day she tells you that at any moment you'll be transferred to the hospital where they'll be able to sew up the hole in your back, which they can't do anything about there in the ER because you don't have medical cover. She also tells you that the governor asks after you daily and that he's promised to get you medical attention and a grant so you can finish college.

Eight days you've spent face down on that stretcher with the flies buzzing around your head and no one taking you up to the ward or transferring you. They give you drugs and insert drips, and are constantly injecting you. Antibiotics, mostly, to make sure the wound doesn't start festering. It's covered by a dressing and they won't let you touch it, but that doesn't stop you trying, and sometimes, when your aunt isn't looking, when the nurses disappear to care for the other patients, you twist your arm back and reach out to touch the hole the dumdum left at the base of your shoulder blade.

'Two inches deeper and you wouldn't be here to tell the tale,' the doctor told you.

The pain gets worse at night, when the drugs have less effect and the silence of the hospital reminds you that your mother is dead, that the same bullets that wounded you killed her while the two of you rode in a taxi along Calle La Fragua, eight days ago.

And then you cry, even if your aunt is there with you, even if she strokes your head and asks you to stop, your *mami* would be sad to see you suffering so. You're crying because it was your idea to go out for *tortas* after the La Arrolladora Banda El Limón concert at the Auditorio Benito Juárez, because you chose the car that would drive straight through the shootout.

And you couldn't even go to the funeral, you couldn't even take her flowers and ask her forgiveness. That's why you're crying, because it's all your fault.

DOUGLAS HERASYMUIK

LINE OF CONTROL

one hour in
I knew
the god inhabiting this arid mountain pass
intended to kill us

air too thin for breathing
hardscrabble scree almost silver with sun
a snow leopard paw print
scat bristling with fur
and relics of rodent teeth
bleached white as a *Stupa*

nowhere anything living

an unmarked trail
imagined remnant of a Silk Road
was instead simply the way
farmers and *Changpas* with their nomadic sheep
navigated the two-day walk to town

a fallen tree bridged the desert and wild roses
improbable apricot and apple orchards
the other side of a swollen river
splintered with rapids
then the barley fields
and a village
cut into the lunar landscape of the Himalayan plateau

100-year-rains came
three nights in a row
severing the mud seams between wooden joists
and rammed-earth bricks of the farmhouse ceiling and walls
we awoke soaked
then the incense smell from a willow wood fire
heating the blackened kitchen stove
All India Radio
static rising like a call to prayer
reported the lone road linking the distal boundaries of the state
was washed out
mountain stones and rivers had come coursing
searching for the villages
and buried them in a communal grave

We started walking
to find a way out
the muddy water furious
folding the stone retaining walls
and submerging the bridge deck
each step
our boots shattering asphalt eggshells

but it wasn't serious yet

cars and transport trucks lined the remnants of the highway into Khalsi
drivers squatted and searched the horizon
for distant flares of lightning
or some indication that the army was releasing the road

Reza was willing to risk going home
and agreed to sell seats in his pockmarked taxi

Srinigar for 10 000 Rs

we must have been the only ones let through
into the bruise of dusk
the exhausted soldiers
dressed in water-blue fatigues
thumbed our damp passports
and waved us on
we skidded down the mucky road
then started to climb
past tourists
wrestling their sputtering Royal Enfield motorcycles
stranded, slick with rain

the Indus river, brown as dried blood
roiled beside the road
chewing chunks off the shoulder
the Chevy hit a stone
and left the ground

WE'RE GOING IN

impossibly
the front wheel caught a rut
and the car was righted

om mani padme hum om mani padme hum om mani padme hum
I clung to the obligation of silent prayer
and strangled the soft throat of each endless moment

It all came apart at Zoji La
11, 575 ft above sea level
heavy machinery pushed the last kilometre of slurry off the road
we were left vulnerable to the yawning vacuum of the Kashmir Valley
when Reza parked on the naked shoulder of the cliff
to allow the shuddering carnival of lorries to pass

2,000 people lost their lives in flooding in Pakistan
20 million more lost their property and livelihoods

on this side of the Line
Hilde – in the seat behind me – started screaming
LETMEOUTLETMEOUTLETMEOUT

N.B. the *Line of Control* is a de facto border established between Indian and
Pakistani controlled parts of the 'former princely state of Jammu and Kashmir'
following a ceasefire agreement signed in 1972. It is distinguished by an electri-
fied fence, motion sensors, thermal imaging devices and alarms. It is considered
to be one of the most dangerous places in the world (*Wikipedia*).

GRANDFATHER'S HOUSE

Remember the rain barrel, the slow-sinking plastic boat?
cherry trees beside the victory garden
the metal downspout
our playground an abandoned stone foundation, jagged as rotten teeth
in the vacant lot beside Dido's house

Sundays the people were free
Ukrainian farmers, railwaymen, cobblers
tools downed, dressed in wedding suits and laughing in the park
picnic baskets (cabbage rolls and garlic pickles, sweet beets)
and too much to drink (potato vodka or crabapple wine)
a picture of Dido wearing a wide-brimmed hat, Baba sitting on the ground with
   their son and twins
her dress spread like a royal cape
our people said *John's madness came because he hit his head on a wall during a fight*
but they turned after a while and whispered *it was her fault*
Baba became alone with her children in the world
and the war was coming

Uncle was a boy when he saw the RCMP beat his father to the ground in front
   of the house
they took Dido to the provincial hospital to set him straight
and surgeons split his skull, scraped part of his thinking brain out
nurses dumped him into an ice bath and kept the doors locked
then psychiatrists snowed him shoulder-deep in Chlorpromazine
and the days abandoned their difference

We'd see Dido once a year
driving all day to the north as the snow melted in the brown Easter fields
led by the hand, he'd sit under a tree and eat chocolate bars one after another
yellowed fingers, feral nails
picking and pulling the brown polyester of his suit pants, his oversized suspenders
if Dido spoke, it was about money taken from him
an immigrant's looping lament
at first he couldn't recognise Mom, she'd always remained a child in his endless days
and he didn't remember Baba was gone
or that she'd spent their married life working – washing and folding laundry at the
   hospital
one of the few jobs she could get
he'd dissolve into tears and needed reminders to eat potatoes with his spoon
instead of herding them like caribou with his hands

It was too much to take Dido home

We left

walking past the locked ward and silent chapel
in the bleak bunker hallways
a tree of a man, silent as falling snow
stepped out from the wall
and mutely offered handfuls of golf balls lime-slick with algae

I was gifted a 1-lb chocolate bunny
so I wrapped it in a funeral shroud of Kleenex
and hid it behind the back seat under the concave windshield glass
it melted and fused together into a distorted hulk
and could not be salvaged
I remember crying

One year we came back to take Dido to be buried beside his wife
church vespers then the frigid stone field
the hospital chapel hand-built in 1913 by a patient
a stonemason similarly lost to days
it's soon to be demolished

FIREFLIES

top-knot
tourist burns fist
full of rupees to claim
god, a guru pats his pockets
empty

emptied
of all pretence
night-orphaned promises
bright blue camel dung coal embers
burn clean

burning
ghat pyre combusts
blossum-shrouded body
children float ash dusted diyas
downstream

Ganga
swallows aeons
a cricket ball stroked 6
solitary sunrise aarthi
septic hymns

THE RUSSIAN MAN
CLAIRE-LOUISE BENNETT

FICTION

Many years ago a large Russian man with the longest tendrils of the softest white hair came to live in the fastest growing town in Europe which at the time happened to be in the southwest of England. Very little is known about why he came there or what he did with himself but one thing relating to his daily round that can be set down with utmost confidence is that whenever the Russian man needed groceries he'd fold himself into his small maroon car and drive to a retail park in the suburbs to get them. And probably the reason he went to that retail park and not another was because there was a very pleasant supermarket in that retail park which aside from Saturday mornings naturally never got too busy and as such there was always an available parking space up near the exit and entrance doors and this in all likelihood suited the Russian man very well because he would likely have had tremendous difficulty finding his own car if it was only shoved haphazardly in there somewhere among all the other cars parked one after the other with cracking midday sunlight spreading out all over them diluting their already indistinguishable roofs in the practically endless carpark. The Russian man's car was fairly distinguishable for the reason that it was ancient which meant it was a distinctly vintage colour and had the finish furthermore of an old immoveable garden gate which meant it could hold its own against the suburban sun's brash emanation. But in all likelihood the Russian man did not in any case know what his own car looked like so the only way he could find it was to be certain of where he left it and this perhaps explains why the Russian man liked to park his small maroon car up near the entrance and exit doors of the supermarket which despite its commodious proportions had the familiar feel and botherless charm of a corner-shop. Right there on the perimeter of this booming yet visionless town in the southwest of England.

Once inside the supermarket the Russian man would seize a basket from the pile that could always be counted on to be neatly stacked and regularly replenished right there on the left of the entrance and immediately he'd taken the basket he'd look alarmed and off-balance just as if it were a grim pail full of headstrong and incompatible eels swinging perilously in his hand. Holding the basket at arm's length, off he'd career, light on his feet, orbiting the aisles at full tilt, the empty yet possessed basket swinging to and fro out in front of him, ghostly wisps of white hair tapering off into the air behind him. Round and round the Russian man went. Making frantic laps of the store's circumference. Plunging headlong through the shining fruits and scrubbed vegetables, hurtling past the bakery the deli the butcher the fishmonger, bypassing all the little paper plates perched up on the respective counters offering samples of gluten-free Kaiser rolls scamorza affumicata award-winning blood sausage special offer undressed spider crab, barrelling back up the booze aisle then rushing by the checkouts one to fourteen at such a terrific rate they might very well have been checkpoints as far as the Russian man was concerned. There he was, back at the start, up by the entrance and exit doors, right where the baskets were stacked. And off he went again, faster this time. And again, and again. Faster and faster.

Plunging headlong through the shining fruits and scrubbed vegetables hurtling past the bakery the deli the butcher the fishmonger bypassing all the little paper plates perched up on the respective counters and all the while the wired basket swinging cagily out in front of him until at last it steered him off down one or another aisle and on into the next and here and there along his lurching passage grocery items predominantly of the long-life variety found their way into the Russian man's basket and he would stand the large Russian man with the now pacified basket swung up and out to the left right in the middle of this or that aisle facing the shelves on one or another side half-bowed just as if the splendidly arrayed shelves of pickled vegetables were in fact the stalls of a magnificent Viennese auditorium and he stood before a prestigious audience who had travelled especially from the grandest domiciles of Europe to witness him perform an exquisite sequence of sublime prestidigitation that of course the Russian man would execute with vigorous precision and a rhythmic tenderness so perfectly pitched that the gentlewomen in the audience bolt upright and agog would hold their breath would part their lips would follow hungrily through narrowed eyes every miraculous yet seemingly inevitable turn of his astonishing hands would think my god what this man could do for me he could turn it all upside down and it would simply feel like everything was at last the right way around and I would flourish flourish yes attain a fullness at last of flesh and spirit experience at last the divulging pleasure I suspected was there somewhere all along all along but have so far myself never twined with directly and the man seated beside her would look down involuntarily at his wife's hands and see that they are squeezing the long burgundy gloves that he did not notice her remove but which are now nevertheless being twisted this way and that between her pale ensorcelled fingers. The man clears his throat to get her to stop that at once but the wife is uncharacteristically oblivious to her husband's characteristically tactful prompting so the man somewhat reluctantly casts a hand over to her lap. Settles it down around her agitated fingers. Bringing them together easily. Pliant yet stilled. There, there.

Like the tapered petals of a pair of cool fresh tulips.

The man's hand relaxes, he does not withdraw it, why not leave it there. His hand stays heavy in his wife's placid lap upon his wife's motionless fingers as if it were no longer attached to him at all. And that was precisely how it felt to her in fact. As if a hand belonging to who knows who from who knows where had plummeted willy-nilly into her lap. Soon her fingers begin to stir again. Like rippling luminaria digitata they turn over and reach through the unflappable fingers of this unsuspecting hand and lift it up to where she can see it. Before he can stop himself the man turns to look at his wife and that is a mistake. Too late. Already his head is turned in order to search out his wife's eyes. The eye contact which he impulsively sought would have surely only made these strange matters worse, had it been established, but eye contact with his wife was not established in fact for the reason that she is peering quizzically at his hand, which she is holding there in mid-air between them. What is she doing now? She is tilting her head to one side now. She is looking around the hand at her husband as if to say, is this yours? There is nothing he can do except let her have the hand and watch as she pushes the first two fingers back and her mouth opens wide. Keeping his hand exactly where it is in mid-air between them and her mouth wide open she brings her head towards the hand and draws her mouth around the two extended fingers without touching them and when at last she feels the tips of the fingers come into contact with the back of her throat sending sudden fluid up up to revel in the crescents of her eyes she closes her mouth around them both. The man can do absolutely nothing except watch his fingers disappear into his wife's head and be appalled at how hot the inside of her mouth is. It is practically industrial and this is very disturbing. It is like a furnace in there and who, who exactly, is responsible for stoking and tending to and maintaining this furnace? Her tongue is nowhere. Her tongue is lying low. Waiting. Waiting for what or who exactly? Between the underside of the man's fingers and his wife's lurking tongue is a torrid vacuum that pulls at him. His gut his ribs his perineum the backs of his arms are particularly susceptible to the abysmal demands of the shockingly insistent and accusatory void brought about by the smouldering abeyance of his wife's tongue.

His wife's tongue.

Where is it? Where is it? The edges of her teeth behind her lips press down on the base of his two fingers and he detects a jolt, a spasm. She presses down firmly, trying to stifle this engrossing bout of cadent gagging. Or perhaps she is pressing down firmly in order to bring it on? He attempts to inch his fingers out but it is impossible. In addition to her lips clamping the base of them her hand hampers his wrist with the indolent strength of a nothing-else-to-do-in-the-world constrictor. She will never let go. She will perhaps discreetly choke to death on his fingers. Slump down into his lap. And he will perhaps push his left hand into the amaranthine coils of her fastened hair. Come into contact thereupon with the ethereal beauty that is surely immediately emitted by a shapely cranium no longer stippled by the hell-bent drub of sequestered and unfathomable yearnings. And perhaps while the ethereal beauty of this smooth and peaceable skull permeates his fingers and moves onwards unperturbed towards his chest where it will collect into a propitious pool within which the man's heart will be bathed and anointed the man will look about the auditorium and see that yes the head of every wife has come to rest in the lap of the man beside her and he will also note that every man has one hand pushed into the elaborate updo forever fastened upon the stilled head there in his lap while the other hand reposes on the narrow velvet armrest there to the left of where every man sits. And look don't the first two fingers of every man's hand glisten wetly upon the velvet armrest there to the left? And look, hasn't the Russian man come to a standstill at the front of the stage? Doesn't he stand there, smiling, triumphantly, and aren't his two fingers held aloft for all the men to see? As the man's heart makes its decorous descent into the scintillant pool of ethereal beauty drained from the recently mollified dome lolling heavy and unloaded upon his knees he experiences lapping waves of awe and gratitude at the sleight of hand this Russian man has performed which has surely unfurled all the riddles, all the riddles, all the riddles have been unfurled. Their intractable convolutions thrown to the breeze, the Sphinx at last is laid to rest and how beautiful she is. How very beautiful. More beautiful now it goes without saying than she has ever been. She is letting go. The man's wife drags her lips away from the base of his two fingers. Pulls them along their renowned length. Just as she is about to run out of finger her tongue rises from its dip and flickers between the two tips. Fleetingly cajoles the two fingertips with lubricious delight before the tongue and the lips, her whole mouth, departs from the hand completely. The winding grip around his wrist eases. But she does not let go. Her hand moves upwards. Glides over his hand. Clasps the two long embrocated fingers. The man's wife holds his fingers up in front of him, she flashes her dark sparkling eyes in surprise, and mouths the word 'Voilà'. And still she does not let go. She leans in towards him. She looks directly into her husband's eyes. She presses his two fingers against her stretched throat and with her vocal apparatus thus slightly impaired she says very quietly, 'It's all yours.' The Russian man comes to a standstill at the front of the stage. He stands there. Smiling, triumphantly. His hands moving slowly through the tumultuous air.

Caressing the air in fact.

For it is absolutely altered. It is mottled mercurial aflame. The gentlewomen in the Viennese auditorium are on the edges of their seats their ductile kidskin gloves of various regal shades squirm and slide like tossed offal beneath the small heels of their small encrusted boots they are beating their unclad hands together with so much ferocious excitement their hands sting, their hands are burning, their hands are on fire, and all at once they begin to sing, feel my breast, how it burns, brilliant fire, holds fast my heart, it twists within, and surrounds me. Wagner – of all things! The Russian man runs his hands all over the air's beseeching currents and indeed he can feel oh so clearly that the women are emboldened, that the women are ready for anything. Anything! Is this why the Russian man is smiling so triumphantly? Because he knows very well that the most distinguished women of Europe are primed yet at the same time they do not have the faintest idea what it is they crave? Because he knows very well that they have preserved and finessed a diaphanous and titillating cluelessness and in doing so have foregone developing the natural wherewithal and cultivating an unflinching curiosity that surely would conduct the unbridled appetite that is tearing hell for leather through their breast towards an expedient and gratifying erotic scenario? There will be one or two here and there who are perfectly capable of course. Those débrouillard women however would have been sitting in the Viennese auditorium with something or other up their sleeve from the off. Doesn't the Russian man know very well that for most of them all this has been rather too much, all at once, and as such their urgent and blind fervour will be coaxed and exploited in all manner of abominable ways? Ways that will thrill and send them over the edge of course, the impulse for transgression and a taste for abasement is not so difficult to locate and arouse. Because of course it is thrilling to be astutely defiled. To have every revered trait and inimitable asset compromised, undermined, and subverted. Yet the Russian man knows these fine demure women cannot abandon themselves completely. Once and for all. It is not possible! Reality will right itself, roles must be resumed and all things nice must take their place once more. Oh, and all things nice! Lace, opal, gypsophila, rose oil, meringue, gardenia, pearl powder, mink, sugared almonds, pas des chat, beeswax, tarot, orange blossom, Liszt, calisthenics, Venetian talc, parakeets, baklava, cameo, amber, calamine, broderie anglaise, whalebone, honeycomb, rabbit, polka, damask, pot pourri, crystal, Chrétien de Troyes, lavender, mah-jong, gymkhana, tortoiseshell, filigree, silk, liquorice, curling tongs, terrapins, pineapples, bathwater, plumes, tinctures, tazze, candelabrum, the cherry moon – and what then, what then? Surely the Russian man knows very well that they will be mortified by the unspeakable acts they were complicit in carrying out and will henceforth be cowed and contrite to the core of their besmirched bodies and chequered hearts? It is quite impossible to know in fact which side the Russian man is on as he stands there, smiling, jubilantly, stirring the fractious air, smiling, smiling, now reaching forward, one irrepressible hand coming to rest first of all on a jar of pickled cucumber then moving impishly along to a jar of pickled cucumber containing dill and the Russian man is very fond of dill especially in his pickled cucumber because he likes to eat pickled cucumber as an accompaniment to red salmon and red salmon and dill are natural bedfellows and it is this very jar of pickled cucumber containing dill in fact that the Russian man is settling into his basket when I enter the condiment aisle with a pen in my hand and my hair twisted back into a French plait on my way to checkout fourteen where I will sit myself down upon a lopsided swivel chair and commence yet another nine-hour shift because these are the summer months and in the summer I work all the hours the devil sends so I have a sizeable wedge squirreled away for when I return to the college equidistant from the woeful library and the marooned casino slap-bang in the centre of the fastest growing town in Europe in order to resume my studies in three subjects pertaining to the humanities come September. The Russian man is alone in the aisle. His hand is again moving deftly through the air and I cannot get past him because in an instant he has pulled a book from out of nowhere and delivered it directly into my path. 'Here – all yours!' he exclaims, and I take the book from the Russian man's hand without stopping and say thank you kindly and keep walking to checkout fourteen with my head up and the book held close against my thigh and when I get to the checkout I immediately stash the book on a shelf beneath the small beige machine that prints out receipts. There it is next to the till rolls there it is next to my obdurate seat there it is brooding beside me until I take my lunch break and I don't give it a single glance in all that time. Whether I look at it or not makes no difference. I've seen the title, I know what it is. The book the Russian man has seen fit to give me is by Friedrich Nietzsche and the name of it is *Beyond Good and Evil* and I am beyond unnerved because it is abhorrently clear that the reason why the Russian man has seen fit to give me this book is because despite time and again rolling his jars of pickled vegetables and tins of omega-rich fish across the scanner deliberately without uttering a word more than the amount due, a minor yet far-reaching aspect of my disposition wavered in the periodic presence of the Russian man nonetheless and has given me away, unveiled a secluded modicum of my deeper substance, for there is the proof, right beside me, that the Russian man has seen through my ruffled yet unbroken flesh. Straight into the quickening revolutions of my supremely wicked imaginings.

RACHAEL ALLEN's first collection of poems, *Kingdomland*, is published by Faber & Faber. She is the co-author of a number of collaborative artists' books, including *Nights of Poor Sleep* with Marie Jacotey, published by Prototype, and *Almost One. Say Again!* with JocJonJosch, published by Slimvolume. She hosts the Faber Poetry Podcast and is the poetry editor for *Granta* magazine and Granta Books.

CLAIRE-LOUISE BENNETT is the author of *Pond* (Fitzcarraldo, 2015) and *Fish Out Of Water* (Juxta Press, 2020).

THOMAS BUNSTEAD has translated some of the leading Spanish-language writers working today, including Agustín Fernández Mallo, Maria Gainza and Enrique Vila-Matas. His own writing has appeared in publications such as *The Brixton Review of Books*, *>kill author* and *LitHub*.

REVITAL COHEN & TUUR VAN BALEN (b.1981, based in London) work across objects, installation and film to explore the process of production as cultural, personal and political practices. Recent solo shows include *Luna Eclipse, Oasis Dream* at Stanley Picker Gallery, Kingston; *Trapped in the Dream of the Other* at Mu.Zee, Ostend, and *Assemble Standard Minimal* at Schering Stiftung, Berlin. Their first survey show opens at Z33 Kunstencentrum in Belgium in summer 2020.

ZHANG ENLI was born in 1965 in the province of Jilin in China. In 1989, he graduated from the Arts & Design Institute of Wuxi Technical University and relocated to Shanghai to teach at the Arts and Design Institute of Donghua University. Zhang Enli's paintings have been featured in numerous important exhibitions, with recent solo exhibitions at Galleria Borghese, Rome, Italy (2019), K11 Foundation, Shanghai, China (2019), Firstsite Gallery, Colchester, England (2017), Moca, Taipei, Taiwan (2015).

JOHANNA HEDVA is the author of the novel *On Hell*. Their EP *The Sun and the Moon* was released in 2019. Their collection of poems and essays, *Minerva the Miscarriage of the Brain*, will be published in September 2020. This essay is from their book in-progress, *The Mess*, writings on music and mysticism.

DOUGLAS HERASYMUIK is a healthcare worker, community activist and emerging Canadian poet who writes about social justice, freedom and beautiful sadness. This is his first published work.

DAISY HILDYARD is the author of *Hunters in the Snow*, a novel about farmers, and *The Second Body*, an essay on the Anthropocene.

SOPHIE HUGHES has translated some of the finest Spanish and Latin American authors at work today. In 2019 she was shortlisted for the Man Booker International Prize for her translation of Alia Trabucco Zerán's *The Remainder*. In 2018 she was named one of the Arts Foundation '25' for her contribution to the field of literary translation.

ZOSIA KUCZYŃSKA is the author of *Pisanki* (The Emma Press, 2017). Her work has been published in *The Tangerine* and is forthcoming in *Poetry Ireland Review*. In 2019, she was shortlisted for the Mairtín Crawford Award for Poetry and highly commended in the Patrick Kavanagh Poetry Award. She is currently an IRC postdoctoral research fellow at University College Dublin.

ROBERT MCKAY writes about literature and film in which animals' ethical demands pose aesthetic as well as political and social problems. He is Professor of Contemporary Literature at the University of Sheffield where he co-directs the Sheffield Animal Studies Research Centre. He is series co-editor of *Palgrave Studies of Animals and Literature* and his publications include *Killing Animals*, *Against Value in the Arts and Education*, and *Werewolves, Wolves and the Gothic*.

ROSANNA MCLAUGHLIN is a writer and editor from London. Her book *Double-Tracking*, a collection of satirical essays and short fiction on middle-class duplicities, was published by Carcanet Press in 2019. She is an art editor at *The White Review*.

FERNANDA MELCHOR (born Veracruz, Mexico, in 1982) is widely recognised as one of the most exciting new voices of Mexican literature. In 2018, she won the PEN Mexico Award for Literary and Journalistic Excellence and in 2019 the German Anna-Seghers-Preis and the International

Literature Award for *Hurricane Season*, published by Fitzcarraldo Editions.

LISA OPPENHEIM (b. 1975, New York, USA) lives and works in New York City and Berlin. She studied for a BA at Brown University in 1998, and later an MFA from the Milton Avery Graduate School for the Arts at Bard College in 2001, and is a graduate of the Whitney Museum's Independent Study Program and the Rijksakademie van Beeldende Kunsten in Amsterdam. Recent solo exhibitions include *The American Colony*, The Approach, London (2019), *Spine*, MCA Denver, Denver, Colorado (2018) and MOCA Cleveland, Cleveland, Ohio (2017).

HANNAH ROSEFIELD studies and teaches literature at Harvard University. She is a contributing editor at *The White Review*.

SANKI SAITŌ (1900-1962) was a leading figure in the avant-garde haiku movement of the 1930s. He began writing in his thirties as a practising dentist, and was imprisoned for his poetry in the Second World War. His collections are: *Flags* (1940), *Night Peaches* (1948), *One Hundred Haiku* (1948), *Today* (1952), and *Transformations* (1962). 'Sanki' is a nom de plume that means 'Three Demons'.

SAMARA SCOTT lives and works in Dover. Solo exhibitions include *Belt and Road*, Tramway, Glasgow (2018), *Silks*, Eastside Projects, Birmingham (2015), and *Poems*, Almanac Projects, London (2013). Recent group exhibitions include *Day Tripper*, Focal Point Gallery, Southend-on-Sea (2019), and *The Happy Fact: A Popular Mechanics of Feelings*, La Casa Encendida, Madrid (2019). Forthcoming projects in 2020 include a solo show at CAPC, Bordeaux, and a book with Loose Joints.

PATRICK STAFF is an artist based in Los Angeles, USA, and London, UK. Through a varied and interdisciplinary body of work, they interrogate notions of discipline, dissent, labour and queer identity. Their work has been presented internationally, including solo shows at Serpentine Galleries, London (2019), Irish Museum of Modern Art, Dublin (2019), Dundee Contemporary Arts, Dundee (2019), MOCA, Los Angeles (2017), Spike Island, Bristol (2016), and Chisenhale Gallery, London (2015).

JEREMY TIANG is the translator of novels by Li Er, Zhang Yueran, Chan Ho-Kei, Yeng Pway Ngon and Yan Ge, and was named the London Book Fair's inaugural 'Translator of the Fair' in 2019. He also writes and translates plays (most recently Chen Si'an's *Ocean Hotpot* for the Royal Court's International Climate Crisis Plays at the Edinburgh Festival). He is the author of a novel, *State of Emergency* (Singapore Literature Prize, 2018) and a short story collection, *It Never Rains on National Day*.

SABINA URRACA is a writer and journalist. Born in the Basque Country, she spent her childhood in Tenerife and has lived in Madrid for over a decade. She is the author of the novel *Prodigal Daughters* (*Las niñas prodigio*), published by Fulgencio Pimentel in 2018. Sabina Urraca writes regularly for *Vice Spain* and *El País*, and is widely hailed today as an exciting new voice in Spanish letters. She is currently writing her second book.

ELVIA WILK is a writer and editor living in New York. Her writing has appeared in publications such as *frieze*, *Artforum*, *Bookforum*, *Granta*, *n+1*, *BOMB*, *Mousse*, *Flash Art* and *art-agenda*, and she is currently an editor at *e-flux Journal*. Her first novel, *Oval*, was published by Soft Skull in 2019. She is the recipient of an Andy Warhol Arts Writers Grant and a 2020 fellow at the Berggruen Institute.

HSU YU-CHEN was born in 1977 in Taiwan. He has published the story collection *Purple Blooms* (Ink, 2008) as well as short stories and book and film reviews in journals such as *Ink Literary Monthly* and *UNITAS A Literary Monthly*. His short stories have won Best Story in the United Daily News Literary Awards (2008), and First Prize at the New Taipei City Literature Awards (2010).

PLATES

ON MEAT

Adams, Carol J., *The Sexual Politics of Meat* (New York, NY: Continuum Books, 2010).

Berlant, Lauren, and Jordan Alexander Stein, 'Cruising Veganism', *GLQ: A Journal of Lesbian and Gay Studies*
(21:1), 2015, pp. 18-23.

Calarco, Matthew, *Thinking Through Animals: Identity, Difference, Indistinction* (Stanford, CA: Stanford
University Press, 2015).

Cassidy, Rebecca, *Horse People: Thoroughbred Culture in Lexington and Newmarket* (Baltimore, MD:
Johns Hopkins University Press, 2008).

Chen, Mel Y., *Animacies: Biopolitics, Racial Mattering, and Queer Affect* (Durham, NC: Duke University
Press Books, 2016).

Connor, Steven, 'Smear Campaigns' <stevenconnor.com/smearcampaigns.html>

Douglas, Mary, *Purity and Danger* (Oxford: Routledge, 1996).

Giedion, Sigfried, *Mechanization Takes Command: A Contribution to Anonymous History* (Minneapolis, MN:
University of Minnesota Press, 2014).

Gossett, Che, 'Blackness, Animality, and the Unsovereign', Verso Blog, 8 September 2015,
<versobooks.com/blogs/2228-che-gossett-blackness-animality-and-the-unsovereign>

Haraway, Donna, *Staying with the Trouble: Experimental Futures* (Durham, NC: Duke University Press Books, 2016).
— *When Species Meet* (Minneapolis, MN: University of Minnesota Press, 2007).

Hayward, Eva, 'Spiderwomen', in *Trap Door: Trans Cultural Production and the Politics of Visibility*
(London: MIT Press, 2017).

Reines, Ariana, *The Cow* (New York, NY: Fence Books, 2006).

Schneemann, Carolee, *Meat Joy*, 1964.

Shukin, Nicole, *Animal Capital: Rendering Life in Biopolitical Times* (Minneapolis, MN: University of Minnesota
Press, 2009).

Smith, Julie Ann, Beyond Dominance and Affection: Living with Rabbits in Post-Humanist Households,
Society and Animals 11:2, (2003), pp. 181-197.

The Animal Studies Group, *Killing Animals* (Urbana and Chicago, IL: University of Illinois Press, 2006).

Tyler, Tom, 'Meanings of Meat in Videogames', in *Literature and Meat Since 1900*, ed. by Sean McCorry
and John Miller (London: Palgrave Macmillan, 2019).

Hurricane Season by Fernanda Melchor (tr. Sophie Hughes)
is published by Fitzcarraldo Editions on 19 February 2020.

'Brutal, relentless, beautiful, fugal, *Hurricane Season* explores the violent mythologies of one Mexican village and reveals how they touch the global circuitry of capitalist greed. This is an inquiry into the sexual terrorism and terror of broken men. This is a work of both mystery and critique. Most recent fiction seems anaemic by comparison.'
— Ben Lerner, author of *The Topeka School*

Fitzcarraldo Editions

'Truly dazzling' *Scotsman*
'Exemplary' China Mieville   'Wickedly clever' *Guardian*

salt
slow

julia
armfield

'A writer whose next move you wouldn't want to miss' *Observer*
'A gut-wrenching talent' Daisy Johnson

'Her work has a timelessness to it, and a generosity of emotion
that's brave and affecting.'
Chloe Aridjis

'A distinct new gothic, melancholy, powerful and poised.'
China Miéville